MURDER IS A SMOKING GUN

A KELLY ARMELLO COZY MYSTERY BOOK 5

DONNA DOYLE

PUREREAD.COM

CONTENTS

JARROD'S BACK IN TOWN

Kelly Armello was at the circulation desk, taking care of a patron, when the front door to the library opened and Jarrod Zabo entered. He made a point of catching her eye, not a difficult thing to do as Kelly was conscientious about making sure that every person who came into the library was acknowledged upon entrance with, at the very least, a welcoming smile.

Her smile froze in place as she handed the stack of children's books to Mia Shaw.

"I'm sure Mason and Lucia will enjoy them," Kelly said.

"I know they've heard the Dr. Seuss stories dozens of times," Mia said, "but they still like to hear them, and I like reading them."

"That's why they're classics," Kelly said. "They never get old."

Jarrod was idling in front of the display of new books. She knew it was only a pose; Jarrod didn't read fiction. How had she ever been engaged to him?

"These books will count toward their summer reading prizes," Kelly said. "Just add them to the list and at the end of the summer, we'll be awarding prizes to the kids who've read the most books—or, in Lucia's case, had the most books read to them."

Mia smiled at that. But Kelly thought she looked careworn. She resolved to bring the question up to Troy Kennedy, an officer in the Settler Springs Police Department and a friend to Mia's father, Leo Page. Leo had been unfairly suspended from the force after accusations were made that he had coerced a murder confession from a suspect who happened to be Mia's ex-husband.

Thinking of Troy, particularly with Jarrod, her ex-fiancé, brought its own complications. Troy was so many good things: he was honest, conscientious and compassionate, hard-working, unimpressed by the trappings of affluence, respectful of people who struggled. He was also good-looking, with blazing blue eyes and thick black hair and the physique of a military veteran who kept himself in fighting shape even though he'd left the Army.

Not that Jarrod, with his impeccably styled blond hair and alert green eyes, wasn't good-looking, she was forced to acknowledge. But somehow, Troy in his jeans and tee-shirts bested Jarrod in his tailored suits. Maybe that was why she and Jarrod had broken up, Kelly thought. She was just a jeans-and-tee-shirt kind of woman. Provincial, Jarrod had called her. Small-town. He'd said other things, too, hurtful, insulting things, about her strict morals and her ethics. But he had given her an engagement ring.

Troy showed no signs of wanting to have Kelly if it meant getting married.

"Hello, Jarrod," she said evenly after Mia left.

"Hey, Kelly," he said, sauntering to the circulation desk. "How are things?"

"Fine. What brings you to Settler Springs?"

When they'd broken up a year ago, Jarrod had said that he couldn't wait to get out of the dead-end town that Kelly loved. She'd refused to leave with him, just as she'd refused to move in with him until they were married.

"New job," he said with a casual manner that didn't deceive her. "I've been hired by Representative Eldredge to manage his re-election campaign."

He'd left to find employment in an arena where he could be among the influential powerbrokers in politics. He didn't intend to stay in local politics for long, but by choosing Eldredge, Jarrod was hitching his star to a man regarded as a rising leader in the state, someone who would eventually seek national office. Kelly's views on the state representative were somewhat conflicted by a suspicion that he was entirely too involved with Roger and Lois Stark, the reinstated police chief and his wife, who, she and Troy knew, had connections to the disturbing rise of drug use in Settler Springs.

But that wasn't something to share with Jarrod.

"And what are you doing here?"

"I came to invite you to lunch," he said with a winning grin that seemed as if it had been modeled after a politician's sculpted smile.

"I'm covering the desk while Carmela is at lunch, sorry," she answered.

"What about dinner?"

"It's my late-night working."

"Another time?"

"How long are you in town?"

"I can be in town whenever I want if there's a reason to be here," he said, leaning on the desk and making sure that Kelly perceived that his comment referred both to her and to his position on the campaign staff.

"That sounds very accommodating," she replied noncommittally.

The side door opened to admit Lois Stark. Ignoring Kelly, as she preferred to do, she spotted Jarrod and immediately an expression of pleasure transformed her features into welcome.

"Why, Jarrod, I didn't know you were around," she said. "Where is the Congressman?"

"Working, Mrs. Stark. You know how it is. Even with a campaign, the people's business doesn't stop."

"I was so pleased when I heard that he had gotten rid of that useless Keith Rigowski; promoting him to campaign manager was not a good decision. He's back where he belongs, filling out forms and staffing the office."

"Keith isn't a bad guy," Jarrod replied, his tone indicating that he agreed with her, and the other man had his place, an inferior one in the hierarchy of political staff members. "He's just not meant for the front lines of a campaign."

Mrs. Stark's gaze drifted over to Kelly briefly. "He's better out of the limelight," she said. "There's too much bad publicity being generated out of foolish speculation and idle gossip."

Jarrod wasn't dim. He caught the glance and the undertone of criticism, and his features sharpened as if he wanted to ask more. But Jarrod wasn't a man to get caught in the middle before he knew who was on either side.

"If I hadn't just gotten back from lunch," Mrs. Stark said, "I'd have invited you to join me and Roger."

"Maybe another time," Jarrod suggested, making it clear to Kelly that even with her refusal of his invitation, he didn't lack for dining company.

"Definitely. Are you in town long?"

"No, just setting up a campaign headquarters in town."

"Yes, the Congressman said something about that. It's going to be exciting to be at the center of things."

The telephone rang, to Kelly's relief, and she broke away to address a complaint from a patron who wanted to know why she was being charged for an overdue book she swore she had returned a week ago. Kelly addressed her questions, but didn't relent on the overdue book. The woman was appeased by Kelly's manner and agreed to look "one more time" to see if she could find it.

"Sometimes, the kids put them somewhere and don't remember doing it," Kelly suggested. "That happens all the time."

The patron laughed. "With my gang, that could very well be. I'll look again. Thanks, Kelly."

When Kelly hung up the phone, Jarrod was gone and Mrs. Stark was at her customary spot at one of the tables in the middle of the library, halfway between the front door and the circulation desk, so that she was near enough to both if there were any conversations or arrivals that were worth her attention. But everyone who knew that Mrs. Stark had her own reasons for expanding the role of the library board president to maintain a daily presence knew that if they wanted to tell Kelly something important, the library was not a secure place to divulge information.

When Carmela returned from her lunch break, she ignored Mrs. Stark, as she usually did and went into Kelly's office.

"I heard that Jarrod is back in town," she said in a low voice. Mrs. Stark was engaged in a conversation with one of her friends and the chatter made good cover for Carmela's topic.

"I know. He's working for the Eldredge campaign. He came by."

"To see you or her?"

Kelly shrugged. "With Jarrod, who knows? He's always on the lookout for an opportunity and Mrs. Stark is much more influential than I am."

"Maybe," Carmela replied with asperity. "But she's not young and pretty and a former fiancée."

"That's over."

Carmela grinned. "Jarrod is nice looking, but Officer Troy, now that's a real man."

"Troy and I are good friends," Kelly said, not for the first time. The library clerk had been won over by Troy Kennedy when he'd been supportive of her during an investigation that had her briefly included among the suspects in the murder of Lyola Knesbit.

Now Travis Shaw, Mia's ex-husband and former Police Chief Leo Page's ex-son-in-law, was awaiting trial for the murder, but he'd recently stirred things up with a television interview asserting his innocence and Leo's culpability in the arrest.

"Jarrod isn't involved in any of that, is he?" Carmela asked.

Kelly doubted it. Jarrod was an opportunist and a social climber, but he didn't use drugs and he wasn't likely to get involved in illicit actions that could get him into trouble. At least, she didn't think he was.

2

SPREADING THE NEWS

Troy wasn't Kelly's boyfriend. They both understood that. He wanted a relationship that didn't end at the bedroom door, and that wasn't Kelly's way. They hadn't actually discussed their views on intimacy, but each knew where the other stood. The stand-off left them in a state that neither could describe; they knew they were friends; they were even partners in the crusade to get to the bottom of what was going on with Chief Stark, the drug traffic in town, and the truth about the murder of Sean Claypool, Troy's army buddy, whose death had been conveniently identified as a suicide by the authorities. But to the people of Settler Springs who saw the pair out on the Trail for their Saturday morning run, or spotted them afterwards at The Café, or who decided that a man and a woman who spent that much time together must be more than friends, Troy and Kelly were a couple.

Which was why Troy had only been on his afternoon shift for a few hours before he learned from three different people that Kelly's former fiancé was back in town.

"Looks like you've got competition," teased Tia Krymanski when Troy stopped at The Café for supper.

Assuming that she was referring to Chief Stark, Troy's supervisor and nemesis on the force, Troy just grunted assent, decided that he'd have the fish sandwich and fries, and put his menu down so that Francie would know he was ready to place his order.

"That means it's time for a ring," Tia said.

"What?"

But Tia was heading back to the kitchen, where she did the cooking for the restaurant.

"I hear that Jarrod Zabo stopped at the library this afternoon," Francie said when she came to take his order.

"Who?"

"Jarrod Zabo. You didn't know that he and Kelly were engaged until they broke up last year?"

"Oh, yeah, him. Yeah, I know that. Instead of coffee, I'll have a Coke. It's hot out there."

"It's heading for July," Francie replied. "It's always hot when the re-enactors come for the Fourth. I don't know how they stand wearing those heavy uniforms. Personally, I think they're crazy."

"Just so they're not as wild as the Memorial Day veterans," Troy said. *Jarrod Zabo? What was he doing around town?* Kelly said that was over and Kelly wasn't the kind to equivocate about her emotions.

Francie sobered, remembering that Troy's friend from the army, a relative through marriage to Tia, had committed suicide during the Memorial Day celebration. Tia didn't believe that he'd killed himself; she denied that he was despondent and said that he'd been in great spirits as he reconnected with the Krymanski side of the family. But suicide was what the police ruled it, and Francie didn't see that there was any reason for them to lie about something like that, although she could understand why family members might have a hard time accepting the news.

"I'll be back with your Coke," she said.

By the time he'd been told a third time, before he'd finished his meal and paid the bill, that Kelly's ex-boyfriend was in town, Troy was baffled and irritated. Why were people telling him that? Kelly and Jarrod were past news, not current. And why was the guy back around, anyway? He wanted to ask Kelly but that would be breaking the unspoken rules of their relationship. They weren't a couple; therefore, asking about an ex-fiancé would blur the lines between friendship and romance, and neither Kelly nor Troy, for different reasons, was ready to deal with that.

With the murder of Sean still very much in the forefront of his thoughts, Troy wasn't in the mood for an ambush from another direction. Skip Krymanski was pressing him to do something about Sean's death and Troy was trying, but Chief Stark had the state police on his side—at least one of the troopers—and Troy couldn't make a dent in that alliance. He considered stopping by the state police station to see if Trooper Callahan, new to the force and, as far as he could tell, neutral in the line-up of officers linked to Stark and one who stayed out of the battle. But he decided against it; he'd gone out there last week to see if she knew anything. Then Trooper Meigle had returned while he was there. Upon seeing Troy, he'd demanded to know what business he was on, reminding him that the Settler Springs force worked through the police chief, not the officers. Trooper Callahan had maintained her impassive expression during the exchange, giving away nothing and doing nothing to indicate support for either side. So far, she was staying out of it, but Troy was hoping that eventually, she'd see the lay of the land and realize that she'd become a state trooper to uphold the law, not to ignore it or bypass it.

He drove past the field where the re-enactors would recreate their French & Indian War battle over the Fourth of July weekend. Crews were busy preparing for the event, setting up grandstands, mowing the lawn and getting the parking lot in shape for the out-of-towners who would be coming for the event. Kelly wasn't involved in the planning and that was a bright spot; she'd been so engulfed with Memorial Day preparations that they hadn't been able to spend much time together. But when he needed her, after Sean's death, she'd been there for him.

It was the way she was made.

Why was her ex in town? Kelly didn't have anything to do with the Eldredge campaign, so Jarrold whatever-his-name-was had no business going to the library to see her.

He headed back to the station. Chief Stark ought to be gone by now. He wasn't one for staying past quitting time, despite his protestations that being the police chief was a 24/7 job.

As he unlocked the door and entered the office, he saw Mia Shaw crossing the street and heading in his direction.

"Hi, Mia," he said. "Everything okay?"

"No," she said bluntly. "I just got off work and I wanted to come here before I go home. You know jury selection is going to get underway for the trial."

He didn't know that, but he was expecting it. Mia followed him into the office. "I'm worried about Dad."

"Leo didn't break the law, no matter what Shaw claims," Troy reminded her.

"I know that. But Travis has this high-powered lawyer who keeps the story in the news. Dad's going to get an ulcer over it. He's taking some flack over it at his job."

"At the security job?" Troy asked. That wasn't good. Leo had found other employment after being suspended, getting hired by a security firm in Pittsburgh. The position was a good one, despite the longer commute that came with having to work in the city, but Troy had thought the distance would be a good thing, providing Leo with some anonymity from the Shaw trial. Apparently, that wasn't the case.

"Yeah. He said his boss has asked him a couple of times if Dad is going to have to testify."

"Of course, he'll have to testify," Troy said angrily, "but that doesn't make him guilty of forcing Shaw to confess."

"I know. But his boss said that the company's clients don't like that kind of publicity. I'm afraid they're going to get rid of him."

There wasn't anything Troy could do about that, but he could give Leo a call and stop by over the weekend and try to rally his former colleague's spirits.

"What about you?" he asked. "How are you doing?"

She shrugged. "I don't know. I feel like no place is safe, you know?"

Troy didn't blame her for the way she felt. There had been several incidents—her son being abducted for a few hours and Chief Stark claiming that Mason had just made up the story because he was late getting home; a dead rat left in her mail box; a broken bicycle left on her porch that was meant to scare her into thinking it was her son's—that were enough to worry her. Mia Shaw was putting her life back in order after drug addiction, marriage to Travis Shaw, a drug dealer, and then rehab, and she couldn't afford any mistakes. Her parents had custody of her kids, and they were vigilant in looking after the children. Mia visited them often, and was close with her family, but Troy knew that she yearned for a normal mother's life, when her children were with her and she wasn't fearful that her ex-husband was pulling the strings to harass her from behind the walls of the prison where he awaited trial.

"You've got my cell number," he reminded her. "Call any time, night or day, if something isn't the way it should be. Even if you can't pinpoint what's wrong. Call."

"Thanks, Troy," she said gratefully, and he was glad to see that a little bit of her anxious expression seemed to ease. But he knew that wouldn't last. Mia had a lot to handle these days and her ex-husband seemed to have a way of getting to her, despite his imprisonment, that indicated he was not on his own. He had help. But whose? The Starks were a local power couple, but they wouldn't have been able to arrange for Shaw to get all of the pre-trial attention he was receiving from the media. That had to come from higher up.

From Representative Eldredge? But why? What did the state representative have to gain from coming to the assistance of a drug dealer who was accused of murder? The Starks were generous contributors to Eldredge's re-election campaign; Troy knew that much because Doug Iolus, who wrote for the weekly Settler Springs paper, had sources on all levels of local and state government. Maybe Doug had some new information.

3

FALLOUT FROM A COUNCIL MEETING

Before Troy was able to ask Doug if there was anything new on the Eldredge front, he got a text later that night, just before he went back to the police station to finish up his final reports for the night. It was from Kelly.

Just heard that Tia Krymanski was at the council meeting tonight. She lit into the mayor about the drug problem. Chief Stark was there, said there's a drug problem among certain parts of town, with certain families. Tia was furious.

Troy pulled into the parking space in front of the station. The lights in the council meeting room were still on, although the meeting should have been over well before now.

Looks like it might still be going on, he texted. *Lights are on.*

No, the meeting is over, but maybe Stark and Mayor Truvert are still there. Don't take any chances.

Troy decided that he'd pretend he hadn't read the last sentence. There was no danger of anyone hearing him unlock the police station door on the bottom floor; the council meeting room was on the second floor of the municipal building. He went in and climbed the stairs, making as little noise as possible.

"I saw the lights on," he said, opening the door to the meeting room and looking surprised to see the police chief and the mayor in conversation.

Chief Stark's face revealed a flash of anger, but not before a nuance of alarm showed itself. "Isn't your shift over?"

"I thought so, but then I saw the lights on and figured I'd better check and see if something was going on that shouldn't be."

"Nothing is going on, Kennedy. We're just finishing up some council matters."

Troy smiled genially at both men. "Good night, then."

He descended the stairs making no effort to be silent, clocked out, and returned to his car. He'd learned how to be silent in motion in the army, one of many useful tactics in training, although he hadn't expected it to be of use as a civilian. But he'd overheard a few seconds of the conversation between the mayor and the police chief.

"See if Meigle can set anything up," from Stark.

"And soon," from the mayor. "We don't need any more screw-ups."

It wasn't conclusive. It could have meant anything, referred to anything. But as Troy stood on his porch, waiting for Arlo to finish his last outdoor call for the night, his instincts told him that Tia Krymanski's outburst at the council meeting must have triggered something, and whatever that was indicated that State Trooper Meigle was, as Troy had suspected, in with Stark. It remained to be proven what being in with Stark actually involved.

The next step was finding out directly from Tia what she had said at the meeting. She must have felt strongly about speaking up; she worked long hours at The Café, so she either rearranged her schedule or had gotten the okay to leave early in order to attend. Asking her at the restaurant wouldn't be fair, he thought; she deserved privacy at her workplace.

Kelly's plan of action was already in motion when she went into the library the following day. If the council meeting had been as volatile as her neighbor had told her it was, then people coming into the library were bound to bring the subject up with Mrs. Stark when they saw her.

She went to work an hour earlier than usual so that she could have a reason to be out at the circulation desk, rather than in her office, when the library opened. When Carmela arrived, only fifteen minutes after Kelly, it was apparent that she, too, had heard about the council meeting and she was eager to discuss it before Mrs. Stark arrived.

"I heard that Mrs. Krymanski really went off on them," Carmela said. "She said there's drugs on every street in this town and the police need to stop looking the other way."

"Did you hear anything about what Chief Stark said?"

"I guess he tried to calm her down by saying that the drug problem isn't as bad as people claim. He said it's a problem everywhere, but it's not as bad in Settler Springs as it is in the bigger cities. Mrs.

Krymanski—you know how she is—fired back 'That's just because we don't have as many people who live here.' I guess he didn't like that. She said a few other things, and then he started making pointed remarks about some families in town being more prone to substance abuse because they tended to come from families with criminal records. You know what he was trying to say."

Kelly knew. He would have tried to paint the drug problem as something that wasn't suffered by the "good" families of the town, only by those like the Krymanskis, who were more likely to be picked up by the police for even a misdemeanor than the offspring of the prominent citizens. It was the sort of stance which the police chief had perfected in his role, reinforcing the notion cherished by the town's more affluent and influential members that the social problems of the times would not strike at them because the other families—the ones who struggled to make ends meet and needed public assistance to pay a utility bill or food stamps in order to feed their families—those were the ones who were already entangled in the web that vice wove around.

But what had made Tia go to the council meeting in the first place to voice her concerns? Kelly wondered. Tia was busy with work and her five kids; she wasn't one of the citizens who made a point of attending meetings. She didn't have the time.

"It just seems like too much is going on," Carmela stated as she put a pile of returned books on the cart to put back on the shelves. "And with the trial coming up . . . "

Her voice trailed off. Kelly knew that Carmela was anxious about the trial, about being called to testify about what she had seen and done on Groundhog Day, the day that Lyola Knesbit had been murdered, and the subsequent investigation. Carmela, too, had been targeted for harassment, presumably as a warning from whatever allies of Travis Shaw were attempting to reinforce his claims that he was guilty of robbery, involved in drugs, but not a murderer. Her tires had been slashed in front of her home, and that had cowed the usually belligerent woman. It had, in the end, been part of the process that had transformed Carmela into a less dour person and a more welcoming library staff member, but Kelly would have preferred a less-intimidating means for the alchemy.

"I know," Kelly reassured her. They both spotted Mrs. Stark outside the door, inserting her key into the lock and by common design, Carmela went off to the stacks and Kelly logged into the automation computer.

Mrs. Stark, it was quickly apparent, was in a foul mood and eager for a target. She criticized Kelly for not having opened the library before Mrs. Stark had to use her key to get in. Kelly deflected the criticism; there was no reason to unlock the front door when Mrs. Stark was doing so, and the other entry doors were already unlocked. She found fault with Carmela's re-shelving the books; the new books should have been put back first, she told her, because those were the ones most likely to get checked out again. She even found a reason to berate Chloe, the student who worked as a part-time children's librarian, in the girl's absence; Chloe, she said, needed to find something for the parents to do downstairs while they were waiting for the children's program to end in the children's center. They were noisy and they talked too much, disrupting other patrons.

Kelly simply said that she would mention this to Chloe.

"You're the director, aren't you?" Mrs. Stark demanded. "Don't 'mention it' to her, tell her!" Twin red spots of color showed up on Mrs. Stark's cheekbones like crimson spotlights, indicators of her temper.

Kelly looked up and met the board president's gaze, saying nothing and letting her expression speak volumes. The other woman glared in silence.

Kelly returned to her task, unruffled by Mrs. Stark's demeanor. She felt as though she could have said more, even if only to repeat the statement that she was the director. But maybe it was better, right now, to hold her fire and see if the day brought forth anything new.

4

WHY IS JARROD BACK?

M*eet for supper?*

Troy texted back. *Six, The Café?*

Six is good, Kelly replied. *Not The Café. The Pizzaria?*

That meant that she didn't want to take the risk of being overheard by diners in the closely connected booths. Which meant that she had learned something.

Ok, Troy responded. *See you at 6.*

Kelly was already at a table when he arrived at the crowded Pizzaria. Two televisions were showing the evening news on opposite ends of the restaurant. It was a popular eating place across the river from Settler Springs, and one which was well-suited for a private conversation in a public place.

Troy's pizza tastes were changing. They compromised on a margarita pizza; Kelly order iced tea with hers, and Troy had the same.

"You're influencing me," he responded when Kelly raised her eyebrows with regard to his menu choices. "So, what's new?"

Kelly unfolded her napkin and placed it over her lap. "Mrs. Stark was in a nasty mood today," she confided. "She couldn't even manage her usual plastic cheer when people came in to ask about the council meeting last night. She said that Tia Krymanski has a lot of nerve complaining about what she calls a 'manufactured' drug problem when 'everyone knows that the Krymanskis are responsible for most of the crime in Settler Springs.' She pretty much said that to everyone, and she wasn't . . . she wasn't her usual composed self when she said it. And she left the library at lunch time and didn't come back."

The waitress brought their drinks; Troy waited until she left before responding. "I wonder what made Tia go to the council meeting," he mused.

"I don't know. Maybe we'll see her on Saturday after we run and we can ask?"

"I don't know . . . I wonder if something is going on with her kids? If we see Lucas, we can try to find out. I don't like pumping the kid for information, but Lucas doesn't generally need to be pumped. If he's thinking it, he's saying it."

"I can ask him, if he comes in and Mrs. Stark isn't there. He doesn't come in as often during the summer, but if I see him, I'll try to find out without doing too much probing. We can at least ask Doug what went on at the meeting; he covers council business for the weekly."

"When I went into the building last night, the lights were still on in the council room. So I went upstairs —hey, it could have been a break-in, you know, and it's my job to arrest criminals—" he said when Kelly's countenance turned to wide-eyed alarm. "It was Stark and his brother-in-law. Relax, they aren't going to just shoot me right in the municipal building."

"Trooper Meigle shot Eddie Kavlick," she reminded him.

That was out in the open, by the cemetery. Different circumstances entirely."

"You need to be more careful, Troy," Kelly advised him, her brown eyes vivid with concern. "They both

29

know where you stand on all of this, and you just can't trust people who've already made the choice to sell their souls and serve the Devil."

"Whoa, that's a little heavy, don't you think?" he queried, somewhat uncomfortable with her wording.

"Call it what you want. Call it going to the dark side. Call it bad choices. But they're in this, we both know that, and once people have made the choice to forsake their conscienc there's nothing they won't do to achieve their own ends."

"You sound like a fire-and-brimstone preacher from another era."

"No, just a Christian from the 21st century," she answered. "But I know evil when I see it. Carmela said it today . . . things are going on. They seem to just be happening independently, but they aren't. Tia speaking up at the council meeting—"

"Mia Shaw says that her dad is getting grief at work for the publicity about Shaw accusing Leo of forcing him to confess to murder—"

"Sean's murder."

Troy didn't want to think about that. "The murder of Kavlick. Mason being temporarily abducted. The incidents at Mia's apartment."

"Carmela's tires being slashed."

"But what's the connection? I still don't see how Travis Shaw can be pulling strings from prison. He's not that high up in the trade and he's certainly not that influential."

"We don't know that it's being initiated by him," Kelly said.

"Speaking of, I hear that your ex-fiancé is back in town. He works for Eldredge now, doesn't he?"

"Yes, but I don't see Jarrod as a cog in a drug trafficking wheel. I wouldn't call him a man of noble principles," she admitted, "but he's not likely to be tempted by drug money."

"You haven't been in contact with him since you broke up with him, right? How do you know he hasn't changed?"

The pizza arrived, putting the conversation on pause until the waitress had served them and left.

"I don't know for sure, but . . . he wasn't venal when I knew him. Turning to making a profit off drugs, that's a pretty deep step. I don't think he'd do it."

"Would he close his eyes if Eldridge is somehow shielding the Starks and authorizing Shaw to have media contact?" Troy challenged.

"I don't think so . . ."

"But you can't say for sure!" Troy chose not to ask himself whether his insistence on making Jarrod Zabo a likely convert to corruption was because he wanted to dig for the truth or because he wanted to make Kelly's fiancé appear compromised.

Kelly finished chewing the bite of pizza she was eating. "I don't think he would," she repeated, "but I don't know. In politics, how much is it possible to 'not see' some things that might look obvious to people in the inner circle?"

"Why was Jarrod hired by Eldredge? Seems kind of abrupt, doesn't it?"

"I have no idea. I only follow the re-election like any other voter. I don't know why Keith Rigowski was removed from being campaign manager; I wouldn't even have paid attention when it was announced on the news, except that the name was familiar because it was his car . . ."

"That Sean was killed in, yeah. Because Rigowski was away visiting his kid and he'd left his car at home, and Eldredge would have known that. But what, except you, is the connection between your ex-fiancé and this whole Stark-Eldredge web?"

"I don't have any connection to Representative Eldredge," Kelly pointed out, "and my connection to the Starks is mostly through the library."

"You're connected to Lucas Krymanski; you supported him when he was a murder suspect back after Scotty Stark's girlfriend was found in Daffodil Alley," Troy said brusquely. "And," he added, "you're connected to me."

"Jarrod doesn't know that," Kelly said after a pause.

"Can you say that for sure?"

"What do you mean?" Kelly sounded genuinely mystified by his question.

"What if the Starks got Eldredge to hire your ex because they know that you and I are . . . good friends, and they think he might be able to weasel his way back into your good graces? Maybe even get engaged again?"

"I wish you'd stop referring to him as my 'ex'," Kelly answered. "He's not my anything now. And it's not like I've been languishing for Jarrod to come back into my life. I didn't even know he was around until he showed up in the library yesterday."

"But he did show up," Troy pressed. "That says something."

"It doesn't say anything," Kelly retorted, sounding peevish, even to herself. Why was Troy making more of this than was there? "Jarrod just wanted to brag about himself and his new position. He was always like that. It used to drive me crazy. It still does."

"Is being the campaign manager for a state representative that important a position?"

"It would be to Jarrod. He wants to move up, to be influential, to be someone who gets to shake hands with important people. And wear expensive suits and drive an expensive car," she added.

"What does he drive?" Troy demanded.

"I don't know, how would I know? He used to drive a Mustang; he was always complaining about the payments. It was used and that bothered him. I suppose he still drives it. I don't know," she said again in exasperation. "I didn't go out to the curb to check what cars were out front. Now, can we talk about something else besides Jarrod?"

Troy was more than willing to talk about something else, but he couldn't help thinking about the arrival of Kelly's former fiancé in town, and what that might mean, not only in terms of the Starks and their connection to Eldredge, but what it might mean in connection to Kelly.

5

SCENES FROM THE CEMETERY

Doug rolled over onto his belly and aimed his camera down the slope from the statue of General Porter. The night was still, and the cemetery had been quiet as usual, its out-of-town isolation ideal for the ambience that was expected for a graveyard. But its setting was also ideal for other purposes and Doug had been spending nighttime hours here, waiting to see if the visitors that had shown up the previous month would make appearances again. As he'd suspected, they were back.

Doug shot his photos with furtive skill, using a camera chosen from his vast store that was flawless in taking photographs at night without a giveaway flash to reveal his presence.

The Settler Springs Cemetery wasn't just the final resting place for the town's citizens; it was also a secluded spot where the drug trafficking, which had been stymied by the exposure of past locations, could continue without being observed by concerned citizens or such law enforcement that might be interested. Which didn't include the police chief, but did include Officer Troy Kennedy.

He watched and waited as the cars trickled in, stopped, and left a short time afterwards. Then he watched while the vehicle, a black pickup truck that had been there the entire time, backed up and drove out of the cemetery, its lights off.

He waited another hour. Only then did he leave the cemetery, crouching behind the tombstones and trees until he was on the road. He had walked, not driven to the cemetery in order to prevent anyone from seeing him arrive, not long after the sun had gone down.

He had called Troy earlier in the evening to let him know what he was doing. If the night was productive, did Troy want him to stop by with photos?

Troy did want him to stop by, no matter how much later. Doug was instructed to enter Troy's property from the back yard and come around to the front porch and sit on the far end of the porch swing. Behind the forsythia bush.

Doug was surprised by the precise details and the clear instructions to conceal himself, but he followed the directions and sat down on the porch swing, once again waiting. He didn't have to wait long. The front door opened, and a German shepherd trotted out, pleased at the nocturnal opportunity to attend to calls of nature in his yard. He was followed soon after by Troy, wearing the rumpled tee shirt and gym shorts that, Doug assumed, he had been sleeping in before Arlo alerted him to the arrival of a presence on the porch.

If he had been sleeping, that is. Troy hooked Arlo to his leash so that he could have the freedom of the yard without being hurried to finish and come back inside. Then he sat down on the porch.

"You can be seen, but I can't?" Doug queried.

"It's my porch," Troy answered in an alert tone of voice which made Doug doubt that he'd been asleep at all. "No one would be surprised that I'm out here. But no one would expect me to have visitors."

"No one being . . ."

"Anyone. My neighbors are attentive. I don't want someone casually mentioning to someone else that I was out on the porch after midnight talking to a reporter."

"Someone else being . . ."

"I've seen Stark drive by here a couple of times, for no real reason."

"It's a small town," Doug reminded him. "People drive by without a reason on their way to somewhere else."

"Maybe."

"And there are a lot of old people on this street. They go to sleep early, and they wake up early. Why would they see anything?"

"Old people go to the bathroom during the night. They look out their windows, they notice things. But they don't know whether what they're noticing is important and they might mention it."

"Okay, you've convinced me. You're already working so that Stark doesn't know that you're investigating him." Doug removed his camera from around his neck. "Press here; you'll see the shots. I'll print them out tomorrow so you can get a better look."

"Any matches to the ones you took last month?"

"I'll wait until they're printed to be sure, but you'll notice that the vehicles are the same, a lot of them anyway."

Troy viewed the images. He'd wait until he had printed copies before making his own judgment.

"Thanks," he said, handing the camera back to Doug.

"And now?"

"You ever go running on the Trail?"

Doug gestured to the camera around his neck. "Run with these? And I'm always with these. I'm a walking man. Why would I be out on the Trail?"

"I want Kelly to see them, see if she recognizes anyone. We run on Saturdays."

"Yeah, I know."

"You know?"

"Everyone knows," Doug said. He shrugged. "It's a small town."

"I wouldn't expect something like that to be public knowledge."

"You'd be surprised by what's public knowledge. But don't knock it," Doug said. "People noticing things—like your old people with weak bladders—are going to make a difference in us finding out what's going on here. But why would you want me to go out to the Trail to show Kelly the photos? I can see her anytime."

It was Troy's turn to shrug. "Excess of caution, I guess," he said. "Or paranoia. Sean Claypool was murdered. Whoever did it—or hired Eddie Kavlick to get it done before they killed him—isn't going to want loose ends. I want to find out more about the council meeting when Tia Krymanski had her outburst, and I want Kelly to be there. One more question—Jarrod Zabo."

"Kelly's ex? Yeah, he's back in town. He already stopped by the library, but I guess she wasn't bowled over by his new position, so he didn't get a trophy."

"Does he want one?"

"Jarrod always wants a trophy; it's how he's made. Anytime you look at Jarrod, you know he's checking the reflection in his mental mirror."

"Doesn't sound like Kelly's type."

Doug grinned. "Nope," he said. "I'm not her type either. Not for lack of trying."

"You two went to the prom together."

"As friends, not as a couple. I wouldn't have minded it turning to something more, but I'm not a church guy. That's important to Kelly."

"Was Jarrod a church guy?"

"He went with Kelly. I don't think it was deeper than that. Jarrod likes being seen, and church is a good place for that, especially if a guy is ambitious for a political future. I don't know. I'll be talking to him about the campaign, but I doubt if the subject of Kelly will come up. I might ask him about his car, though."

"What about his car?"

"He's driving Scotty Stark's red Aston Martin Vanquish."

"The one that's registered in Lois Stark's name? You're sure?"

"You think there are two Aston Martin Vanquishes in Settler Springs?"

"Not likely. I wonder why?"

"I don't know. That's why I'll be asking."

"You'll ask carefully?"

"No, I'm going to ask him how he got his hands on the car that a drug-dealing murderer used to drive. Of course, I'll be careful. I've been driving my Volvo for ten years. No male is going to be surprised when I admire his fancy car, and I'll make sure that it's where I can see it before I bring it up in the interview."

"Jarrod driving Lois Stark's car . . ."

"One of the many strands in the skein," Doug said cheerfully.

"What?"

"Not a knitter, I take it?"

"You are?"

"I'm a lot of things. But a runner isn't one of them. So, what's the plan for meeting Kelly and you without violating any of your covert ops procedures?"

Troy ignored Doug's jocular reference to his insistence upon caution. Maybe Doug was right, and he was being overly careful, but it was better to be careful and alive than reckless and dead. Until they had a mountain of evidence to present to prove that the Knesbit murder, the drug problem, and the Starks were all entwined, he wasn't going to take any chances.

But it was hard to find a trul private place in a small town like Settler Springs, where everyone knew everyone else and noticed where they were and who they were with.

"I'll let you know," he promised.

"When?"

"I'm off on weekends now; Kelly's off. Sometime this weekend."

"Better be Saturday," Doug recommended. "She's pretty tied up on Sundays with church stuff. I think they do some kind of special service on the weekend before July 4."

"They're always doing a special service for something. Last week, Kelly told me there was a blessing of the beasts service."

Doug stood up. "I know," he said. "I brought my hedgehog."

"Your what?"

"My hedgehog."

"You have a pet porcupine?"

"Yep. Spike's his name."

"Of course."

"I have to hand it to Reverend Dal, he never hesitated. He's a good guy. If I ever did decide to join the Sunday set, I'd go to First Church because of him. Anyone who blesses a hedgehog has some powerful faith."

6

LOOSE THREADS

Troy drove past the field where the re-enactors would stage their battle. Some of them had already arrived and had set up their tents along the parameter of the grounds. From the road, he could see men in colonial dress greeting one another. Kelly said it was a big event in town, but all that meant to Troy was the potential for trouble, like he'd experienced for Memorial Day. Maybe the frontiersmen confined themselves to eighteenth-century rowdiness, he hoped; or maybe they stayed in character and didn't leave the grounds. He wasn't eager for a sequel to the Memorial Day madness.

He wondered if Doug was right. Was he being too cautious about anyone seeing him talking to Doug? Was his desire for secrecy excessive? Driving him was the knowledge that Sean had been killed because he hadn't been distrustful enough. Sean was a tough guy, physically fit, alert . . . but he'd been shot. If Sean could be caught off guard, that meant that everyone had to stay on their guard. It was as simple and as plain as that.

Too many deaths . . . too many unexplained incidents . . . too many unanswered questions. Doug was right: there were people in town who might notice things that were important, things they didn't realize were important. Troy thought back to the help that had been given by Mrs. Hammond, a cheery, chatty senior citizen who had noticed the goings-on outside her apartment window down in Daffodil Alley. Her observation had helped to nail a killer. Mrs. Hammond's friend Rosa had been useful in observing the activity in the senior citizen high-rise parking lot, where Travis Shaw had taken to selling drugs from his car, convinced that old people wouldn't notice. Carmela Dixon had noticed that Lyola Knesbit's purse was in the hands of a stranger and she'd challenged him; the stranger turned out to be Travis Shaw, Leo Page's drug-dealing son-in-law. Jimmy Patton noticed that there were ambulance calls to the road by the cemetery; Jimmy didn't know that drugs were being sold there. At least, he didn't know yet.

How could all these people be pulled into a cohesive group that could be relied upon just to notice things that might not, of themselves, seem significant, but which, when connected to other observations, would reveal the pattern Troy was trying to find? It wasn't a book or a movie, this was real. He needed help.

Kelly could help by finding out more about Jarrod's connection to the Starks through the Eldredge re-election campaign: why was Jarrod driving the flashy car that Mrs. Stark owned, the one that had been driven by her son until he was sent to prison? But Troy wasn't comfortable with the idea of asking Kelly to probe her former fiancé for information and he knew that his reluctance did not spring from altruism. He didn't want Kelly spending time with the guy, period. What if—

Kelly had denied that there was any chance that she and her ex would reconnect; she'd gotten irritated with him for even suggesting that it could happen. Doug had verified that Jarrod Zabo was an opportunist looking out for himself, enhancing his own image and reputation, not overly concerned with integrity. That made him shallow, but it didn't make him a criminal.

Tia Krymanski didn't get involved in local politics. Something had goaded her into showing up at the council meeting to voice her views and she hadn't held back. Kelly had told Troy that Mrs. Stark had been so annoyed that she hadn't stayed in the library past lunchtime.

And why was Lyola Knesbit killed? Travis Shaw was now claiming that his murder conviction was forced out of him by Leo Page because Leo held a grudge against his daughter's ex-husband. People who knew Leo knew better, but Troy knew that Shaw's attorneys would be able to make a potent case against Leo because human emotion was volatile. Even though Carmela Dixon had been in the vehicle with Troy and Leo the night that Shaw was arrested, and even though Mia Shaw had been in the police station when Leo brought Shaw in, there wasn't anybody who was neutral, who had no ties to Shaw at all, who could testify.

Mia Shaw was uneasy; the harassment had done what it was intended to do. Frighten her by making her feel that her kids were vulnerable. Carmela had been intimidated by the slashing of her tires. Would their fear make them unreliable on the witness stand? Would Leo's outrage make him too volatile in testimony?

Why had Lyola Knesbit been killed . . . it kept coming back to that. If the attorneys could make the jury doubt that Travis had been treated fairly, and that he didn't deserve to be charged with the murder, he'd serve a lesser sentence, minus the time he had already served. Mrs. Knesbit's murder would be put down as unsolvable; someone in the Groundhog Day crowd had tried to rob her, she'd fought the killer, he drowned her and left her body by the river; Shaw had come by, noticed the purse, figured that it might be worth something since it was made of leather, and taken it with him to sell for a few bucks to buy drugs. It all seemed plausible from a jury's perspective. Lawyers of the caliber that Shaw had—through means that no one seemed able to figure out—could make that kind of case so easily that deliberations wouldn't take long and Shaw would beat the murder charge. Which would mean he'd be out on the streets all too soon. Mia Shaw's life would be controlled by fear of him; he'd demand some kind of visitation with his kids, and who could say what that would turn into? Leo and Millie Page had custody now, but if Shaw pushed it . . .

Why was Lyola Knesbit killed?

Troy realized that he'd driven out of town and was on his way to the state police station. That wasn't in the plans. But he kept driving. When he arrived, he saw that the squad cars were gone.

Quickly, he got out of his car and went into the station. Trooper Susan Callahan, as usual, was expressionless as she waited for him to explain why he was there.

"Look," he said, "I know I'm a pain in the butt about coming out here. And I don't know how much you know or how much you want to know or who's side you're on—"

"I'm not on anyone's side," she interrupted. "I have a job to do. If someone is a criminal, I'm supposed to arrest him."

"They don't let you out of the office, though, do they? You're a veteran, you're comfortable handling weapons, you've been in dangerous situations, but they keep you here."

"I'm the new kid on the block," she said.

He couldn't tell by her tone whether that irked her or whether it didn't matter. She gave nothing away, either in her visage or in her voice. It occurred to him that she'd be a good witness in giving testimony. Nothing flustered her.

"I just want you to know that I'm not on Trooper Meigle's Christmas card list. And I'm not on Chief Stark's Christmas card list either. There may come a time when you'll have to decide if you want to be on the Christmas card list or not. Some things are going on around in the area that are dead wrong. I can't prove any of it, but I'm keeping my eyes open. I'm not asking you to take sides. I'm asking you to keep your eyes open. Can you do that for me?"

She considered him as she waited. He didn't know if she was going to answer or not.

"I can't linger here," he said. "I have to get back. But I need to know your answer."

"I keep my eyes open because it's my job," she said. "If someone is a criminal, it's my job to make an arrest. I already told you that."

"If something is wrong," he continued with a feeling of desperation. This officer worked with Meigle every day; she would be able to tell if he tried to cover something up. "You won't look the other way?"

She looked, just for an instant, as if he'd gone too far. But the moment passed, and the angry expression vanished. Once again, her face was impassive.

"If someone is a criminal," she said again, "he should be arrested. If I'm the one that catches a criminal doing something that's against the law, it's my job to arrest him."

He nodded. "I'm going to hold you to that," he said.

"Officer Kennedy, you can't hold me to anything. I'm the one who does the holding."

7

QUESTIONS ABOUT JARROD

Although the battle re-enactment wouldn't take place until the following weekend, Kelly had made arrangements for the summer reading program participants to meet with some of the re-enactors who had arrived early for the event. The children would be able to see the tents where the re-enactors were sleeping, watch a display of musket marksmanship, and learn more about the lifestyles of long ago. Some of the re-enactors were also going to provide a cooking demonstration so that the children could sample foods that would have been common several centuries ago.

Parents had been eager to come along to help, recognizing that corralling sixty children of varying ages and grade levels was too much for just Kelly to handle. The children rotated from site to site, talking freely with the re-enactors who relished the opportunity to share their love of the historical past with the young.

"Hey, Kelly!"

Kelly turned at the sound of her name. Doug Iolus was coming her way, cameras as usual draped around his neck.

"I didn't expect to see you out here," he said when he reached her.

"I talked to some of the re-enactors that I know, the ones who come every year, and they were fine with us bringing out the kids to talk to them. It ties in with the summer reading program, 'A Blast from the Past,' and I've always wanted to tie in the re-enactment with reading."

Doug grinned. "You want to tie everything in with reading. Not that I blame you. Too bad Troy isn't here; we could meet and look at the photos I took from the cemetery the other night. Troy wants us to meet but he doesn't want anyone to know."

"Yes, I know. He texted me."

"Is he right, Kelly?" Doug asked, his intonation unusually serious. "Does he really think that we're being watched?"

"I don't know if he thinks we're being watched, but he thinks that the people who are involved with the drugs—and with Sean's murder—are ruthless."

"Killing an out-of-town visitor with a history of post-traumatic stress disorder is a lot different from offing the local librarian," Doug said. "Or the local reporter. You know small towns; strangers are strangers, but locals are extended family."

"It's better to do it Troy's way, I think," Kelly said, pondering Doug's words. *Where did Troy fit in the town's family tree? He was a newcomer, but was he still a stranger? And if so, did his life mean less to people? If that were true, would his death also mean less?* It was a disturbing thought.

"I suppose they'd want to kill him first anyway," Doug said. "You can't be surprised to hear that," he said, reacting to the startled alarm in Kelly's eyes. "He's the problem, at least the way they would see it. And it's all too easy to arrange for something to happen to a cop that wouldn't look suspicious."

"I think you've just convinced me that Troy is absolutely right in all of us making sure that we don't attract attention."

"Maybe so. What about Jarrod?"

Kelly sighed. "What about him?"

"You know he's driving Scotty Stark's Aston Martin?"

"Troy told me, but no, I don't know it personally. I haven't seen him since he came into the library on Monday and I don't plan to."

Doug raised his eyebrows. "You're not enemies, are you?"

"No, of course not, and I wish people would stop asking me about Jarrod as if I'd somehow have answers. We're not engaged."

"Sounds like you're not even friends anymore."

"I'm not sure we ever were friends," Kelly said thoughtfully.

"You were engaged, weren't you?" Doug reminded her, incredulity plain in his tone.

"Yes, but . . . sometimes, when you think you're in love, you don't consider friendship as part of the deal. It takes a wrong choice to make you realize that what's important is more than the trappings of being engaged."

"Sounds pretty deep to me."

She shrugged. "No. I was younger then."

"Right. By a whole year."

"A lot changes in a year."

"Like a new man in town?"

But she wasn't going to answer that. "You don't think I can re-evaluate a broken engagement on my own?"

Doug smiled. "I think you're a smart woman, Kelly, and Jarrod knows what he lost when you broke the engagement."

"Trust me, Jarrod will get over it. He'll find someone, and he's moving in the right circles. There's someone out there with a Michael Kors purse, Oakley sunglasses, and the right car for Jarrod; he'll find her."

"Designer wife?"

Kelly smiled at Doug. "I feel like I'm being interviewed. Should I tell you that everything I say is off the record."

Doug laughed in response. "No need for that," he said. "Troy has me wondering how Jarrod fits into all of this."

"Troy is working overtime on this. Jarrod likes the nicer things in life, but I don't believe he'd support drugs or murder as part of the process."

"If he asks to see you, will you go?"

"Now, I definitely feel like I'm being interviewed. I'm going to get back to the kids. I'm sure you, Troy and I will be meeting soon to go over the important things—and that doesn't include Jarrod. And since you're here, why don't you take a few photos of the kids talking to the re-enactors?"

"Already did, Kel, I'm way ahead of you."

"Take a few more," she advised.

The children were chattering excitedly on the way back to the library. The muskets fascinated some of the older boys, who found it hard to believe that such a clumsy weapon could have been used in battle. Everyone agreed that food had definitely improved since colonial days, an opinion that was reinforced when the bus pulled into the Sloppy Joes parking lot, as Kelly had arranged, so that the kids could have lunch.

Mia Shaw was working, and her eyes immediately went to her kids, who were excited about seeing their mom at her job. Lunch was sandwiches and a drink. Kelly asked Joe, the proprietor and a member of First Church, and Mia to come out so that the kids could thank them for their help and generosity. She took a photo of the kids and the adults to post on social media; Kelly always made a point of promoting local businesses that supported the library.

During the commotion intrinsic to any engagement involving so many kids, Kelly found a minute to go over to Mia, who was cleaning off the tables.

"How are you doing?" she asked.

"This trial hasn't even started and I'm already anxious about it," Mia admitted. "Mom is careful with the kids, she takes them to their friends' houses and picks them up; the mothers know about Travis so they're cooperative, even though they don't know everything that's happened. I'm lucky that everyone is so patient with me. I'm all nerves these days."

Kelly patted Mia on her arm. "I know; this has been especially hard on you and your parents."

"When's it going to end?" Mia asked, her voice low but imbued with a sense of urgency that bordered on panic. "If he gets a lesser sentence because that attorney of his makes it sound like Dad made Travis confess, he'll get a shorter sentence and we'll never be free of him. How does Travis manage it? His attorney must be costing a fortune and Travis doesn't have that kind of money."

Kelly could only listen in sympathy; she had no words of hope that would bolster Mia's state of mind. Mia was doing everything she could to make a new start so that, one day, she could regain custody of her kids. But if Travis served a shorter sentence instead of doing time for a murder charge, he'd find a way to challenge Mia's custody, if she got it. And if she didn't, would Leo and Millie suffer, should the legal system penalize Leo on the belief that he had abused his power and forced an innocent man to confess to a crime he hadn't committed?

Kelly knew that Troy was trying to devise a way for all the disparate threads of this situation to be brought together into a single, smooth seam that would clearly identify the guilty and the innocent. But how could anyone persuade Settler Springs residents that there was a diabolical conspiracy in progress that intended to allow the Starks, and their adherents, however high up in power they might be, to call the shots even if it meant that innocent people were destined to suffer? There had to be a way. There just had to be a way!

8

A NEW FACE ON THE TRAIL

A s Kelly and Troy finished their Saturday morning run on the Trail, they turned around for their usual walk back to the parking lot. The day promised to be hot and humid, typical July weather; unlike in the other seasons, when a run was immediately followed by breakfast at The Café, a summer run would require showers in between, which was the reason that they met a half hour earlier.

As they began the easy, loping walk that allowed them to cool down while still staying active, Troy seemed to suddenly turn and lose his balance. Quickly, Kelly moved closer and Troy draped his arm around her shoulder.

"I think I turned my ankle," he said.

"Lean on me," Kelly instructed. "I can give you some support. Just take it easy; you can wrap it when you get home and ice it."

"Yeah, I guess I'll have to," Troy said, limping at her side. They went on a few more yards, Kelly dispensing advice on how to handle an ankle sprain. But then, in the middle of her explanation of heat versus ice, Troy said, "Did you notice the guy who passed us on the other side of the Trail?"

"Who? No, I wasn't paying attention. Why?"

"Trooper Meigle. He was dressed for a run, but he kept looking over at us."

"Why?"

"I don't know. I'm guessing he thought we'd just be starting out, which we would have been if we'd met at seven instead of six-thirty."

"Is that why you 'sprained' your ankle?" she asked, cued to his rationale.

"It seemed like the best way for us to be together, without talking about what we really want to talk about. Doug said everyone knows that we run on Saturdays; I suppose Stark knows too."

"Lots of people run on Saturdays," Kelly countered, both impressed and surprised that Troy had been paying attention to both sides of The Trail's paths, which were separated by a long, narrow field of wildflowers. "You seriously think he came out here to spy on us?"

"I don't know. Why is he here? We've never seen him out here before. He doesn't live in Settler Springs."

"The Trail is a popular place," she reminded him. "People take walks here, they walk their dogs here, they have lunch at the picnic tables . . ."

"This is Meigle," Troy insisted, an edge to his voice. "Yes, I think he came out here to see—or hear—what we're up to. It's not hard to hear conversations on the other side of the path; we tune them out, but the voices carry."

"Well, if that's the case, all he knows is that you have a sprained ankle. You'll have to baby it for a while to make the story hold."

"I'm a fast healer," Troy grinned. They had reached their cars. He scanned the parking lot; no police cars were parked there, so Meigle must have come in his own vehicle.

They agreed to meet at The Café in an hour. Troy fully expected to see Meigle show up at the restaurant; before he left, wearing shorts and a tee-shirt from his Army days, he took the time to wrap an Ace bandage around his ankle, which was devoid of any swelling or signs of a sprain. But the bandage concealed its healthy condition; all anyone who bothered to notice would be able to see was the bulge beneath the sock caused by the bandage.

Kelly was taken aback when Troy asked the waitress, a new girl instead of the familiar Francie, if he could look at a menu.

"Why do you need a menu?" she asked. "It's breakfast, we know what they're serving."

But Troy didn't answer, although he periodically looked up from the menu so that he could see who was coming in the restaurant.

"Troy," Kelly said warningly, "you're acting like we're in a spy—"

"Your usual, the Hungry Man's Breakfast?" Troy interrupted smoothly. "Trooper Meigle, what brings you to Settler Springs?"

The state policeman looked as if he might not be in the best of moods. His jersey was damp with sweat and his hair was disheveled. Although he looked to be in good physical shape, it seemed that running was not his preferred form of exercise.

"I thought I'd try someplace new for breakfast," he said.

"You couldn't pick a better place than The Corner Café," Troy said cheerfully. "Kelly Armello, meet Trooper Don Meigle; he works with Chief Stark a lot. Kelly is pretty well known in town, Meigle. You might have heard the Chief mention her. Kelly and I run every Saturday on the Trail; we'll probably see you some time. You're welcome to join us for breakfast; we come here every Saturday too. Although we do stop at our homes to shower first," he said.

Meigle scowled. "I just came in for coffee to go," he said. "I'm going to need to shower, myself. Nice to meet you, Kelly."

"Next Saturday, 6:30," Troy called as Meigle went to the counter to order a coffee. "We just have one rule; no talking shop."

Meigle didn't answer, and when he had his coffee, he left the restaurant without acknowledging Kelly or Troy.

Troy, who had been in the midst of a discussion about the re-enactment weekend, broke it off quickly when he saw Meigle leave.

"That was brazen," Kelly commented.

"Why?"

"You more or less taunted him with innuendo: 'works with Chief Stark a lot,' 'you might have heard the Chief mention Kelly' and then, you invite him to join us and all but make it plain that he needs to shower."

She wasn't annoyed, just amused. It was a different side of Troy that she hadn't seen before, instead of the cautious, methodical police officer, Troy had been daring and cocky.

"There's no sense in playing innocent," Troy said after their breakfasts arrived. "But it's best to be on our guard. He'll try something else."

"Now he thinks you have a sprained ankle, okay, that might fly. But he'll never believe that we don't talk shop."

"Maybe not. But he didn't hear us saying anything that couldn't be overheard."

"I'm curious; where do you expect us to be able to go to discuss things that cannot be overheard?"

"Doug has photos from his cemetery surveillance; he also was at the council meeting to let us know what Tia Krymanski said. Those are definitely not subjects for public consumption. Any thoughts?"

"What about your house or mine?"

Troy shook his head. "I've seen Stark's car drive by my house. Maybe for no reason, but I don't want him to speculate. Unless he thinks we're shacking up," he said, just to bait Kelly.

She didn't rise to it. She didn't even acknowledge the comment. "We can't wait a lot longer, Troy, just to find a meeting place. I saw Mia Shaw this week and she's almost a wreck over this. Between worrying about her dad and how he's going to be treated during the trial, and her fear that Travis will get a lighter sentence and be able to press for some rights with his kids, she's on edge. And people who were former addicts have enough stress in their lives."

"I know that. And you're right; I'm dithering over this."

Kelly's voice softened. "I know that it's because of what happened to Sean that you're so concerned about something happening to one of us. We have to meet somewhere. And I think I know where!"

"Where?"

"First Church," she said. "We have a meeting room that people use for . . . well, for meetings."

"That doesn't seem right, meeting in a church and lying about the reason."

"We're not lying. I can let Reverend Dal know."

Troy shook his head. "No, it's better not to do that. Not until we have more proof. There's no sense in dragging him into this until we have conclusive evidence."

"Well, think of somewhere soon. Tomorrow we're having a heritage service at church for the re-enactors and there's a picnic afterward. But I'm free after that, say around 3 or so. What about Leo's camp?"

"We wouldn't know for sure that Mayor Truvert wasn't up there."

"Oh, yeah . . . I forgot."

They were silent for a while, eating their breakfasts but not really paying attention to the food. Troy was frustrated with the realization that in a small town like Settler Springs, nothing was private. Kelly was aggravated that Troy's caution, the reason for which she couldn't fault, was making it almost impossible to move forward on their efforts to get this solved before the Travis Shaw trial began.

"I just wish there were a way to get everyone who has a stake in this working toward the same objective," Troy said, keeping his voice low so that no one would hear. The Saturday breakfast crowd at The Café was a noisy one and it was unlikely that anyone would hear his conversation with Kelly, but he was definitely hyper-vigilant since Sean's death. He realized that it made him seem paranoid, but he couldn't think of a way for everyone to stay safe and still share what they knew, putting the pieces, however small, together to make the puzzle complete.

"The photos," Kelly said. "We have to look at them. Soon. In the midst of all of this, people are dying. Jimmy Patton is going to burn out as a paramedic if this doesn't stop. He takes those deaths seriously."

"I know. He's a good guy."

"Good enough to join the First Responders Bowling League in the fall?" Kelly teased.

"Maybe not that—maybe that's it . . . a town bowling league."

"What do you mean?"

"Jimmy could expand it from first responders to public servants," he said. "Journalists, police . . . librarians."

"How does that move us forward?"

"We have to plan, don't we? Let's go see if Jimmy is at the ambulance center after we eat."

"But we can't wait until fall to look at the photos," she objected.

"No, but we can start planning for the league. And if the planning starts with you, Doug and me, who's to say it won't grow into meetings to share what we know about the drug trafficking, the murder of Lyola Knesbit, and whether Eldredge is involved in any of this? We'll get in touch with Jimmy, put up signs . . . and see what happens."

Kelly wasn't at all sure that Troy's plan made any sense at all, but he seemed to think it did.

"Just so you know," Kelly said. "I'm a lousy bowler."

9

CONGRATULATIONS ON YOUR ENGAGEMENT?

J immy Patton, with no concept that the Public Servant Bowling League had an ulterior motive in its formation, was enthusiastic about the idea and agreed that he'd contact the first responders in other communities to enlist their support in broadening the original premise. He created signs encouraging people to join up; Troy, in a puckish mood, posted one of the signs on the police department bulletin board on Sunday morning. Kelly promised to do the same for the library and said she'd also talk to Reverend Dal about posting the sign in the church social room.

Doug, when he learned of the plan, just raised his eyebrows quizzically. "I haven't bowled in years," he said. "But I'll give it a try anyway. I hope that by the time fall gets here and we're actually supposed to be bowling in competition, we have this mess figured out. In the meantime, I'll meet you and Kelly at five o'clock this evening. I printed the photos; some of them are of kids. Teens," he corrected. "Kelly might recognize them. I could go through high school yearbooks to match them up, and I will if I have to, but it might be quicker to ask her."

"Where are we meeting?" Troy asked.

"My studio," Doug replied. "I share it with another photographer. I told Amber I'd need the place for about an hour and a half this evening. I explained to her that I'm meeting with a couple who are planning to get married and need a photographer for the wedding." Doug smiled brilliantly. "She was really happy to learn that you and Kelly are planning to tie the knot."

"What?" Troy thought he must not have heard correctly. It sounded like Doug had said—

"That you and Kelly are planning to tie the knot."

"You're joking, right?"

"Nope. The way I see it, we need a reason to meet. We need a place to meet. You two are the obvious connection."

"You can't just manufacture an engagement—Kelly will be ticked off when she hears."

"Kelly is a sport, she'll understand. Let her know, okay."

"About the meeting in your studio? I'll let her know. But you're going to explain about this engagement you've hatched up."

Kelly, unaware that she had become an engaged woman, showed up at Doug's studio a little early. Doug answered the door, but before he'd had a chance to do much more than let her in, Amber Andrini, the other photographer who rented the studio with Doug, hurried over to Kelly.

"Kelly, congratulations! I'm so happy for you!"

Kelly mentally ran through the recent events in her life, but nothing inspiring congratulations came to mind. Her expression was quizzical. "What—"

"Amber is on her way out," Doug said firmly, putting his hands on the other photographer's shoulders and steering her toward the door of the studio, just as Troy opened it.

"Troy, what great news!"

Troy, spotting Kelly in the studio, looked puzzled, managed a weak smile. He wasn't at all sure that this was going to go over very well. "Yeah . . ." he said.

"Home, Amber!" Doug said.

"Oh, I'm going, but if you need a videographer, I do that. Here's my card," she said, handing a business card to Troy before Doug could stop her.

"Thanks," he said, stepping beside them to go inside.

"Amber congratulated me," Kelly told him. "I'm not sure why."

"Oh, well, she just found out that we're engaged," Troy said, deciding that he might as well not waste time while waiting for Doug to come back into the studio. "Actually," he said, as Kelly's brown eyes grew darker, as if a storm were brewing somewhere in her pupils, "she found out before I did. Funny how things work in small towns."

"What are you talking about—"

"I'm not sure, but Doug here can fill you in. But quickly, okay? And lock the door. We don't want to be interrupted."

It was probably Troy's reminder that time was fleeting that abbreviated the lecture that Kelly delivered to Doug, who listened patiently as he put albums out on the table for the prospective engaged couple to view.

"In case anyone walks by and peers in the window," he said when Kelly finally took a breath. "They'll believe that you're here to go over the arrangements."

"Nice work," Troy said amiably, browsing through the albums. "If we were getting married, we'd definitely want you to do the photos, wouldn't we, Kelly?"

"What are you talking about?" Kelly demanded. She'd had a busy day with the Heritage Day service. The air conditioning in the church social room hadn't been working, and after the luncheon, she'd been part of the clean-up crew doing the dishes in a steamy kitchen that felt like a sauna. Only the fact that they needed to meet and look at the photographs of the cemetery visitors had kept her from going home and staying there, comfortably ensconced in her living room with an iced tea and a book, seated by the window where she could glance out at the street in between pages.

Her expression revealed that she was not amused by the levity in Troy's tone.

"You want us to pretend to be getting married so that we have an excuse to meet? That's preposterous."

"Not really," Doug said, pointing to one of the chairs at the table where the wedding albums were spread out. "It's really a perfect idea. If you and Troy are together, no one will be surprised. You're engaged. If you're sitting on his porch, and Stark drives by, no big deal. You're engaged. Now can we get down to business? I'm as sentimental as the next guy, but I've got photos and I want you to identify the people in them."

Kelly sat down after giving Doug a sideways look that was not designed to inspire bonhomie.

"Here," Doug said, putting the photographs on the table. "Recognize anyone?"

Kelly studied the photographs. Some faces were completely unknown to her. At her side, Troy was jotting down the makes and models of the cars, noting license plate numbers where they were visible.

"I couldn't get close up," Doug said by way of apology as he noticed Kelly peering intently at the images. "I have a clear shot at them from behind

General Porter's statue, but I don't dare get any closer."

"No," Troy said firmly. "It's not even safe for you to have been there to take these. They've already proven that they'll kill to keep this quiet."

His words and his inflection reminded both Kelly and Doug that Troy had already suffered a personal loss with the death of his friend Sean Claypool, one which had hit him particularly hard because of his conviction that Sean had been killed as a warning to Troy to back off from his unofficial investigation.

"I'm not aiming to be a hero," Doug said with a grin. "I just want to find out what's going on. Settler Springs is being undermined by drugs. If it's Stark who's involved in it, or running it, the town needs to find out. If Representative Eldredge is involved, then people need to find out before the election."

"If we can find out why Shaw killed Lyola Knesbit," Troy said evenly, "we've got our

answer."

"You really think that's the key?" Doug asked. "You think she was murdered by Shaw for a reason, not just theft?"

"I think that Shaw has some powerful friends," Troy said. "They want it to look like a random murder on Groundhog Day, so that Shaw just comes off as a petty drug pusher and thief."

"Dealing drugs isn't going to be ignored by a jury."

"Ignored, no. But compared to murder . . . especially if the jury thinks the confession was coerced by an ex-father-in-law looking for vengeance. Juries can be manipulated, and Shaw has a good attorney. A very good attorney. Mia says there's no way he could afford someone like that. And if a campaign against police brutality becomes part of Eldredge's re-election, it can dovetail with the trial. That won't be good for Leo. Or Mia, in the end, if Shaw comes into town wearing the mantle of a victim. Kelly and I have both talked to Mia, and she's agonizing over this."

Both men looked to Kelly, waiting for her to add her views, but she was staring at one of the photographs, holding it in front of her, a frown on her face.

"Troy . . . look at this photograph. Not at the guy in the foreground, look behind him. To the left. Look at the girl. That's Carrie! Carrie Krymanski!"

It made sense. Tragic, alarming sense. It explained why Tia had gone to the council meeting to berate Chief Stark for not doing enough to combat the town's drug problem. Carrie had broken up with her boyfriend during her senior year in high school and in the ensuing months, her grades had fallen off, she'd lost her job as a server at Sloppy Joes, and she had to take summer school classes in order to receive a diploma. The school had let her take part in the graduation ceremony, but only on condition that she make up the failed credits over the summer so that she could receive her diploma.

Somewhere during that time, Carrie must have turned, as too many young people did, to taking drugs as a way of deflecting the angst of her senior year. But Troy wondered if it might have started before the break-up with her boyfriend. He recalled how troubled she'd been when her brother Lucas was falsely accused of the murder in Daffodil Alley. Carrie had gotten into a fight at school and the police had been called. Troy had driven her home after the incident, trusting that her mother would administer the brand of Krymanski tough love that kept her brood under her control and out of real trouble. But this was something beyond Tia's ability to manage. And even though she was a Krymanski by marriage and a divorced one at that, Chief Stark had found her an easy target at the council meeting when he nurtured the myth that it was families like the Krymanskis, not good, upstanding people, who ended up taking drugs.

"What do we do?" Doug asked quietly. He hadn't noticed that Carrie was in any of the photographs. He knew many of the high school kids and he was the photographer who took the school class pictures, but it had taken Kelly's keen eye to spot the girl in the background.

"Lucas hasn't been in the library lately," Kelly answered. "He's not in as often in the summer, and with Mrs. Stark there every day, he's even more likely to avoid us. But even if he came in, I don't know how I'd bring up the subject. When something is wrong, Lucas usually brings it up himself."

"What about asking his mother herself?"

Kelly hesitated. "She works a lot, but I don't want to ask her about something like this at The Café."

"Home?"

Kelly sighed. "I could, but that's not usually where I'd see her. I'd feel like I was invading."

Doug looked at Troy, who shook his head. "The last thing she needs is a cop knocking on her door. No, this has to be done another way. Tia went to the council meeting and from all we hear, she didn't get much satisfaction."

"She got branded as a Krymanski," Doug recalled. "It was smoothly done. Chief Stark knows his audience. They want to believe that only certain people are vulnerable to drugs or crime or getting in trouble and that's what he tells them. I'm just now starting to put the pieces together myself, but if you and Troy hadn't filled me in on some of the background, I wouldn't have known what's going on. I know that Chief Stark has always been too slick for my tastes, but I don't think I'd have gone further than that. It's you two who got Lucas free of a murder charge."

"He could never have been charged," Troy argued. "Kelly and I pushed it, I agree, but if it had come to trial, no jury would have swallowed the story."

"Maybe not," Doug said, "but there wouldn't have been anything tying Scotty Stark to her murder. Boyfriend-girlfriend, yes, and he'd have had to get out of that. But his family would have gotten him out of it. They couldn't because Lucas saw Scotty dump the girl's body, and your friend Mrs. Hammond saw what was going on in the alley. That came from what you two found out. How do you know that getting Carrie hooked isn't part of the plan?"

"That seems a little far-fetched," Troy disputed. "I'm willing to believe almost anything about Stark, but that's a little beyond my reality orientation."

"Sean Claypool's suicide as a murder is beyond most other people's reality orientation," Doug said. "But you don't find that hard to believe."

"They're not the same—"

"Maybe they are. And maybe it's time we started realizing that this is even more unsavory than we would have thought. Troy, you said that what we need is a whole group of people noticing things." He smiled. "The First Responders Bowling League is part of it. Your engagement is part of it. Jarrod Zabo is part of it."

Kelly began to object. "Jarrod is an opportunist, yes I admit that. I should have seen it from the beginning. But I don't believe he's involved in murder and drugs."

"I didn't say he was," Doug replied. "But someone has to find out just what he is involved in with this campaign and you're the obvious one."

"Isn't that going to be a little peculiar," Troy said, "if we're engaged and Kelly is suddenly chatting up her ex?"

"I wish you'd stop calling him that," Kelly said angrily.

"Well, he's not your current," Troy said. "Do you suppose you could start wearing your engagement ring that he gave you? Angela never gave mine back, so I can't—"

Kelly stood up. "No, I don't suppose I could start wearing the engagement ring that he gave me," she said, "because I gave it back. Of course, I gave it back. I don't have it, and I wouldn't wear it if I did. Marriage isn't a pose, it's a covenant. I'm not sure I want to play pretend this way. I want to solve this as much as you do, and you too, Doug, but I'm not going to do it in a way that makes me feel like I'm playing a part in an amateur theatre production."

She was mad. Really mad. Troy could tell and he knew that he had to make amends. Kelly took things seriously, he ought to know that.

"Kelly," he said. "I'm sorry. I wasn't mocking marriage. I was just—"

"Being a jerk?" she offered.

He deserved that. "Yeah, I guess I was being a jerk," he said. "And it probably won't be the last time I'm a jerk. But I don't mean to be. I . . . " it was hard enough to express himself around her, never mind having the local town reporter on the scene as well. "I'll try not to be a jerk," he said. "I'll try not to make this any more uncomfortable than it's going to be. I know that pretending to be engaged to me isn't something that sits well with you. But for now, for this, we're all going to be called upon to show a public side that doesn't match what we really are. Can you do it?"

Kelly didn't know what to say. How could she tell Troy that part of the reason she was resistant to the ruse was because she could happily imagine herself being engaged to marry him? But their concepts of commitment and intimacy were poles apart. Putting a false masquerade of an engagement on view for all eyes to see only made the true separation between them all the more apparent.

"Please."

Strange how that one word could alter a moment. Troy wasn't someone who liked having to ask for help. He wasn't like she was, willing to reach out for aid whenever she felt that she needed it. Troy was independent and rugged, used to depending upon his own wits and his own abilities. He liked it that way. Now he needed help.

"Okay."

"Well," Doug said briskly as he gathered up the photographs, "I'm glad that you've weathered your first quarrel as an engaged couple. Kissing and making up are all part of the romance."

"Don't push it," Kelly warned.

Doug gazed at her beatifically. "I don't know what you mean," he said.

"Yes, you do," she retorted. "By Monday morning, news of our engagement is going to be all over town and you're not going to do anything to prevent that from happening. We're going to have to pretend to be talking about marriage when we're really trying to bring criminals to justice. So we'd better have our stories straight and we'd better know exactly what it is that we're trying to do because there's too much at stake for us to get it wrong. There's Carrie and her family; there's Mia and her future; there's Leo and his reputation."

"And," Troy added, "there's an election coming up with a candidate who might be an accessory to murder."

APARTMENT BREAK-IN

Settler Springs adjusted to the presence of men in buckskins as it always did for the week of the Independence Day festivities, but Troy had to tell more than one living history purist that he could not bring his musket into the town. It was one thing, he explained to an earnest, bearded young man wearing a coonskin cap and carrying a musket, for the colonial reenactors to have their firearms in the designated area. But not in town.

"But sir," the young man persisted, "I daren't go without my weapon, lest I be set upon by wild critters or Injuns." He lifted his cap. "I'm partial to my pate, you see."

Troy fixed the young man with a stern eye. "I outrank you, soldier, and I'm telling you, go back to your tent and leave your musket there."

"If I lose my scalp because I lacked proper defense, it'll be on your soul," the young man said as he turned.

"I'll take that risk."

"They're kinda funny, aren't they?"

Lucas Krymanski had come up to Troy early enough to catch the exchange, but Troy hadn't noticed his presence.

"They're really into their history," Troy said diplomatically.

"Yeah, but do they want to live like that? No TV, no video games, no potato chips, nothing," Lucas shook his head as he listed the achievements of the modern era as he prioritized them.

"I don't know. I'm glad to have hot running water and indoor toilets, myself." Which reminded Troy; he needed to stop by the field and make sure the company in charge of delivering and emptying the portable toilets was on schedule; the police station had gotten a complaint that there was a smell coming from the latrine area, as the reenactors called it, and Chief Stark had assigned Troy to that task. Kyle had given him a look of sympathy as he left the station, his shift over.

Troy was well aware that the assignment was deliberate, but it was a legitimate concern and he didn't take it with hostility, perhaps disappointing the police chief if Stark had hoped to demean him.

"I'm going up to the encampment now," Troy said. " Want to join me?"

Lucas looked dubious. "Why?'

"No reason. I haven't seen you in a while. How's everything at home?"

It wasn't necessary to be subtle with Lucas. "Carrie is in trouble, Mom knows it. She's using stuff. She's— she didn't come home the other night and Mom didn't know what to do. That's never happened before. Mom always knows what to do."

Troy could sense that Lucas, for all his mischief, preferred a world in which his mother was the arbiter of authority.

"Using stuff. Drugs?"

"Yeah," Lucas said. "You won't arrest her, will you?" he asked anxiously, as if his response would get his sister into trouble.

"If I see her using, or buying, or selling, I will," Troy said honestly. "If she's breaking the law, she'd be arrested."

"Mom—she and Carrie fight all the time. I've been hanging around Carrie as much as I can, trying to be there without getting on her nerves. I'm afraid something is going to happen to her."

"I'll keep an eye out for her. Not to arrest her," he said quickly, noticing that Lucas' initial relief was tempered by the realization that being under the scrutiny of a police officer carried its own risk. "I can't ignore it if she's doing something she shouldn't, but if there's a way to keep her out of trouble, I'll do it. And it doesn't hurt for you to hang around her, even if she's not always pleased to have her younger brother there."

"She doesn't seem to notice," Lucas said. "She doesn't pay attention to us."

There was a lament in the boy's voice. Troy felt sorry for him. Lucas was a good kid and Tia Krymanski was a good mother. Carrie had been a good kid too, and probably still was. Except for drugs. That was a different path.

Troy didn't have any words of comfort for Lucas; the boy was a teenager and he knew, maybe in some ways better than Troy knew, what was going on with the kids his age. Tia was firm with her kids, but somehow Carrie had managed to escape her mother's vigilance, and if something didn't happen soon, she'd end up in jail or dead.

Seen from that perspective, checking on the toilet pick-up at the reenactor encampment, while it might have lacked dignity, was almost welcome. He went to the encampment, spoke with the groundskeepers and learned that the company was maintaining their set schedule, but the town hadn't ordered enough of the portable toilets. Budget cuts, they'd been told.

Troy sympathized with the groundskeepers and said he'd pass the word on to the police chief and mayor, but he knew, and they knew, that nothing would be done about it. Even though the annual reenactment brought money into the town, the mayor had been pleased to present a lower budget to the town. This was this result.

He left the encampment, waved at the young man who had returned and was now leaving without his musket, and drove back to the police station. His cell phone rang just as he was pulling into his parking spot.

It was Mia Shaw. "Troy," she said, her voice shaking. "Someone has been in my apartment."

"I'm on my way. Mia, are you in any danger?" he asked as he put the police car in gear and steered back into the street. "Is anyone there?"

"No one," she said on a sob that seemed to catch in her throat. "I got home from work and I know things are different. Nothing obvious."

Troy had his cell phone on speakerphone as he drove out to the apartment where Mia lived. "Okay," he said, not questioning her instincts, even though he knew that, in order to make an official complaint, she'd have to have something more damning that just a feeling that things were different. He believed her.

"I walked in—"

"Was the door locked?" he interrupted her as she opened the door and let him in.

She nodded. "It was locked. But I know someone was in here, Troy, I can tell. Things were just moved a bit . . . my coffee cup, I always put it in the sink in the morning. It's on the counter. The remote, I always leave it by the TV and it's on the couch."

"Anything else?"

"Isn't that enough?" she demanded angrily.

"For me, yes. I believe you. But that doesn't mean it's something that rises to the level of a break-in. What about the other rooms? Your bedroom?"

She began to cry. "Someone was in there. My bureau drawers, someone . . . someone was in them. My clothes are moved around."

"Messed? Tossed around?"

She shook her head. "No. Just . . . just moved. I know they're moved. I've gotten into the habit of putting everything away neatly—it's a rehab thing. A way to bring order into our lives. I've kept it up even though I'm out now. And they're moved around."

"Underwear?" he asked crisply, knowing it was an uncomfortable question but also knowing that this was where someone who wanted Mia to know that he could invade her private space at will was likely to leave a sign.

Her thin face seemed to crumple into tears. She nodded.

"Show me."

She led him into her bedroom. It was a utilitarian room, no frills or flourishes, just the kind of order that wouldn't have been out of place in a military barracks.

She opened the drawer. Underwear was personal and Mia was a young woman and like any young woman, she was going to dress for her age, even if no one was going to know that she liked lace and silk. He could tell that she was embarrassed and in response, he maintained a matter-of-fact demeanor.

"What's been moved?"

"They're not in their places . . . I keep everything in place."

It looked as though someone had hurriedly rifled through the stack of undergarments. If anyone were arrested for the break-in, a judge would find it unlikely that Mia was so neat that she could tell for certain that someone had been searching through her bureau drawers. It was, again, a cunning way to leave a sign that someone could get into her apartment without her having recourse to accuse anyone.

"Do you feel unsafe staying here?"

"This is my home! I have to be safe here."

Troy nodded. "You have a deadbolt lock?"

"Yes, I lock it at night, but I can't lock it when I go out."

The intruder had probably counted on that. Troy remembered when Mia's son Mason had been abducted, he'd been returned with a key that he said was a present from his father. Travis Shaw. Stark had refused to follow up on the trail, and thus far, Troy's efforts had been in vain. And the abductor, Eddie Kavlick, was dead.

"You could stay with your parents," Troy suggested.

Mia shook her head. "No, I can't. I'm a grown up, I can't go running back home. Besides . . . I like it here. I want to stay, and I want my kids to be able to come here eventually."

"Ever thought of getting a dog?"

"I don't know if we're allowed pets," she said.

"It might be worth asking. A dog's bark is a pretty effective warning to stay away for someone trying to break in. I know the woman who runs the shelter over in Lamont."

"I'll check with the landlord," she said, looking relieved at the thought that she might have an option other than moving back in with her parents. "Troy, how long is this going to keep happening?"

He suspected that the harassment of Mia Shaw would go on through the trial. After that, who knew? It depended upon the verdict.

"I don't know," he lied. "Find out if your lease allows you to have a dog."

"Who's doing this?"

He didn't know the answer to that either. But he had a hunch that Chief Stark knew.

OVERDOSE AT THE LIBRARY

P olice Chief Stark and Mrs. Stark had been the guests of Representative Eldredge at a 4th of July gathering to celebrate the French and Indian War battle that the reenactors would be commemorating on the holiday weekend. It had been an evening of red, white and blue, full of florid speeches from local politicians and county leaders congratulating one another on their role in the continuation of the patriotic fervor. Fresh off that event, Mrs. Stark was in an exceedingly good mood the next day when she arrived at the library in the morning, and Kelly knew why. It was good publicity, not just for the candidate but for his supporters, especially those as visible as the Starks.

Her friends who came into the library complimented her on the coverage, eager to chat about the event and the part she had played in bringing attention to their town. It seemed to Kelly that their praise was so fulsome as to be absurd, but Mrs. Stark didn't seem to see it that way. Mrs. Stark replied with polished modesty that it was wonderful to be part of one of Settler Springs' most cherished traditions and that she and Chief Stark were honored and humbled to represent their town in such a patriotic way.

"She sounds like she's running for office," Carmela muttered as she went into Kelly's office to hand her the mail.

Kelly smiled in sympathy. Carmela and Kelly had enjoyed the respite of the previous days, when Mrs. Stark had not been in the library after the uproar at the council meeting. But apparently the library board president was restored to good humor by hobnobbing with the political crowd. If Kelly hadn't been so busy putting together the end-of-the-month statistical reports, she'd have spelled Carmela at the circulation desk, but the reports needed to be done.

"I might take an early lunch," Carmela muttered darkly.

Kelly nodded. "That's fine." An early lunch, joined with Mrs. Stark's lunch hour, would give Carmela two hours of reprieve. Although Kelly had a lot of administrative work to do, she knew that Carmela's tolerance for Mrs. Stark was limited. She'd get her work done one way or the other, but in the meantime, she needed to make sure that Carmela didn't give way to her temper when Mrs. Stark's goading got underway. "What's that noise?"

"Kids coming in," Carmela said, glancing toward the front door. "Older kids."

It was unusual to see the older kids in the library during summer, when they didn't have school assignments, especially in the morning. Carmela would definitely be taking an early lunch, Kelly knew. Although her demeanor was vastly improved over what it had been in the past, she was not particularly fond of the adolescent patrons.

"What are you doing here?" Mrs. Stark's voice was strident, making no effort to present herself as the polished and professional businesswoman in Settler Springs. That meant that the new arrivals at the library were not anyone that the Starks regarded as having influence.

Kelly rose from her chair. Whatever it was and whoever they were, Mrs. Stark would only make things worse. She left the office and went to the circulation desk.

There were four or five kids in a group, wandering around the library; they weren't causing any trouble, but they didn't seem to have a real purpose for being there. Then Kelly noticed Lucas Krymanski, hovering on the edges of the group as if he didn't quite belong.

"Hello, Lucas," Kelly said, her tone as alm as Mrs. Stark's was belligerent.

"Hi, Miz Armello," Lucas said, but his eyes weren't on her. Kelly followed the direction of his scrutiny.

"Hello, Carrie," Kelly said, noticing Lucas' sister among the group. She looked disheveled, as if she'd slept in the clothes she was wearing and had just gotten out of bed without changing.

Carrie's gaze slid over Kelly and past her. "Can I use the bathroom?" she asked.

The bathroom door was kept locked when not in use. Kelly took the key from the drawer and unlocked the door. "Go ahead," she said.

Carrie mumbled her thanks.

Something wasn't right. Kelly looked at Lucas, who was trying to make his way to the restroom aisle of the library without being noticed by Mrs. Stark, who was standing like a sentinel watching the other kids, waiting for them to do something wrong so that she could have a reason to eject them.

Carmela might not have been a fan of the teen patron, but if Mrs. Stark was opposed to them, then Carmela welcomed them. "Anything I can help you with?" she inquired of one of the kids.

The boy shook his head. But his eyes weren't on her; he, like Lucas, was intent upon the entrance to the restrooms. The direction in which Carrie had gone.

It was just a feeling . . . and she hoped she was wrong. "Carmela," Kelly said quietly. "Can you bring me the Narcan?"

Alarm was plain in the older woman's features. "Where is it?" she whispered.

They had hidden the anti-overdose medication after Mrs. Stark had voiced her opposition to the library having any pharmaceutical which, she said, would encourage drug addicts to come to the library. Kelly had gotten into the habit of hiding it in a new place each week, just in case Mrs. Stark went exploring.

She tried to make sure Carmela knew where it was each time, but Carmela had probably forgotten the most recent place of concealment.

"In the bottom drawer of the filing cabinet with the past year's auditors' reports."

"You, there!" Mrs. Stark called out to a girl who was standing in front of the DVD racks. "What do you want? There's no loitering allowed in here!"

"I'm just looking to see what you have."

"The cases are empty," Mrs. Stark told her with a note of triumph. "There's nothing in any of them. We keep the disks locked up in back."

"I wasn't going to steal them—"

Kelly saw Lucas dart into the restroom. Quickly, she followed him, her heart beating furiously, first grabbing the key from the drawer.

Carrie was on the floor. She looked to be unconscious. Carmela came into the restroom, the Narcan in her hand.

"Do you know how to use it?" Carmela asked, handing it to Kelly.

Kelly nodded. She'd been to a conference on the subject the previous year. "Go call 911," she said to

Carmela. "Tell them that we have an overdose in the library."

Mrs. Stark, having noticed the sudden rush of activity in the vicinity of the restroom, appeared in the doorway, saw Carrie's slumped body, and shrieked as Kelly, kneeling on the floor, was administering the nasal spray to the girl.

"What are you doing!"

Kelly didn't answer. Carmela and Lucas, standing like a phalanx between Kelly and Mrs. Stark, did not move.

"She can't do that here! Not in the library! What are you doing? Kelly, I told you to get rid of that—that— it'll just encourage addicts to come here to die! The library will get a bad reputation, you'll ruin—"

Kelly was paying no attention. She was barely aware of Mrs. Stark's ranting, so intent was she on Carrie's condition. If Carrie died—

"Kelly, what have you got here?"

Jimmy Patton was in the doorway. He hadn't wasted any time. Everyone moved back to let him in. "You gave her Narcan?"

Kelly nodded.

"Good. You've saved her life. We're taking her to the hospital."

"Carmela, can you cover? I'm going in the ambulance with Carrie," Kelly directed. "We'll call your mom, Lucas, and let her know that you're here."

"Get her out of here," Mrs. Stark, her voice shrill, was yelling. "She's going to give the library a bad name. And Kelly, I'm going to see that you're fired. I told you to get rid of that—that drug addict saver, and you deliberately disobeyed me."

"Stand back, Mrs. Stark," Jimmy directed. "We'll take over now. Kelly, thanks for doing what you did."

"Kelly, if you leave, you're fired. How dare you do this to the library? This is an upstanding institution, not a haven for junkies. If she's a drug addict, then she might as well die. She's not serving any purpose. You're making this library a byword for criminals."

Kelly wasn't paying any attention. She had grabbed her purse and was following the stretcher out the doors while Mrs. Stark continued her diatribe against Kelly and all that would result because of what she had done.

Mrs. Stark didn't notice the expression on Jimmy Patton's face as he and the other paramedic took Carrie out of the library on a stretcher, but Kelly did. He looked as if he were in the company of Medusa, avoiding the eyes of a monster whose gaze could turn a person to stone.

JIMMY PATTON'S CONCERNS

top by the ambulance station sometime today on your shift?

S   Troy knew why Jimmy Patton was texting him. Kelly had filled him in as soon as the ambulance arrived at the hospital and Carrie was taken to the emergency room yesterday. She'd stayed with Lucas and Tia in the waiting room until the doctor came to tell them that Carrie was okay, scared to death, but okay, and the doctor had added that fear was probably a really good result.

He and Kelly had talked that night when she got home. The doctor wanted Carrie to go to rehab, but Carrie was reluctant. She wasn't going to do it ever again, she vowed, her eyes filling with tears. Kelly had told Troy that she didn't want to intrude on a family crisis, but she thought that it would do Carrie good if she talked to Mia Shaw. Tia had looked relieved at the idea and Carrie seemed to find this acceptable. But Carrie wasn't getting off that easily; once she was okay, Tia was restored to her familiar posture as the mother lioness. She told Carrie she was going to rehab, she was going to get her credits and her diploma, and there wasn't going to be any more of this going on. Then Tia had burst into tears, startling both of her children, who were used to seeing her as the ever-calm, implacable ruler of the house. "I'm not going to lose you, Carrie!" Tia had cried out. Somewhere between the tears and the exclamation, Tia had reinstated herself as the head of the household and Carrie hadn't balked.

Troy wasn't sure it would last, but he figured it was a good start and might save Carrie's life in the long run.

Sure, he texted. *I'll be by around 4.*

Mindful of the fact that paramedics had little control of when they'd be out on a call, Troy showed up just after 3:30. The crew had just gotten back from an ambulance run. When Eli Jansen took the ambulance to fill up the gas tank, Jimmy and Troy were alone.

Jimmy looked tired, his genial features showing lines that Troy didn't recall seeing there before. Maybe he just hadn't slept well, Troy reasoned. Jimmy wasn't old enough for lines in his face.

Jimmy poured two cups of coffee from the carafe that had just been filled with a fresh pot. "First of all, congratulations," he said.

"What—oh, thanks," Troy replied. He was going to have to do better at remembering that he was, at least for the purposes of the investigation, engaged to Kelly.

Jimmy managed a grin. "Not having second thoughts, are you? Kelly's a great gal; anyone who marries her is a lucky man. I've known her a long time. She was in my wife's Girl Scout troop back in the day. So, congratulations. You're a lucky guy. You two set a date yet?"

"Uh—no, not yet."

Jimmy nodded. "I guess you just got started planning."

"Barely even that," Troy said honestly. Why was Jimmy stalling?

Jimmy looked down at his coffee cup. "Kelly . . . did she tell you about yesterday? At the library?"

"She told me. Carrie's going to be okay."

"She needs to get treatment. I think her mom will stick to the plan. Every parent is overwhelmed when they find out their kid is using. Tia, give her credit, didn't dodge it. She tried to light a fire under the council at the meeting, but . . ."

He looked up to meet Troy's gaze. "Chief Stark cut her down. He pretty much said that it's people like the Krymanskis who have drug addicts in their family. I know that's not true, but it's what people want to believe."

"Maybe what happened yesterday is a good thing."

"Maybe. Mrs. Stark won't really fire Kelly, will she?"

"Kelly has heard from a couple of board members who heard about what happened. They aren't going to let her try to fire Kelly. They were pleased that Kelly did what she did. But I don't understand. Why was Mrs. Stark so opposed to Kelly using Narcan on Carrie? It saved the kid's life."

Troy knew that Jimmy had to come to the realization on his own that the Starks had their own reasons for what they said and did when the subject of drugs in Settler Springs came up in a conversation.

"Kelly did the right thing," Troy answered. "That doesn't mean that everyone thinks someone using drugs should get a second chance."

Jimmy shook his head. "This was more than that," he said. "I've seen those people; they feel that if a person is an addict, they're going to die anyway so why waste a second chance on someone who's going to need another one? I don't agree, but I hear it all the time. This was different. If you could have heard Mrs. Stark, seen the look on her face . . . it was like she had a personal reason for wanting Carrie to die of an overdose. It was—you remember back around Memorial Day, when you were at The Pizzaria and I was picking up pizzas for my crew?"

"I remember."

"I asked you if there was bad blood between you and Chief Stark, you remember?"

"I remember. And I asked you what you thought about the drug trafficking in Settler Springs."

"And I didn't really answer." Jimmy took a sip of coffee. "I've thought for a long time that Chief Stark was burying his head in the sand. He knows there are drugs in town; he gets the report from our calls. Not names, not on all calls. But if we don't get there in time, and there's a death, we call the police. So, he knows it's not just a few nervous Nellies overreacting. But I figured he just didn't want the town to get a bad rep. I didn't agree with his approach, but I got it. Today, I saw his wife's face . . . Troy, there was not an ounce of compassion in that woman's eyes. Not an ounce. And I don't get it. Whether you think Narcan should be used to bring an addict back from OD'ing or not, that's not the point. You should feel something—pity, fear, sadness, something. I know Mrs. Stark is well thought of in town. She's a businesswoman, and she's good at her work; she's my insurance agent and she's on top of things. I know she's big in her church; she's the treasurer over there at LifeLight Church, finally got the position she wanted, although it's a shame Mrs. Knesbit had to die so she could get it. But—"

"What did you say?"

Jimmy looked abashed. "Bad choice of words; I know murder isn't a joke. It's an open secret that Mrs. Stark wanted to be the church treasurer, but it was Mrs. Knesbit's job, and the church council wasn't pushing her out. She needed the extra income and Mrs. Stark didn't, and churches tend to go by that."

"I wasn't faulting your choice of words. I didn't know that Mrs. Stark wanted the job."

"Oh, we hear all the gossip here at the station. How do you think I heard about your engagement?"

"I probably don't even want to guess. Sorry for sidetracking you. You were talking about Mrs. Stark."

"Oh, yeah. I just never thought I'd see the day when a church-going woman, pillar-of the-community person like Lois Stark would give her true feelings away like that. It got me to thinking about Chief Stark. I thought he didn't want to face the truth about drugs. Now I'm wondering if he wants to hide it."

Troy concealed his reaction. If Jimmy was ready to start questioning the commonly held truth, then maybe others would be as well.

"Then I got to thinking about the Mayor. You know, Chief Stark's brother-in-law. Mrs. Stark's brother. And I wondered about him. Nothing to go by, but he doesn't seem to be paying attention to what we're telling him, what teachers in the school district are telling him . . . this isn't just a prank. This is a crisis. He's the mayor. He should be listening."

"Maybe he is listening. To his sister and his brother-in-law."

"Maybe we need louder voices," Jimmy said.

Again, Troy kept his emotions in check, although he couldn't help but feel a brief surge of euphoria that finally, someone else perceived how deeply rooted the problem was, and how the network of power between the mayor and the police chief jeopardized the citizens of Settler Springs by lulling them into a completely false sense of safety. Drugs? They were a problem for other families in town, not the good families. Chief Stark was keeping the town safe. Mayor Truvert didn't get distracted by low-class social problems. Did no one think of Scotty Stark, now in prison for murder?

He looked Jimmy straight in the eye. "Maybe we need to know who's willing to speak up," he said. "Who's willing to find out what's going on and not let the police chief and the mayor hide behind feel-good slogans."

"I'm willing," Jimmy said.

Troy put down his coffee cup. "Then I guess we're ready to have the first planning meeting of the Settler Springs Public Servants Bowling Team."

14

THE SETTLER SPRINGS PUBLIC
SERVANTS BOWLING TEAM

Kelly would be there, of course. And Doug, who said that journalists were public servants, too, even if people in power thought they were troublemakers. Jimmy was coming. Mia Shaw wanted to come; maybe waitresses weren't public servants, but she felt that she could contribute. But she was going over to the Krymanski house that evening to talk to Carrie, and Troy agreed with her; that was more important right now. Carmela Dixon was coming. She belonged to her church bowling team and boasted that she was the "Strike Queen" of the church league.

Troy made a point of mentioning the meeting that afternoon before Kyle left, while Chief Stark was still in the office. Kyle shook his head. "My bowling days are behind me," he said candidly. "If this thing gets off the ground, let me know and I'll keep score."

"Good enough," Troy said. "I don't know what kind of interest any of the other towns are showing. We'll find out what kind of publicity we need to do tonight."

The meeting was going to be held at Jimmy Patton's house. Since he'd been the initial one to suggest a First Responders Bowling League, it was logical that he'd be the ringleader for the expanded Public Servants Bowling League. But tonight's meeting, while it would lay the groundwork for an actual bowling league, had a much more local purpose.

Chief Stark had okayed Troy having the night off. The State Police would cover, he said. He might even join the league himself, he said amiably; he used to be a pretty good bowler in years past. Troy encouraged him to join. It was a way, Troy said, for Settler Springs to get to see the policemen, ambulance crews, and other civic workers in a more casual setting. Neither man was lulled by the other one's response, but Troy made sure that the police chief had no reason to be suspicious of a bowling team.

"My wife is at her book club meeting," Jimmy said as he welcomed the arrivals. "But she didn't want us to starve, so here are some crackers to go with her buffalo-chicken dip—she makes great buffalo-chicken dip."

Kelly had brought a veggie tray and a plate of brownies. Carmela came in with her specialty, something she said she made for all her church functions, a vegetarian pizza appetizer. Troy hadn't intended to bring anything until Kelly mentioned what she was taking to the meeting; at the last minute, he'd stopped at the store and picked up a salami and cheese platter and a box of crackers.

"Well," Doug said as he surveyed the table, "I'm a bachelor with no woman around to advise me on these things, so I didn't bring anything."

"Now that Troy is engaged," Carmela said, "he's learning fast."

Carmela had been annoyed that she'd learned about the engagement from a library patron and Kelly had been quick to explain that she hadn't planned to announce the engagement until she and Troy had picked out an engagement ring. That explanation mollified Carmela and bought Kelly time, even as she fumed at the position she was in, having to lie over an engagement that was in itself a lie.

Troy, wisely, didn't rise to Doug's jibe, although he shot the cheerful photographer a warning look across the table.

Once they had all helped themselves to the snacks and were seated around the table, Jimmy spoke. "I went to the bowling alley and told them what we're planning," he said. "We need to pick a night when we'd bowl. I told him that we'll have those details before the end of August; leagues get started up again in the fall and we have to pick a night that doesn't conflict with anyone's."

"You mean we really are going to bowl?" Doug said.

"Of course, we are," Jimmy said. "We have to. It's as good a cover as anything for people getting together for a reason that isn't going to be obvious. And we all know why we're here, and why we're doing this. Don't we?" He looked across the table at Troy. "Maybe you can fill in some of the missing pieces?"

"Everyone here is aware that something isn't right in town," Troy said. "We've all either experienced it," he nodded at Carmela, who nodded back with a somber expression on her face, "or we're witnessing it, like Jimmy and Kelly did yesterday, or our gut instincts are telling us something. It goes without saying that what we discuss here tonight, and every night, goes no further than the people here. I might sound like I'm overreacting, but a good friend of mine is dead and I know he didn't kill himself. I believe Sean Claypool was killed as a warning to me to back off. I can't prove it. Not yet. But if each of us starts to pay close attention to what's going on around us, and we share what we know, I think we might be able to put a stop to this before Settler Springs just becomes the personal fiefdom of the Starks and the Truverts."

Everyone's eyes were on him. Even Doug, who was energetically refilling his plate with the offerings on the table, was intent on Troy's words.

"We think it started on Groundhog Day, with the murder of Lyola Knesbit," Troy said. "Carmela and Mia Shaw were pulled into that. They've had to deal with harassment as a result of Travis Shaw being in prison. Leo Page has been accused of forcing a confession out of Shaw. We know it's not true, but the circumstances are against Leo, and Shaw has a good attorney who's going to play on any doubts he can stir up among the members of the jury. We need to find out why Mrs. Knesbit was murdered before Shaw's defense team makes a convincing claim that she was killed by a random thief, and Shaw just happened to find the purse and decided to grab it in case he could sell it. He'll use the drug addict angle because it's a workable distraction against the murder charge. Carmela, you know the people at the church where Mrs. Knesbit was treasurer."

"Mrs. Stark is the treasurer there now," Carmela reminded him, her lips twisted as if she'd eaten something that tasted bad.

"I know. Jimmy, you said something interesting when we talked. You said that Mrs. Stark wanted the treasurer's job at LifeLight Church."

"Well, yeah, but I didn't mean that she'd kill for it," Jimmy shifted in his chair uncomfortably. "She—everyone knew she wanted it. She'd wanted it for a couple of years."

"They joined LifeLight a couple of years ago and she's wanted it since then. She was always making a big deal about how she had a business background," Carmela said. "She said she could do a better job than Lyola Knesbit, because Lyola had never done any real bookkeeping."

"Was there ever any accusation that Mrs. Knesbit was dishonest?"

"Lyola? No, of course not," Carmela replied, looking shocked at the mere thought.

"Lyola Knesbit fussed over the church finances like they were her own. She did everything by hand and Mrs. Stark wanted things to be computerized. That was one thing that came up all the time. Mrs. Stark claimed that it was old-fashioned. Maybe it was, but no one seemed upset with her work."

"What about the pay?"

"The pay?"

"Churches don't pay a lot," Kelly said. "People who do it do it as part of their service to the church. Most of the time, they need the money, even though it's not a lot, but they put a lot more hours into the work than they ever expect to be paid for."

"So why would Mrs. Stark want the job? She has her own business, Chief Stark is the police chief, they aren't in need of money. Why did she want the job so badly that people in town knew about it?"

He looked around the table. Blank faces stared back at him.

"I suppose . . . I suppose she wanted things to be more modern," Carmela said.

"How does she do the library finances, now that she's taken over the task?"

"She keeps a ledger," Kelly answered.

"Does anyone see what she puts in it?"

"Not anymore," Kelly said, frowning as she tried to follow his logic. "She keeps the ledger and then she records things in the library accounting system."

"Why does she do double work?"

"What are you saying?" Jimmy asked.

"I'm wondering why a woman who complained that the bookkeeper at her church was out-of-date and unqualified uses a ledger at the library to record finances."

"But . . ." Kelly began and then fell silent.

Troy let the words sink in. He understood that it was a huge leap to perceive Lois Stark as someone who would have a self-serving purpose, and perhaps even a criminal one, for taking over finances for two local nonprofits where no one would suspect that anything nefarious was taking place.

"Mrs. Stark is very worried about identity theft," Kelly said. "She gave a generous donation to the library, then, when the check was lost, she said she would replace it with cash. She did replace it," Kelly said.

"She accused Lucas Krymanski of stealing the check," Carmela recalled.

"That was absurd. Lucas was in my office only minutes and he'd have had no idea that there was a check in the lockbox, even if he somehow had the time to take it. Mrs. Stark said he was doing it as a prank," Kelly explained to the others, whose befuddled expressions revealed their confusion. "He wouldn't do that."

"But it's not the first time the Starks have made a false accusation against Lucas," Doug said. "They were going to let him be accused of murder—in fact, he was accused of murder—until Troy and Kelly dug into the details and found out that it was the Starks' son, Scotty, who killed his girlfriend in Daffodil Alley on Halloween."

"So, this doesn't start on Groundhog Day," Jimmy said. "It goes back to Halloween."

"Yes and no. The murder goes back to Halloween. Evidence that Scotty Stark was making money dealing drugs goes back that far. But that evidence didn't come up in the trial. It was a murder trial; there was no reason to find another mark against

Scotty Stark. We first become aware that the Starks weren't all they were made out to be then. That's when Chief Stark was first suspended. But nothing was pursued; he was suspended because his son was in prison. At least that's how it seemed. But then, as we've seen over the summer, the spotlight fell on Leo Page and he was suspended, while Chief Stark was put back in his position. When Carmela was unfairly under suspicion for Lyola's murder, Mrs. Stark expanded her position as library board president to first, get Carmela suspended, and then to come in daily to the library, taking over some of Kelly's authority as director. When Carmela was no longer under suspicion, Mrs. Stark didn't stop coming into the library daily to work on finances. We're now in a position where Chief Stark has the power to decide how the drug issues in town are addressed, and Mrs. Stark controls the finances for two of the town's nonprofits."

"You're saying they have a reason?" Jimmy asked.

"I'm saying that we need to find out. Jimmy, you see the effects of the drug problem in town firsthand. You see the bodies," Troy said bluntly. "Carrie Krymanski could have been one of those bodies."

"It's thanks to Kelly here that she isn't," Jimmy said.

"No thanks to Mrs. Stark. She doesn't want Narcan in the library. She says it encourages addicts to come in. She threatened to fire Kelly," Carmela recalled the scene in the library after Kelly left with the ambulance crew and Carrie. "She meant it. When library board members heard about what happened and came by to say that they were glad for what Kelly did, Mrs. Stark tried to make the case that Kelly was abetting criminals. She was laying the groundwork for getting Kelly fired. It won't work," she said, giving Kelly a reassuring look, "but it'll come up at the next board meeting."

"Maybe I'll show up at the board meeting," Jimmy said, "to thank Kelly for being a conscientious citizen."

Kelly smiled. "You don't have to do that, Jimmy. I'm glad, like we all are, that Carrie didn't overdose. I think—I hope—that she's realized how much she has to live for. Mia Shaw is with her now, over at her house, to talk to her about rehab."

"Put me on the agenda for the board meeting, Kelly," Jimmy said stubbornly. "I want to make sure people know that in Settler Springs, we have public servants who care about the people in this town. We're about saving lives here, not letting them be lost."

15

LUNCH AT THE CAFE

There were advantages to being engaged, Troy thought as he walked into the library with a smile. Mrs. Stark glowered at him, but that didn't diminish his smile.

"Just wondering if you can join me for lunch," he said to Kelly, who was at the circulation desk while Carmela was putting books away. "We've got some planning to do. Doug wants to know what we're deciding about engagement photos, and we still haven't picked out a ring. Then there's the wedding, my family is all over the place and your folks are in Florida—"

"Carmela, can you cover the desk?" Kelly asked quickly, more to silence Troy's wedding talk than out of a sudden eagerness for lunch.

"I'll be right down," Carmela said. "You go on ahead."

Carmela's good mood was only enhanced by the fact that in fifteen more minutes, Lois Stark would go out for lunch and the library would be minus her presence for an hour.

Kelly grabbed her purse from her office and began walking out of the library ahead of Troy rather than beside him.

"You know," Troy commented when they were outside, "you're not acting like an eager bride-to-be. Anyone who saw you in there might have thought you were trying to get away from me."

"I was," Kelly said, "before you went into any more details about this bogus engagement."

"It serves a purpose," he said as he opened the door of his Suburban for Kelly. "I can go into the library to see you any time I want, and Mrs. Stark has no reason to be suspicious. How was she toward you?"

"Polar vortex cold," Kelly said. "I expected it. But she hasn't said any more about firing me. Other board members have been in but so far, they've supported me."

"They'll be even more supportive if Jimmy Patton comes to the next board meeting."

"I don't want to be singled out," Kelly said. "All libraries have Narcan now. Librarians are expected to do their part to save someone from an overdose."

"I'm not talking about other libraries. Just this one. Jimmy coming to the board meeting will create support not just for you, but for what you believe in. What all of us are fighting for. It's a way of making a crack in the Starks' defenses."

"You think so?" Kelly asked him doubtfully.

"I do."

They were in front of The Café. They got out and went inside. Their usual booth was taken; the lunch crowd was a busy one and the seats were full.

"We'll have to sit at the counter," Kelly said unhappily. There was no way to talk in private at the counter, not with servers constantly going past and other customers coming and leaving.

But then Francie spotted them. "Hey, you two, good to see you! Kelly, we're so grateful for what you did at the library. Give me a couple of seconds and I'll have your booth cleaned off for you."

"Aren't there people sitting there?"

"They're just lingering," Francie said. "We're too busy at lunchtime for dawdlers."

"Don't argue," Troy advised when Kelly began to protest. Francie had already left on her mission. "She's right about the lunch crowd and dawdling. And she works with Tia," he added.

He didn't need to say any more. Kelly already knew how grateful Tia Krymanski was. Tia was a proud woman, determinedly self-sufficient and independent, but she wasn't too proud to express her gratitude or to give credit to someone.

They had given their orders and their drinks had been served when Tia came out from the kitchen. She reached into the booth to give Kelly a hug.

"Kelly, I just can't thank you enough," she said. "Carrie talked to Mia Shaw and she's agreed to go to rehab. Mia . . . she was honest. I think it was what Carrie needed to hear. Carrie and I have an appointment at the school tomorrow afternoon with the principal. I think he'll be receptive to Carrie finishing her missing credits while she's in rehab. It's not going to be easy, we both know that. But if it brings Carrie back to where she should be, it's worth it."

"She's a good kid," Troy said. "So is Lucas. So are all your kids."

"I know. I just never thought Carrie would give me trouble. She was always so responsible. I don't know what happened. And Lucas—watching out for her . . ." Tia shook her head. "You think you know your kids and then they go and surprise you."

"I think there's a lot of their mom in those kids," Kelly said.

Tia shook her head. "I don't know about that. But we didn't lose Carrie. That I do know. And I have you to thank. And I have both of you to thank for not letting us lose Lucas. I'm going to warn the others that you two are going to get burned out rescuing the Krymanski brats from trouble!"

After she left them to return to the kitchen, Kelly was thoughtful. "Carrie could have died. Mrs. Stark would have let her die. I can't get rid of that thought."

"Neither could Jimmy Patton. That's what brought him over. He said he'd never seen a woman with less compassion."

Kelly nodded. "I wasn't paying much attention to her; she was kind of in the background. Troy, do you really think that the Starks have a deliberate plan going on? I mean with the church treasurer position, and Mrs. Stark managing the library's finances? Churches and libraries don't bring in a lot of money, you know."

Troy knew that his idea was outlandish. He'd mulled it over for a considerable time in his own head before voicing it to the others. "Not much money, but there's always cash," he said.

"True, but not a lot. What do you think?"

"I think that the Starks are dealing in an area they don't really know a lot about. If they are dealing drugs—and I think they are, I just don't know how all the pieces fit together—then they have a considerable amount of cash to hide. Why not use the library and the church, substitute the cash that's already being given, for their drug earnings?"

"But why? Cash is cash."

"Drug addicts who are paying for their drugs use cash. There's possibly evidence of drugs on the bills. If the Starks can substitute church and library cash for drug cash, they've created a decoy, if anyone ever wanted to follow the trail. But no one is likely to, because who would suspect library and church deposits of having a dirty background?"

"It doesn't seem very efffcient."

"It's not. As money laundering goes, this is clumsy. But the Starks aren't rubbing elbows with the criminal element; they aren't experienced in these things. They're doing the best they can to get rid of the cash and keep the money. Make sense?"

"I suppose so, but it makes me . . . I don't know. I feel like we're country bumpkins trying to deal with slick big-city urban problems."

"The Starks aren't any more sophisticated than we are," Troy said reassuringly. "I think they're crooked, but I don't think they're particularly skilled at it."

"What if they have Rep. Eldredge on their side?"

"Let's assume that he's a supporter of the Starks. He may not know what they're up to, maybe he just likes the fact that they support him generously."

"Do you think they give him cash? That would be a little weird for campaign donations, wouldn't it?"

Troy's expression showed admiration. "Can't beat a librarian," he praised. "I wonder if they do. Weird, yes, but if they've convinced people that they're just worried about identity theft, it's plausible. Your—" he stopped himself just in time before referring to

Jarrod Zabo as Kelly's ex. "Eldredge's campaign manager would know."

"Maybe, but I'm not asking him."

"Maybe Doug can find out," Troy suggested. He wasn't going to push Kelly into an encounter with her ex-fiancé if she really wanted to avoid it, even if he privately thought she'd be the most successful at probing Zabo. But it was for Kelly to decide.

Kelly's relief was obvious. "Doug is pretty resourceful," she agreed. "You didn't mention anything, when we met, about him taking photos at the cemetery."

"No, I think there are some things we don't want to share yet."

"You don't trust Jimmy or Carmela to keep it secret?"

"It's not about trust. It's more about trying to figure out how much they can handle beyond their own part of this. Jimmy can focus on the overdoses, it's what he deals with. It's part of his job. Carmela knows the church network. She'll zero in on that. Get them outside those areas and they start to speculate. That doesn't keep us on the path."

"You sound like you know a lot about all of this."

Troy shook his head. "I've never been involved in anything like this before. There are things in the military, sure, but it's not on this level. This . . . it's more about caring about people than it is about standing at attention or flying the flag. Whatever else happens, Carrie came through her crisis, thanks to you refusing to obey Mrs. Stark's orders, and she can get steered in the right direction. And Lucas, he's shown some maturity too, watching out for his older sister, making sure she stays safe."

"And he's safe now, too," Kelly said, brightening at the thought that, despite all of the dark clouds that seemed to be hovering over Settler Springs, there were bright breaks of light. However small their sphere of influence, she and Troy, and their allies in this endeavor, were making a difference.

THE GLORIOUS FOURTH

"I've served in the Army and I don't think I've ever seen this much red, white and blue," Troy observed as he surveyed the parade route that the band and the re-enactors would take to kick off the Independence Day weekend.

"Settler Springs does it up proud," Kyle nodded proudly. "Of course, we were on the same side as the British for the war the re-enactors fought together against the French."

"Details, details."

The two men laughed. Chief Stark had sent them out to make sure that everything was in order during the parade. After that, they had the day off. The State Police would cover, he said, in case of emergencies. And he'd be on call, after the parade, for he would be driving the police car in the parade.

It was a bright, hot day, with a perfect blue sky overhead and no threat of rain. Both policemen were in uniform, but Troy planned to change as soon as he and Kyle had finished their assignment. Kelly was meeting him for the re-enactment that afternoon. They'd get lunch from the vendors at the re-enactment field who would be selling colonial fare with a modern twist: meat sandwiches which bore a remarkable resemblance to hot dogs; fried potatoes, more commonly known as French fries; and a vast assortment of desserts which gave great credit to colonial culinary skills that had somehow been able to invent brownies, cotton candy and chocolate-covered pretzels. The smells of the foods that were being sold in town already were hanging enticingly upon the air, drawing force from the heat of the day and adding to the aromas.

Early arrivals were already strolling the streets, many of them in buckskins, and many with muskets, but not ammunition. They seemed to be enjoying the festivities and the attention they were getting.

"Funny kind of hobby," Kyle commented, watching as one man, his arms and legs covered in deerskin buckskins, loped across the street. "Living out the way things used to be two-hundred-odd years ago."

"That's pretty much what Lucas Krymanski said," Troy recalled.

"How's the girl? His sister?"

"Good. Out of danger."

"A shame. There's too much of that in this town."

"Yeah."

Troy waited to see if Kyle would add to his remark, but nothing further was said and then the officers were hailed by the band director who had a question; if Kyle had planned to expand upon his observation, the moment was gone.

Before the parade got underway, Mayor Truvert went to the microphone on the grandstand to thank everyone who had worked to bring this 4th of July celebration together. "From the re-enactors, who remind us that we fought for our freedom more than two centuries ago, to the marching band that will be honoring our historical legacy with patriotic songs, to all the vendors keeping us fed while we share in the festivities, to each and every one of you for standing and watching as we bring you a Settler Springs 4th of July, I thank you, on behalf of the borough council and the police department. Happy 4th!"

The crowd, which had suddenly gone from a scattering of people to a throng assembled on the sidewalks, jostling so that they could see, gave a cheer.

Troy joined in the applause with perfunctory clapping. He acknowledged to himself that he'd have been more enthusiastic if someone other than Mayor Truvert had been the one making the remarks. He grinned to himself. Someone like Kelly, for instance. At least he knew that she was sincere when she spoke.

Doug's instinct that announcing a fabricated engagement would provide them with an unimpeachable cover for being seen together was true. It seemed that, wherever he went, he was asked where Kelly was. It gave them more time to talk about the progress of the investigation they were conducting against the Stark network, but it also gave time for them to be together and Troy found that to his liking. Kelly was still irked by the engagement ruse, but he had stopped making jokes about it and she did her best to handle the inquisitive queries from people in town who were so happy for her.

Today, after watching the re-enactment, they had plans to go up to Leo's camp for a picnic and a swim. There would be fireworks to watch at night. It had the makings of a traditional holiday and Troy was looking forward to it.

But he had just gotten out of the shower and was getting dressed when his cell phone rang.

"Troy, it's Mia. Dad didn't come home this morning after his shift ended—he works the night shift this week—so Mom called his boss. Someone hit him over the head last night and knocked him out."

"Leo? Is he okay?" Troy held the phone to his ear with his shoulder keeping it in place while he pulled on cargo shorts.

"His boss took him to the hospital; they're checking him out for a concussion. Other than that, they don't see anything major."

"The place he was working, was there a break-in?"

"That's what's weird. Nothing was tampered with, his boss told Mom. The place wasn't broken into, the door wasn't jimmied or broken . . . I just wanted to let you know. Troy?"

"Yeah?"

"It doesn't seem like it makes sense. Why would someone try to knock Dad out if they weren't planning a robbery?"

Troy had the same question. He pulled a tee-shirt over his head, then readjusted the telephone. "I don't know. Is your dad going to be admitted or is he coming home?"

"Mom says he says he's coming home and we're all going up to the lake. He won't hear of anything different."

"The doctors might want him to rest." In any case, it sounded to Troy like this was a time for Leo to be with his family, not with guests. "Kelly and I won't bother you guys while you're up there. It's going to take all Millie has to keep Leo sitting down."

"No, he specifically said that he wants you to come up, you and Kelly. Mom had told him about your engagement already and he wants to congratulate you."

"That can wait until he's recovered," Troy said hastily. Leo in a hurry to congratulation him for a make-believe engagement wasn't good for a person who had just had a bump on his head.

"He says he's coming home," Mia said. "And he wants you and Kelly there. Really, Troy, he does."

"Does he think he knows who hit him or why?" Troy phrased the question with care; he didn't want to alarm Mia unduly or infect her with his suspicion that Leo had been attacked not because someone planned a robbery of the place he was guarding, but because, with jury selection starting soon, Travis Shaw's supporters, whoever they were, wanted to send a message.

"I haven't talked to him. Just Mom did. I don't think she asked him that. But I will."

"Where are your kids?"

"They're with me. I'm at Mom and Dad's, waiting for them. They're going straight from the hospital to camp, so I'll be going up there too."

"If you can wait," Troy said, "why don't you let me pick you up and you and the kids can ride up with Kelly and me?"

Pause. "You think there's a reason for that?" It was Mia Page, the cop's daughter asking.

Troy didn't want to scare her. But there was no reason to take unnecessary chances. "I don't know if there's a reason," he said. "But since we're all going to the same place, why not go together? I'm just getting ready now, then I'll pick Kelly up to watch the re-enactment. We'll swing by and get you and the kids and all go together."

"Thanks, Troy. I'll feel better if we do that."

"Me, too."

So did Kelly, when he picked her up and explained why they were stopping for Mia and her kids before going up to the re-enactment camp.

"Poor Mia," Kelly said. "It never seems to stop for her. He keeps getting to her through her family; first her kids, then her dad. Does he want her to relapse and start using drugs again because of all the stress?"

It wasn't something that Troy had considered but it made a certain amount of sense. As long as Mia was clean, working, and recovering, she was obviously the better parent, despite her past. But if she fell off the wagon, and if Leo was compromised as a police officer because of accusations that he'd forced his ex-son-in-law to confess to murder, Travis Shaw's lawyer would be able to cast considerable doubt on the Pages' qualifications as custodial parents. Millie's reputation was still intact, but custody could hardly be granted to her when she and Leo were married and living in the same residence.

"I don't know," he answered candidly. "So many things seem to be happening and I can't tell for sure if they're deliberately planned or if they're just experimental ploys. Or if they're entirely unconnected."

"Then it's probably safer to assume that everything is linked to everything else," Kelly said. "We're less likely to ignore something important if we treat everything like it's a clue."

17

"LOOK WHERE WE ARE NOW"

Troy realized that by attending the battle re-enactment with Mia Shaw and her kids, he was more or less announcing his support for the young woman, but she might need protection. Her kids might need it too. So, they all sat together on the bleachers and watched as the colonial forces, with the support of British troops, defeated the French and their Indian allies. But when the battle was over, and the participants and the audience were milling around together, Troy and Kelly, by unspoken accord, headed for the parking lot.

"Mom texted me," Mia said when they were all inside and her kids were occupied with the colonial toys that their mother had bought for them. "They're at camp. The doctors told Dad to take it easy. He can't go back to work yet; concussion protocol. He's worried about losing the job."

"It's not his fault he got hit in the head."

"No, but his boss is worried that this is related to the trial, and I told you he's already uneasy about it. I just wish the trial would start and finish," Mia said in exasperation.

"We all do," Kelly agreed, looking at the back seat from her mirror to make sure that the kids weren't paying attention to the adult conversation. "Once that's done, maybe this will all calm down."

"Maybe. But it's not just the trial. It's the rest of it as well. Troy, will you fill Dad in on what you're doing. You and Kelly and Jimmy and the rest?"

"I will. It'll be good to get him involved."

"I think so, too. He's discouraged about not being able to do anything to help."

"Right now, none of us can do much to help. But at least there are enough of us who realize that something has to be done."

Leo greeted them at the door of camp, but winced at the brightness of the light, and when Millie said she was taking the kids to the lake to swim, he didn't suggest going with her. Mia went with her mother but gave her dad an admonishing finger wagging before she left. "You're supposed to take it easy," she said. "That's what Mom said the doctor said. So keep your cool when you hear what Troy and Kelly are doing."

"They're engaged, right?" Leo said. "What do you mean?"

"You know what I mean."

"Congratulations on your engagement, you two," Leo said when the three of them were alone in the cabin. "I was starting to think you were never going to ask her."

"Yeah, well . . . a little slow, I guess. Leo, what—"

"When's the wedding?"

"We haven't decided," Kelly answered. "Right now, we're more concerned about what happened to you."

Leo gingerly touched the side of his head where a bandage attested to a wound beneath. "I'm not sure what happened to me, to tell you the truth. I make the rounds of the complex once every hour. It's not a high-security place, nothing like that. They just want someone on the grounds to make sure that nothing is going on that shouldn't be. So, I was out making my 2:00 a.m. patrol. Didn't hear anything, didn't see anything. All I know is that I woke up and it was daylight. So, I called the boss, he came over, nothing was touched. Nothing in the whole compound was anything other than what it should be. He took me to the hospital. Millie came. They're checking me for a concussion, but I told them that this hard old head is too thick for a concussion. Now, what's going on? Mia tells me that I need to talk to you but she won't say why."

Troy explained. "And there are enough of us now," he said in conclusion, "who know something's going on. We want to find out what it is."

"You mean you want to prove that Chief Stark is in it up to his badge," Leo said. "You know, I can't believe, back last year, when I didn't believe you when you noticed that things weren't right."

"I can," Troy said. "There wasn't any evidence."

"There still isn't much," Kelly said. "But there's enough now, at least, to warrant questions being asked. We just have to be careful. Most people trust Chief Stark and they'd rather believe that everything is fine. Tia Krymanski's outburst at the council meeting wasn't expected, but Chief Stark tilted the account so that it made it sound like good parents, good people, don't have addicts in the family. And when Carrie almost overdosed in the library, that just confirmed that Chief Stark was right."

"Millie and I were the best parents we knew how to be," Leo said. "But we weren't able to stop Mia from getting involved with Travis Shaw."

"Mia is clean now," Troy reminded Leo.

"And it was Mia who convinced Carrie to go to rehab," Kelly told him. "She was pretty blunt, from what I hear, about what it's like to be a hardcore addict. Now Carrie is in rehab and, with a lot of prayer and support, I think she'll be okay. Not all at once, I know, but when she heard Mia's story . . . she listened. She wouldn't have listened to her mother say the same things, but she listened to Mia. Mia told her about Travis, and she told her about losing her kids. It took a lot of courage for Mia to be that honest."

Leo nodded. "Mia has faced a lot. She's still not ready to get the kids, though. Millie and I talked about that on the way home from the hospital. Until this trial is over and Travis Shaw is sentenced for murder, the kids have to stay with us."

"Leo, I have a question and I want you to answer me as a cop. Do you think that all these things that are happening to Mia—the rat in the mailbox, the broken bicycle on her porch, Mason being abducted, someone breaking into her apartment—do you think someone is trying to get her to turn back to drugs?"

Leo thought. "Maybe," he said finally. "It would rattle most people. Mind you, I don't believe that Mia will turn back that way. But yeah, maybe, that's the reasoning. I thought it was just to scare her into not testifying, but by now, she's so mad at what Shaw's done that it would take the National Guard to keep her from testifying."

"I'm trying to figure out why Lyola Knesbit was murdered. Why did Shaw do it?"

"His lawyer says he didn't do it," Leo said. "Apparently Travis is just a harmless drug dealer who's being railroaded into a murder rap because I'm an overprotective father."

"So why did someone hit you on the head? To keep you from testifying?"

"That won't happen. I'll testify no matter what."

"Do you think whoever did this meant to kill you?"

It was a sobering question and Leo gave it the attention it merited. But he shook his head. "If they'd wanted to kill me, they'd have used a gun or a knife. No. They wanted to leave a message that they can find me."

"Find you for what?"

"For the next time, I suppose," Leo said. There was no drama in his remark; it was a simple assessment of what he thought. But to Kelly's ears, it was the absence of histrionics in the tone that made it all the more chilling. Police officers, she realized, expected danger and threats. But they didn't expect them to be personal.

"I appreciate how you've looked after Mia and the kids," Leo went on. "You've been rational, I've been emotional. That hasn't helped. You've told me before to think like a cop, not a dad. And you're right."

"Of course, he is," Kelly said. "It's almost impossible to keep your emotions out of the way when someone you love and care about is being threatened."

"I don't know what I'd do if anyone hurt my family," Leo said. "I know the law and I obey it. I enforce it. Well, I did," he said, "until all of this. Now, I don't know if I could ever go back to being the police chief. Even if Stark is exposed for what we know he is, I don't want to go back."

Troy was surprised by Leo's attitude. Somewhere in the back of his mind, he'd assumed that if they were successful in uncovering Stark's illicit dealings, Leo would return to being the police chief, just as he had been when Stark was put on suspension. But Leo, apparently, had undergone a metamorphosis of some kind, one in which the position he'd occupied as a police officer with more than a quarter century of experience no longer carried weight.

"I should have seen this," Leo continued. "You did. I didn't see it and look where we are now. I should have spotted how things were, but I kept my eyes closed, like everyone else in town. Now look were we are," he said again. "My daughter is threatened by her ex-husband, who has powerful connections; my grandchildren are at risk; my reputation is smeared. No, I'm not going back, no matter what happens. I messed up the first time. Look where we are now."

18

FIREWORKS

Talk turned back to ordinary matters when Millie, Mia and the kids returned from their swim. Troy manned the grill while Millie ordered her husband to sit down and rest like the doctor had ordered him to do. When it was dark, they sat out front and watched the fireworks illuminate the sky. It was a restful holiday and Troy found himself relaxing, even though he knew this was only a temporary respite.

It was getting late when they decided it was time to leave. Mia and her children stayed at the camp when Troy and Kelly left. The Page family was planning to spend a couple more days there while Leo rested before returning home, a schedule which had the children's enthusiastic approval.

Kelly and Troy were both quiet on the drive back into town. It was a silence which didn't feel brittle or uncomfortable to Troy; he knew that both he and Kelly were likely pondering Leo's words. It was yet another life, in Troy's eyes, that had been marred by the actions of Roger Stark.

He might have been surprised to learn that Kelly was considering Leo's comments from a different angle. If Leo didn't want to return to his former position, did that mean that Troy would be offered the job? She had no doubt that he was capable of leading the police force. He was brave; he'd proven that in his military service, and he was proving it now. But would he want to do it? Even though she sensed a deepening of his sense of belonging in the town, she didn't know if Troy had bigger plans. Jarrod had been open to the point of disdain about his desire to shake the dust of the small town from his Gucci shoes. But Troy never spoke disparagingly of Settler Springs. Nor did he give any indication of what he wanted to do after he got his degree, a process which seemed to be moving slowly, especially since he had decided not to take summer classes.

"Did you know that Leo feels the way he does about going back to the police force?" she asked.

Troy shook his head; then, realizing that the darkness of the night would have made it impossible for Kelly to see his response, answered, "No. I've always thought that Leo would return. He's so much a part of the town that I just assumed he'd want it."

"Is he bitter?"

"Maybe. But I think he's being self-critical. Now he's seeing all of this in terms of how it's affecting his family."

"Is he right?"

Troy hesitated. He didn't want to criticize Leo, a friend and colleague and a man who had an authentic instinct for supporting right versus wrong. But . . . "Yeah, I think he is, but I wouldn't tell him that. Speaking honestly, I'm not sure someone who's been in the town as long as he has would have noticed things. But accepting them . . . even something as typical as telling the officers not to give parking tickets to members of the Stark family. It happens all the time, and it's not a big deal, especially when you think of everything else that the Starks are doing. But it's not right. The first time I saw Scotty Stark's car, that red man-dream that he drove, I was getting ready to write him a ticket. Kyle told me not to. The Starks didn't get ticketed. It was policy. Not official policy, no, but it was policy. It bugged me."

"It should bug you. It's wrong. If someone parks by a meter, she knows she has to put money in it."

"I guess the rules were different for Scotty Stark."

"Don't you think it's weird that he's almost never mentioned? It's like the Starks woke up one day and decided that they just wouldn't think about it anymore."

"I'd like to know if Scotty started dealing on his own and they got involved then, or if they were already into it and he took over."

"Did he really take over? He was running the selling in town but that doesn't mean he ran it."

That was true. Scotty Stark was a college freshman; what would he have known about the intricacies of making a profit out of an illegal trade fraught with dangerous alliances and complicated transactions? On the other hand, what did a small-town police chief and his insurance agent wife know about that other world?

"Maybe the Starks are quick learners," Troy said thoughtfully.

"I suppose they make a lot of money," Kelly said. "Maybe that makes someone a quick learner."

Suddenly the sky burst into color. Brilliant flashes of light took over the night, turning the blackness into vivid images. The world, apart from the noise of the fireworks, seemed oddly serene and quiet.

"Oh, Troy, look, Warren Borough is setting off their fireworks. Can we pull over and watch? I love fireworks."

Happy to oblige, Troy pulled over into the empty grocery store parking lot, where they had a perfect vantage point from which to enjoy the fireworks from across the river. As he watched, Troy stole glances at Kelly's rapt profile. She hadn't been joking when she said she loved fireworks. She was staring up at the sky, her head tilted back, as intent upon the tableau as if she were a child seeing them for the first time. She was wearing one of her patriotic outfits: a red skirt with bright blue sequined stars across it, and a white cloth headband in her hair. She looked gorgeous. She always did.

"You know," he remarked as the fireworks finale thundered and lit up the sky, "engaged couples would usually take this opportunity to do something besides stare up at the sky."

He saw her lips curve in a smile even though her attention never left the sky. "Too bad we're not really engaged, then."

"I don't know . . . we aren't going to be very convincing."

She was still smiling. "We can't be too convincing. Think of what everyone would say when this is all resolved and we break off our engagement."

"Who's breaking it off?"

"Oh, we'll figure it out."

"What if I don't break it off?"

"That would mean we'd be getting married."

"Oh, yeah, that's right."

Would he mind marrying Kelly? What would it be like, starting the day with her and ending it with her? Maybe marriage wasn't such a bad idea. Maybe it was worth some consideration.

He was about to suggest the idea, in a casual kind of way, to Kelly while they were sitting in his vehicle, with no one else around and no distractions, when a pickup truck suddenly drove by at a breakneck pace.

"Don't you have to go after him?" Kelly said. "He's speeding."

But Troy was already putting the Suburban in gear as he followed the speeding truck, reaching out his open window to attach the portable warning lights to the roof of the vehicle as he steered.

"Keep your seatbelt on," he said to Kelly.

The advice wasn't necessary. Her seatbelt was already on and always was whenever she was in a car. Even so, she found herself gripping the side of the seat as Troy raced after the pickup truck which seemed to be getting away.

Troy realized that he couldn't catch the speeding truck, but he wanted to get close enough to read the license plate. However, the truck was going at such a recklessly fast pace that Troy realized it was no use. He'd be risking his life and Kelly's if he pursued.

In disgust, Troy let the Suburban's speed drop and he turned down the street so that he could take Kelly home.

"I wonder who that was?" Kelly mused.

"Some idiot," Troy said. "Probably had too many beers and wouldn't pass a breathalyzer. Not that I could administer one now, from my car. But he could kill someone driving like that."

"I wonder who it was."

"Trying to figure out who drives a black pickup truck in Settler Springs is an impossible challenge." He pulled into a parking place in front of Kelly's house.

The light-hearted banter that had been going on as the fireworks ended was gone. He mentally cursed the pickup truck for ruining the mood between them. She'd been amused by his suggestion they stay engaged, not offended. Maybe she just hadn't taken him seriously, or maybe she was getting to the point in their relationship where she didn't mind him teasing about the engagement that wasn't one. But she had no way of knowing that for a few brief moments, he'd allowed the idea of marriage to float, every so lightly, upon his mental itinerary.

19

LUCAS IS MISSING

"Lucas didn't come home."

It was too early to be awake, but when Troy's cell phone rang, he answered it. Tia Krymanski was on the other end. She was trying not to cry, he could tell; her voice was tight and strained.

"Lucas?" Troy sat up in his bed. He'd gotten to bed later than usual, sitting outside on his porch with Arlo for company after he'd taken Kelly home. "Was he staying over at a friend's?"

"No, he was to come home before dark. He knows my rules. He just wouldn't break them now, not after everything we've just gone through with Carrie. Troy, I'm sorry to call you at this hour, but I didn't know what to do. I should just call 911 but Stark isn't going to do anything."

"The State Police would be covering." Not that they would do anything either, not if Meigle was on duty. "But it's okay that you called. You haven't heard anything from him? No messages, nothing?"

"Nothing. I know that Lucas is a typical kid, he doesn't think about the time, but he knows when it's dark. He knows to come home."

"Did you call his friends?"

"I called them earlier, when he didn't come home like he was supposed to. They told me that they all left the swimming pool together and then went to the park and hung out until it started to get dark. Then they all went home. He left with them and he said he was on his way home. Troy, I know people think Lucas is a mischief maker, but he knows how I feel about curfews and with everything that went on with Carrie, he's really been very responsible lately."

"I know, Tia. I know. You have to call 911 in order to get something started, though. They can't do anything if they don't know. I can follow up with them later this morning. Call, okay?"

"I feel like it's a waste of time," Tia burst out. "They don't care if it's my kid who's missing. They only care about kids whose last name isn't Krymanski."

Troy thought of Trooper Susan Callahan. "Not all of them, Tia. There's a state trooper who's on the ball. I'll talk to her tomor—I mean today. But you call, okay? I'm getting dressed now and I'll be over as soon as I can."

"I'm sorry, Troy, I shouldn't bother you."

"You're not bothering me," he said, getting out of bed and throwing the covers back in a facsimile of a made bed. "This is my job. Lucas is a good kid."

"He is," Tia said, her words interrupted by a gulp that sounded like a sob. He knew that Tia didn't like to reveal her emotions, at least not this kind, so he pretended that he hadn't heard the sound. "He is a good kid. He's been through so much . . ."

They all had. Lucas had weathered the murder accusation surprisingly well, but it had still been a jarring episode in a young teen's life.

"I'll be right over," he promised. "As soon as I'm dressed, I'll be there."

Showering and dressing were tasks he knew how to accomplish without wasted time; the military taught him that. Within less than twenty minutes, he was knocking on the door of the Krymanski house, with only wet hair to reveal that he'd left the house in a hurry.

One of the twins, Alexa or Madison, he couldn't tell them apart, answered the door, her eyes sleepy but still alert enough to show that she was alarmed. He followed her into the kitchen where Tia sat in front of a cup of coffee. Her thirteen-year old, Marissa, was sitting there with her. The other twin had been asleep on the couch as they passed through the living room.

"Did you call?"

Tia nodded. "They took all the information and asked all the questions you asked. They don't believe me."

"Just because they don't believe there's anything to worry about doesn't mean they won't follow through on the report," he said gently. "Now, why don't you—which one are you, anyway?"

"I'm Madison," she said.

"You two need to do something so I can tell you apart. One of you dye your hair pink and the other dye hers green and then I'll know." Troy felt for the kids; they didn't understand what was going on. The family had had too much to deal with lately.

Madison giggled. "Mom wouldn't let us do that," she said.

"Then try a color that she likes and maybe she won't mind. You two need to get to bed," he said. "It's way too late for you to be up."

Madison looked to her mother. Tia nodded. "Officer Troy is right," Tia said firmly. "Alexa has the right idea; she's zonked out on the couch. Marissa, honey, you too. Bed."

When the two had left to go upstairs, Tia said, "Thanks, you're right. I've been so frantic that I wasn't even paying attention."

"I'm not surprised. Not with Lucas missing. You've checked with his friends, with everyone that he was with, and no one knows any reason why he wouldn't be home." Troy stated this, knowing that for all his mischief, Lucas didn't try to get in trouble and he was especially solicitous, in his own way, of his mother after what she'd gone through with Carrie. Now Carrie was in rehab and safe, but the travail that seemed to haunt the Krymanskis had struck again.

"He was out with friends all day, but I expected that. It's the Fourth of July, it's summer . . . Lucas and his friends were out enjoying the parade, the re-enactment. They have a good time and they don't get into trouble. You know that The Café does one of the outdoor grills for the 4th, so I was cooking during the day. But I've never worried about Lucas before. I didn't check up on him; I knew he was with Tyler's family for a cook-out . . ."

"There was no reason to think this 4th would be any different from the others," Troy supplied, realizing that Tia was accusing herself for being lax when she had just followed the normal routine. Lucas spent the holiday with friends while his mother worked. That wasn't neglect on his mother's part, even if she was blaming herself now for his disappearance.

"Troy, where could he be? He didn't run away; he's not hanging out somewhere and not telling me. I know what they're going to say," Tia said wearily. "But they don't know Lucas. They think they can label him because he's a teenager and he's a Krymanski."

"I'll check with the state police," Troy promised, wondering if Trooper Callahan would be more forthcoming or if she was going to stay out of it, in order to avoid hostility from Meigle. Troy sensed that she was honest and a good cop, but he didn't know how far she'd extend herself if she felt that her job were on the line.

"And you'll let me know as soon as you hear anything?"

"You know I will," Troy said.

"Troy . . . I'm really worried this time. There are things going on in this town that aren't right."

"I know."

"The Starks would like to get back at Lucas, I know it. They would have let him take the blame for murdering that girl. They blame him for being innocent, because the way they see things, a Krymanski should be guilty, not a Stark."

Troy knew that Tia didn't know everything that was rotten in the situation, but she knew enough for her fear to be authentic. "Scotty Stark was guilty," Troy said. His voice sounded harsh to his own ears; he wondered how it sounded to Tia. "I don't care what the Starks think; their son is a murderer. Blaming Lucas would have convicted an innocent kid for that girl's death."

"But you know what I'm saying, don't you?" Tia pressed. "It's not safe to be a Krymanski in this town. Sean's death . . . I know, they say it was a suicide, but—"

"It wasn't suicide," Troy interrupted. "I don't care what they try to make it out to be. Sean had no reason to kill himself."

"But why did they have to kill him?" Tia's eyes showed fear. She wasn't a woman who readily succumbed to emotional stress; raising five kids as a divorced single mother had forged her spirit and she was a fighter by nature. But she was vulnerable because she loved her kids. She was, Troy realized, starting to see the threat to her family in broader terms. Sean had been a Krymanski on his mother's side. But that wasn't what killed him. He had been killed because he was Troy's friend. "Skip, he's pretty angry over it. I think it's easier for him to be mad than to admit that he's grieving."

"He thinks I'm not doing enough to find out what really happened."

"Oh, I'm sure he knows that you're doing all you can," Tia said, not denying Troy's assertion.

"There are a lot of pieces to put together. We'll find Lucas, we'll find out what's going on," Troy vowed. "I'll get back to you as soon as I know anything. Tia . . . you probably hear a lot of what's going on in town."

"I'm back in the kitchen, I don't hear much from the customers," she said.

"No, but you hear things, all the same. Keep your ears open, okay?"

"For what?"

For what? That was the challenge. He didn't know.

"Just . . . anything that doesn't seem right. Anything about the Starks, or about Lyola Knesbit's murder. Anything about Mia Shaw . . ."

Tia's expression showed confusion. "You think they have something to do with Lucas being gone?"

"I don't know. I just need to hear anything that seems like it doesn't belong."

"The waitresses, they hear a lot. I'll pay closer attention. Just find Lucas for me."

A BLACK PICKUP TRUCK

F inding Lucas had moved to the top of the list for Troy, but there wasn't much to work with and he didn't know where to start, especially since any investigating that he did would have to be under the radar to avoid attracting the attention of Chief Stark. He needed to talk to Lucas' friends, the ones who had been with him on Independence Day, and any official questioning needed to take place with the knowledge and in the presence of their parents.

Tia had waved this concern away. "You don't need to worry about that," she had told him before he left her house. "The kids all know how things are. His friends know that if not for you and Kelly Armello, Lucas would have gone to trial for the murder that Scotty Stark committed. Most evenings, you can find them playing basketball on the playground court; they're there from around six o'clock or so— after suppertime—until it starts getting dark. I've already talked to them and their parents, but you might think of something that will help find him."

Troy wasn't optimistic that the youths would open up to him if they hadn't already done so with Tia, but the following evening, he drove by the court and found a group of kids there. When he got out of the squad car and walked onto the court, the game came to an immediate halt, as did the conversation.

"Anyone heard anything from Lucas?" Troy asked. "Chris, Tyler?"

The two boys stepped forward immediately, which surprised Troy, who expected the usual reticence displayed by teens when a police officer called them by name.

"Lucas wouldn't run off," Chris said emphatically. "We think someone took him."

Several of the other boys nodded their assent. "Krymanskis get blamed for everything," spoke up another youth. "And ever since Lucas got blamed for murdering that pregnant girl last Halloween, we think that the cops are out to get him."

Troy responded to this with raised eyebrows.

"Not you," Tyler said quickly. "Lucas said it's not you. But Chief Stark, Lucas says he sees him a lot."

"Define a lot?"

"Following him when Lucas is riding his bike home," another boy said. "Kind of like he's watching him to see what he's going to do."

"What about the rest of you? Does the Chief follow you?"

"Sometimes," Tyler answered. "If we're with Lucas."

"When you are with Lucas, what are you doing?"

"Just hanging out."

Just hanging out. A term that could mean nothing or everything and would be impossible to pin down as proof that Chief Stark was deliberately targeting Lucas.

"Does anyone, like Chief Stark, ever say anything? Like let you know if you're out too late, or if you shouldn't loiter, things like that?"

Chris shook his head. "We just see him. Lucas just keeps going on with what he's doing, he doesn't talk to the Chief unless Chief Stark talks to him first."

"But he doesn't do that," Tyler picked up the story. "It's sort of like he's just watching Lucas. You know, to see if he'll do something wrong."

"How long has this been going on?"

Another boy spoke up. "Ever since the police chief got his job back."

"How do you know that?"

"My dad says Chief Stark would rather put a Krymanski in jail than find a real criminal," the boy said.

"Are you a Krymanski?"

"No, but Lucas is our friend."

"Officer Kennedy, are you gonna find Lucas?"

"We're working on it. But we need to know everything about yesterday that you remember. Was anyone following Lucas yesterday?"

"Not a police car," Chris said.

"But someone?" Troy pressed. There was enough ambiguity in the response to warrant a follow-up question.

Chris looked at Tyler. "There was a pickup truck that we noticed. But . . . "Tyler shrugged. "There are a lot of pickup trucks around, my dad says, and with everything going on for the 4th, it doesn't mean anything. That's what my dad says."

"But you noticed it," Troy said.

"Well, yeah, but . . . there's a lot of pickup trucks."

"What color was it?"

"Black."

Black. Troy thought immediately of the black pickup truck that had been speeding by when he and Kelly were in the parking lot watching the fireworks across the river. There were a lot of pickup trucks in town, that was true. It was also true, as Chris noted, that with the Fourth of July celebrations going on, Settler Springs had more than the usual number of visitors.

Troy hadn't been in his police car when the truck raced by. But it had been speeding fast enough that Troy was unable to catch up to it. Had Lucas been in the truck?

"Anyone get a license plate number?" he asked, knowing that it was a forlorn hope.

There was a collective shaking of heads. "But it has a skull in the back window," Chris said.

"A skull?"

"Yeah, it's a skull, like . . . you know, skulls."

"No words, nothing else, just a skull?"

"Yeah," Chris said, not finding the absence of an accompanying organization or cause of slogan to be strange.

"And it was kind of a beat-up truck," Tyler added.

If the owner drove at the speed he'd maintained last night, it wasn't surprising that the truck would show signs of wear.

"If you notice the truck again, let me know, okay?"

"You want us to get the license plate?"

"I don't want the driver of the truck to notice any of you," Troy cautioned. "If it goes by, and you notice it, and you can get the plate number without attracting attention, then sure, get it and let me know. If it's going to cause a problem, don't do it. It might be nothing," he told them, deciding that it was better to douse their enthusiasm than to get them into trouble.

"If we can help find Lucas," Tyler said, "that's what we're going to do."

Again, the collective nodding of heads. Lucas plainly had loyal friends.

Troy joined the nodding heads. "That's a deal," he said, "but remember to stay unnoticed. It's hard enough trying to find one missing person. We don't want any of you to be the next ones."

As he got back into the squad car, he noticed that the boys, instead of resuming their basketball game, moved closer together as if they were holding a meeting. That wasn't a surprise either, Troy realized. Lucas was their friend, and they were old enough to know that a missing kid was likely to be a kid in trouble or even danger. He just hoped that they were wise enough not to do anything that would have Chief Stark following any of them.

He'd already told Kelly that Lucas was missing. He'd known how she would react. This wasn't something to be discussed over supper, this was serious. The library would be closed by now and she would be home, unless she had a meeting to go to, which, with her schedule, was always a possibility.

Ready to check with Doug about those engagement photos? he texted.

She didn't answer right away. She might be annoyed, he knew, but he doubted that she would let her annoyance at the fabricated engagement interfere with her concern about Lucas' disappearance.

Sorry, came her reply half an hour later. *I was at a church meeting after work. Tomorrow at lunchtime? I checked with Doug and he can meet us in the studio at noon.*

Ok. See you then.

There was a lot more that he wanted to talk about with her but, as much as the bogus engagement allowed them to be more visible in public, it also constrained them with the need to behave as if they were engaged. He knew that Kelly probably found the ruse a lot more difficult to bring off than he did. For Troy, it was a way to benefit from a supposed wedding without actually having to do anything about it, but Kelly wasn't the kind of woman who would find that appealing. And with Lucas missing, neither one of them was willing to be entertained by playacting when the safety and possibly the life of Lucas Krymanski was at risk.

RECRUITING TROOPER CALLAHAN

"**K**elly, if Troy didn't catch the license plate number of the truck, how do you think you'd have been able to do it?" Doug asked patiently after the couple came into his studio and, realizing that they were alone with Doug, Kelly began to fret over her failure to notice anything about the truck.

"We don't even know for sure whether there's a connection between the speeding truck we saw and the pickup truck the kids saw hanging around when they were with Lucas," Troy noted.

"It has to be the same one," Kelly said, urgency audible in her tone.

"It might be," Troy corrected her. "At least we know it has a skull sticker on the back windshield. That will help a little to notice it."

"And in the meantime, we pay attention to every black pickup truck we see," Doug said. "Here."

"What's this?" Troy and Kelly asked in unison after Doug handed them each a sheet of paper.

"My rates for engagement photos and wedding photos," he said. "You'll need to have something to complain about so that people believe you're really getting married. Everyone complains about what photographers charge for weddings."

"I'm not surprised," Troy said, glancing at the numbers.

"It gives it that air of authenticity if you have real numbers to quote," Doug encouraged. "Now, with Lucas missing, I'm guessing that all of this goes into pretty high gear. Do you think he's in danger?"

Troy was impressed by the rapid-fire way that Doug shifted roles from wedding photographer to photojournalist. But before he could respond, Kelly was speaking.

"Of course, he's in danger, if Stark has him," she said. "I don't think they've forgiven him for not being the murderer. It wouldn't surprise me if they have some plan."

Both Troy and Doug looked doubtful. Troy refrained from telling Kelly that she was reading too many mystery novels, but he did ask, "What kind of plan do you think he has when his son was arrested and charged six months ago?"

"I don't know what kind of plan Chief Stark might have," Kelly answered, "but there's no reason why they couldn't be planning to get Lucas in trouble for something, just like they've done with Leo Page to make Travis Shaw look like he's innocent."

Troy didn't think Chief Stark had that circuitous a mind. "Finding Lucas isn't going to be easy, but we all know that he wouldn't have run off, even though that's what the official line will be."

"What about your state trooper contact?" Doug asked. "The honest one."

"Susan Callahan. I hope she's honest; so far, she's undeclared. But I know that Meigle is crooked. I think he killed Eddie Kavlick, not because of self-defense but because he and Stark wanted Kavlick silenced. Kavlick knew what was going on, so he was a threat. Lucas isn't a threat and right now, that's probably keeping him safe."

But Kelly didn't think Lucas was safe. She knew that Doug and Troy were trying to pursue this without allowing their suspicions to overrule their logic. However, logic wasn't going to keep Lucas alive.

As she and Troy walked out of Doug's studio, she said, "We need to be proactive on something."

"Like what? I'll check with Trooper Callahan again and find out what she knows and what's being followed up on. It's a missing kid, so they shouldn't be ignoring it."

"Unless they don't want him to be found yet."

"You think they're hiding him for a reason?"

"Why would they abduct him?" Kelly demanded. "I think they need him to be guilty of something."

"You don't think they might just be trying to scare Tia after her accusations at the council meeting?" That was Troy's guess. Chief Stark would want to remind Tia Krymanski that he had the upper hand. It was part of the pattern that was working to success with the way that the perception of Leo Page had gone from him being regarded as a dedicated police officer to a rogue cop who'd forced a confession from his former son-in-law, and Troy thought this was the likely motive for Lucas' disappearance. Mia Shaw was the one paying the price in emotional turmoil as her young son's safety was in jeopardy thanks to the ploys that someone—it had to be Stark even though there wasn't any proof—was using to make her aware of how vulnerable she was. It didn't make Lucas safe, because there was no way of telling what Stark had in mind, but it still seemed more plausible than Kelly's melodramatic assertion that Stark and his cohorts planned to pin a crime on Lucas.

"I think they definitely are trying to scare Tia, but that's not all they want to do," Kelly said. "She's got a daughter in rehab and a son who's missing; there can't be much scarier than that for a mother. But they've also been able to build evidence that supports what Chief Stark said at the council meeting: these things happen to people like the Krymanskis. He's also managed to scare Mia Shaw with the things he's done. Mia is an ex-addict trying to rebuild her life, but Chief Stark can paint her as a drug addict who lost custody of her kids because of her habit. I'm afraid that Lucas might not be found unless Chief Stark can turn it to his advantage."

Troy was silent. He remembered the scene in the cemetery. Self-defense, that was how Stark had justified shooting Eddie Kavlick. Trooper Meigle had claimed that he'd seen the shooting unfold, backing up Stark's claim. No one had asked why Meigle was there in the first place, but Troy suspected that they'd planned the shooting together because Kavlick was becoming an impediment. *Was it that easy,* Troy *wondered, to simply shoot someone because he was inconvenient as long as he was alive?*

Why should he doubt Stark's ability to kill ruthlessly? He'd certainly ordered the killing of Sean Claypool, even if he hadn't pulled the trigger. He'd orchestrated it; Kavlick had likely done it on those orders and then paid the price for knowing the truth.

"Troy," Kelly asked urgently, "would Stark kill Lucas?"

He wanted to say no, that even Stark would draw the line at killing an innocent kid. But Stark had been willing to let Lucas be arrested for a murder that Stark's son had committed. How much of a stretch was it to go from ordering a killing to doing it?

"I think Stark would do just about anything he felt he had to do to keep his secrets safe."

"Then we have to get moving on this, faster now," Kelly said.

She was right. But where were the answers? In the cemetery, where drug transactions were still going on, as proved by Doug's surreptitious photographs? In the prison where Travis Shaw awaited trial? At LifeLight Church, where Lois Stark was treasurer and had control over the bank deposits? In Mia Shaw's apartment, to which someone had access and had already broken in? In Representative Eldredge's campaign, so generously supported by the Starks? At the state police office, from which Meigle operated and aided Stark?

"I'll check with Trooper Callahan again," Troy said.

"Maybe she'd like to join the bowling team," Kelly suggested.

Troy smiled. "Not a bad idea," he said.

He took a flyer with him so that he'd have an excuse if Meigle was there. But he was in luck and when he arrived at the state police barracks, Trooper Callahan was on her own. She greeted him with her usual impassive, measuring gaze when he entered.

"Anything on the disappearance of Lucas Krymanski?" he asked briskly, making it clear that he was there on business.

"Nothing."

"Any leads?"

"Nothing."

"Is Meigle pursuing it?"

A pause. "He hasn't said anything."

Their eyes met and he realized that Callahan had just divulged the kind of information that he was looking for without revealing anything of her own views. A missing kid was a priority, the kind of scenario that had police officers following up on every lead. If Callahan hadn't heard anything, that meant there weren't any leads, and maybe, just maybe, there weren't any leads because Meigle knew exactly where Lucas was.

"Kind of unusual, isn't it?"

He let the question remain, pregnant with the unsaid speculation that, even unvoiced, was inescapable.

"Kind of unusual," she said at last.

"I might have a lead," Troy said. "A black pickup truck with a skull sticker on the back windshield was seen near Lucas several times. If you hear anything, can you let me know?"

"If I hear anything," she said, but her tone indicated that this was unlikely. And that, in its way, was also significant. Did she suspect Meigle of dirty dealing and using his authority in a corrupt manner?

Troy took the flyer out of his pocket. "How's your bowling score?"

Surprise flickered in the officer's dark eyes. "I'm better at golf."

Troy explained the Public Servant Bowling League premise. "Mind if I post a flyer here on your bulletin board for the other troopers?" he asked.

"I'll post it for you," she said. "Maybe I'll give bowling a try."

"Thanks," he said, and meant it. He felt as if he'd just won a victory, however cryptic, in getting Trooper Susan Callahan to declare her allegiance.

After her conversation with Troy, Kelly felt a sense of urgency similar to the way she'd felt after the Halloween murder, when Lucas was unjustly accused of killing the girl found in Daffodil Alley. She'd known that he was innocent, just as she knew now that he hadn't just run away, no matter how Chief Stark intended to smear the boy's character.

But what could she do about it? Mrs. Stark was ensconced in the library, working on the treasurer's report for the upcoming library board meeting. A frown cut a cleft in her forehead as she studied the figures, but Kelly knew that it wasn't the accounts that had caused the treasurer's displeasure.

Jimmy Patton had called that morning to ask to be added to the agenda for the meeting. Kelly had taken the call and added him to the agenda, letting him know that public comments could only be voiced if they were on the agenda and that he would have a limited time to speak.

"It won't take long to say what I have to say," he had said.

She'd told Mrs. Stark that he would be at the meeting. Immediately the treasurer had protested; they didn't have time to let everybody in town speak up at their meetings. Kelly calmly explained that the public had the right to attend board meetings as long as they followed protocol. At her side, Carmela, although silent, was nodding her support.

"That's ridiculous," Mrs. Stark said. She'd left early for lunch and had come back late, something which hadn't bothered either Kelly or Carmela, who had taken the opportunity, when there weren't any patrons in the library, to share their thoughts. Carmela had learned that Mrs. Stark was really irritating the congregation at LifeLight with her very public generosity and the church council was split over whether or not to accept a large donation which would rename the social hall after the Starks.

There was enough money to completely modernize the structure and make it attractive as a wedding venue, creating an additional source of income for the church. But, Carmela said, there were people in the church who just didn't like the idea.

That wasn't advancing any theories that the Starks were using the church—or the library, where Mrs. Stark also controlled the flow of money—as a way to launder their drug profits, but it did merit consideration. How did the Starks, he a police chief in a small town, she an insurance agent in the same small town, have the kind of income that would allow a six-figure donation to a church building project? It was something to tell Troy, at any rate; Carmela said that Lois Stark claimed that she and her husband had a profitable investment portfolio, but maybe Troy would have a way of finding out more.

Kelly was at the public access computers, helping a young woman with her resume, when she heard Mrs. Stark say, "Hello, Jarrod."

Her tone was rather cool. And Jarrod's response lacked his usual ebullient swagger.

"Hey, Kelly," he said, approaching the circulation desk. "I hear congratulations are in order."

Kelly kept her gaze on the monitor. "Look it over before you print," she advised the patron. "You don't want to have any typos. Even if you use spellcheck, remember that it doesn't know how to distinguish between—"

"Kelly," Mrs. Stark interrupted, "you have a patron at the desk."

"I can help you," Carmela, who had been in the workroom processing new acquisitions to the collection, came to the desk.

"I think Jarrod has business with Kelly," Mrs. Stark's tone was dismissive.

"I'll be with you in a moment, Jarrod," Kelly said, "as soon as I've finished helping Amy."

"No problem," Jarrod said hurriedly. "I'll wait."

Kelly continued with the computer patron, running a swift eye over the resume to look for errors. Amy's husband had just lost his job due to downsizing within the corporation and she was returning to work after a five-year absence to stay home with their two young children.

"It looks good to me," Kelly said with a smile.

"Hit print?"

"Hit print. Jarrod, how can I help you?"

Kelly returned to the desk where Jarrod was leaning, some of his insouciance returning.

"I hear that congratulations are in order," he said. "Hey, what's this? No ring? At least I gave you a ring. Maybe your police officer fiancé can't afford it?"

That was bold, even for Jarrod. Kelly stared at him. "I don't think it's any of your business, is it?" she said, reluctant to nurture any more engagement chatter than was necessary.

"Ohhhh, did I hit a sensitive spot? I tell you what, I still have our ring. How about if I give it to your policeman?"

Kelly was about to respond when she noticed that Mrs. Stark was paying avid attention to the conversation. Why?

"I don't think so," she said, "although I'll tell him you offered."

"So how about lunch tomorrow?" he coaxed. "I'll be in town; we're working on a rally for Representative Eldredge next month. Lunch?"

"Go ahead, Kelly," Mrs. Stark said. "I'm sure Carmela can handle things."

"I always handle things when Kelly goes to lunch," Carmela reminded Mrs. Stark.

"In case this is a longer lunch than usual," Mrs. Stark said.

Rep. Eldredge. The Starks. Lucas missing.

"I'll go to lunch with you," Kelly said. "It'll be an hour. Is that clear?"

"Perfectly," Jarrod said. "I'll pick you up at noon." He glanced over at Mrs. Stark. "Give you a chance to see what it's like to ride in a fancy sports car."

Mrs. Stark nodded.

"And that didn't make sense either," Kelly told Troy later that night over pizza. "It was like he was getting her approval."

"It's her car," Troy reminded Kelly.

"I know that, but he's not a teenager asking his mom for the keys," Kelly said impatiently. "I felt like it was all staged."

"Staged?"

"Mrs. Stark's voice when he came in . . . she wasn't welcoming. But once he started with the smart aleck remarks about the ring—"

"Maybe I should rent-a-ring."

"—and invited me to lunch, her tone changed. And she nodded when he mentioned the ride in his car."

"A sports car beats an SUV," Troy acknowledged.

"I have a car," Kelly pointed out. "It's mine and I paid for it. I didn't get it from someone who might have used drug money to buy it for her son."

Troy smiled. That was Kelly; she didn't lose sight of what mattered. If Jarrod thought he could lure her into anything because he was driving an expensive car, he didn't know his ex-fiancée very well. "It might be worth going to lunch for him," Troy considered.

"That's what I thought. He might know something about the Starks and their support of Eldredge. Maybe he knows something about the Travis Shaw interviews."

"Be careful," Troy cautioned. "Don't give away anything, even your suspicions."

"I won't. But I want Lucas to be found."

"So do I. Right now, though, I want to know who broke into Mia Shaw's apartment while she was up at Leo's camp for the Fourth of July weekend."

"A break-in?"

"A real one this time. Someone stole the piggy banks she kept her tip money in. That's money she was saving for the kids' Christmas presents. The window was broken, that's how the intruder got in. She came into the office just as Stark was leaving. He said he'd go out and check things out. That wasn't what she wanted; I don't think she wants him anywhere near her place, but she wants to know who stole the money."

"Poor Mia. Anyone would be alarmed to be robbed like that. How is she?"

"The landlord is fixing the window; in the meantime, she's staying with Leo and Millie and the kids. She doesn't want the kids to know why; she said she told them her landlord is having some repairs done."

"How much was stolen?"

"She's not sure, but over $500. She's saved a lot," Troy said. "She wants to give the kids a Christmas that will make up for the ones she didn't give them. But now the money is gone."

"Having their mom with them is going to be worth a lot more than presents," Kelly said.

"I know that, and you know that, but it's not an easy point to make."

"Did Chief Stark take her seriously?"

"He did," Troy admitted. "I guess because money was stolen."

"He didn't make any nasty insinuations about the money and where it might have gone?"

"No. He said he'd be out there himself to check it out. He'll have been there and back by now."

"Will he tell you what he found?"

"There might not be anything to tell," Troy said. "They'll have tested for fingerprints, but they'll only show up as a match if they belong to someone already in the database."

"I would think that someone who steals kids' piggy banks has stolen before!" Kelly declared indignantly.

"How do you figure that? The piggy banks weren't in an obvious place; she said she keeps them in her bathroom cupboard, so that she can put her tip money in when she's taking off her uniform after work."

"Because," Kelly said. "Anyone who would steal from a piggy bank is a thief."

"Or a kid looking for easy money," Troy argued. "They made quite a haul with this, whoever did it."

"I hope you find out who it is, and I hope you catch them!"

23

LUNCH WITH JARROD

Even though she wasn't really engaged to Troy, Kelly felt inexplicably ill-at-ease the next day when it was time for her to leave for lunch. Her distaste for the ruse wasn't helped when Mrs. Stark entered her office as Kelly was getting her purse.

"You know, Kelly, Jarrod has prospects," she told her.

"For lunch?" Kelly asked, deliberately misunderstanding Mrs. Stark's comment.

Irritation creased Mrs. Stark's features. "I'm sure he can afford a much better venue than The Café or that pizza place across the river," she snapped. "Or that sandwich place."

Kelly took her purse out of the bottom drawer of her desk. How did Mrs. Stark know where she and Troy ate? Was it merely because she was assuming that when they ate out, they chose local places that were close by? Or was it because there was someone watching?

That was a troubling thought.

"It's just lunch," she said.

"Jarrod has prospects," Mrs. Stark repeated. "He's doing very well with the Congressman. You know that Representative Eldredge is a particular friend of mine and my husband's."

"Yes, I think I'd heard something to that effect. You support his campaign."

"He's done very good things for this district. Naturally, as the chief law enforcement officer in the town, my husband maintains close ties with our elected officials."

Very close ties, Kelly thought. But then she heard Jarrod's voice as he came up to the circulation desk, natty and polished in a sleek white shirt, sleeves rolled up to his elbows, and a pair of tan trousers. His sunglasses were on top of his head and he had car keys in his hand.

"Ready?"

She really didn't want to do this. Mrs. Stark had a simpering look on her face, Jarrod's expression was eager and confident, and Carmela was glowering.

"I'll be back in an hour," Kelly said.

"Oh, we might be late," Jarrod said. "It'll take us at least 20 minutes to get there. I have a reservation, but—"

"I told you that I need to be back," Kelly said.

"Kelly, Carmela can take care of the desk," Mrs. Stark said. "You have my permission to take a longer lunch today."

Kelly's lips tightened as she held back a retort. Lucas, she reminded herself. She was trying to find out whether Jarrod knew anything about Lucas.

"What do you think of the car?" Jarrod asked as he opened the door of the sporty vehicle so that she could enter.

"Isn't this the car that the Starks' son drove?" Kelly asked disingenuously. "Scotty, the one who's in prison for murder? How'd you get his car?"

A faint crease of annoyance marred the contours of Jarrod's handsome countenance. "He's not driving it," he pointed out in a manner that he'd likely not have used in front of Mrs. Stark.

"I know that," she said. "But . . ."

"Let's just say it goes with my new position," he said smoothly paving over the obstacles in her question.

"But you work for Representative Eldredge," she said. "Unless Representative Eldredge works for the Starks." She made a point of laughing at this comment as if she recognized the absurdity of a small-town police chief having the upper hand over an elected state representative.

But Jarrod didn't laugh and as he pulled the car into traffic, he glanced at her. "Representative Eldredge is very grateful to the Starks for their support," he said. "They're very generous."

"That's what I hear," she said. "Someone said the insurance business must be very lucrative."

"They've invested wisely," Jarrod said. "That gives them the financial freedom to have political influence and to live the life they want to live."

"Who's their financial advisor?" Kelly inquired. "Maybe I should move my 401k. Has Representative Eldredge mentioned anything about financial advisors to you now that you're working for him?"

She knew that putting the spotlight of the conversation back on Jarrod was the best way to get him talking.

"We're concentrating on the election," Jarrod said. "He has bigger plans than state office, but for right now, this is a springboard. And when he goes to D.C., yours truly will be going right with him."

"I didn't know that you had political campaign experience."

"I've got a lot of experience in a lot of different areas," Jarrod said. "I haven't been letting the grass grow under my feet since I left Settler Springs."

"What have you been doing?"

"I've stayed in touch with people like the Starks, and when they realized that Representative Eldredge wasn't being well served by Keith—nice guy, real nice guy, but not savvy when it comes to the voters —Mrs. Stark suggested that I'd be able to help."

Once again, Jarrod hadn't really answered her. He'd presented her with a response that seemed plausible, but was, she realized, as empty of substance as— well, as Jarrod himself. How had she not realized this before? Or had it taken Troy, who was as genuine and substantive as a man could be, to make her remember to look below the surface?

"What's Representative Eldredge going to do about the drug problem?" she asked.

They were driving away from Settler Springs, confirming that she wouldn't be back in an hour. She knew that Carmela would understand but still, it bothered her that Mrs. Stark had engineered this extended lunch. But why did Mrs. Stark want her to go to lunch with Jarrod?

"The drug problem isn't the main issue facing our area. It's jobs. People are distracted by the drug problem, but let's be honest—the cameras aren't on us—" he grinned as if he were used to media attention "and we can say what we think. People like the Krymanskis are always going to have problems. That doesn't mean that everyone is a drug addict."

"Who told you that?"

"No one had to tell me. I know about the episode in the library; Mrs. Stark told me that. Really, Kelly, do you want a public library to become a center for drug addicts to hang out?"

"They don't hang out at the library. Carrie came there because it's familiar to her. Luckily, I had Narcan—"

"You really took a risk, keeping that anti-overdose stuff around when you were told not to," Jarrod said. "Mrs. Stark was understandably ticked off about that."

"It's not for Mrs. Stark to decide. The board didn't object a year ago when I went to a conference on preventing overdose deaths. Libraries are facing real-life problems; we can't bury our faces in our books and pretend that the issues beyond our walls will stay outside."

"Look, Kelly, Mrs. Stark knows that you have a kind heart. Believe me, I put in a good word for you and told her that you're the kind of person who will go out on a limb for people. But you need to give this serious thought."

"I gave it serious thought when I came back from the conference," she replied, her voice tight.

"Here we are," Jarrod said. "You always liked Chinese food. This is just about the best Chinese in the region. It just opened this spring. I didn't want to take you here right away; new restaurants have glitches to work out. But me and some of the staff came here a couple of weeks ago and I was impressed. I think you will be too."

The Chinese restaurants in the Settler Springs area were small outfits run by recent immigrants; the servings were generous and the décor was fairly standard, but Kelly was comfortable in the environment and she'd included several of the proprietors in a program she had done a year ago on other cultures.

This restaurant was not content with paintings of dragons and photographs of the Great Wall as decorations. The host led them into a private room and Kelly noticed that the entire restaurant was a series of private rooms, with doors that sequestered the diners. No wonder a politician's staff found it promising.

"What do you think?" he asked, waiting for her verdict.

"Very nice," she said, not entirely happy that she and Jarrod would be having such an extremely private lunch. "But I'll wait to give an opinion until I've tasted their General Tso's."

She had forgotten Jarrod's habit of ordering for her. He did so now. The waiter, who seemed to recognize him, seemed to at least remember him from that prior dining engagement.

After the server took their orders and left, Jarrod leaned closer across the table. "I'm glad you accepted my invitation, Kelly," he said.

"It seems as though Mrs. Stark was glad, too," she said. "Why?"

"She thinks highly of you," he answered immediately, "She doesn't want to see you tie yourself down to a small-town cop with no future."

"Who says Troy doesn't have a future?" she demanded, defending him as if he really were her fiancé. He wasn't, of course, she knew, but he was a friend and someone she trusted. "He was in the military, served honorably, and now he's working as a policeman while he goes to college. That sounds like a future to me."

"If he had a future, why'd he come to Settler Springs?" Jarrod made a face. But it might have been a reaction to the tea; Jarrod was not a tea drinker.

"Because his good friend and Army buddy, Sean Claypool, was from here and Sean told him what a nice town it was. That stayed in Troy's mind and when he left the military, he decided to come here."

"Sean Claypool . . . he's the guy who shot himself. The Army vet with PTSD and a police record. Not exactly someone whose opinion I'd seek out when looking for ideas on where to settle down."

"There are some unanswered questions about Sean's death," Kelly said. "He had no reason to kill himself. He was found dead in a car that belonged to someone on Representative Eldredge's staff, someone who was away in Florida and had left his car there. How would Sean have known that?"

"Car thieves take chances, Kelly," Jarrod said. "Don't be naïve."

"He didn't need to steal a car; he could use Troy's whenever he wanted."

"I suppose he didn't want to kill himself in his friend's car."

"What if he didn't kill himself?"

Jarrod stared. "Of course, he killed himself. Mrs. Stark told me all about it. That's what the coroner ruled. Kelly, you can't make up fantasies to suit whatever it is that your police officer boyfriend is telling you. You have to think for yourself. You know, I thought that being apart for a year might make you see things differently."

"See what things differently?"

Jarrod grinned, confident, sure of himself, knowing that he looked attractive in his deceptively casual summer garb and his styled hair. "Me, for one. I've got some solid prospects now, Kelly. I told you I was going to make something of myself. Now I'm doing it. Are you really going to expect me to believe that you'd rather stay in Settler Springs than move somewhere where things are happening? Something like Washington, D.C., for instance?"

24

CHIEF STARK INVESTIGATES

"We might not know where Lucas Krymanski is now," Chief Stark said, "but we know where he was. His prints are all over the place in Mrs. Shaw's apartment. He broke in, took the money, and now he's disappeared." The police chief's smooth features did not quite conceal the expression of satisfaction on his face; a demeanor that might have been interpreted as the professional reaction to a mystery that had been solved. But Troy, staring back at the chief, knew better.

"Krymanski did it," Chief Stark said.

"Then you'll be intensifying the search for him," Troy said.

The barest nuance of irritation appeared in Chief Stark's eyes but didn't last. "That kid is long gone," Stark said dismissively. "He's probably found some friends and they're using the money for drugs."

"Lucas didn't do drugs," Troy said.

"His sister did," Chief Stark countered.

The two men were in the police station. Kyle was still there, preparing to leave now that his shift was over. Troy had just come into the office to begin his shift. It was apparent that Chief Stark had waited for Troy's arrival to reveal the news that the identity of the thief who'd broken into Mia Shaw's apartment was Lucas Krymanski.

"She's in rehab."

"Maybe her brother will join her," the Chief said.

Troy knew it wasn't true. He would have said so, if not for the silent warning that was coming from Kyle as expressively as if the man were speaking. He wasn't, but he didn't need to, and Troy knew that Kyle had the right approach. But it was hard for him to tamp down his anger. The Chief and whoever was involved in this scheme needed a reason for Lucas to be missing, so they'd manufactured one by staging a break-in of Mia Shaw's apartment, complete with stolen piggy banks holding the funds she'd been saving to buy presents for her kids. Troy was surprised that Stark hadn't scheduled a press conference to announce his news.

"I told Mrs. Shaw myself," the Chief said. "I didn't want her to be afraid that the thief would return."

"How do you know he won't?" Kyle asked curiously.

Stark turned his head to frown at the motor-scooter officer, whose temperament and handicap kept him out of the crossfire of discussions between Stark and Troy. "What do you mean?" he asked, uncertain if Kyle was voicing support or challenging his superior.

"If Lucas Krymanski did the break-in, why wouldn't he go back?"

"Because we know he did it."

"How does he know that you know," Kyle went on, "if we're not out searching for him?"

"I told you, there's been no sign of him since he disappeared. He's left the area; you can count on it. He probably has dealer friends to run to and he's with them."

Kyle shook his head. "We've never had drug trouble with him," he said. "Mischief, that's all."

"It doesn't take much before mischief turns into crime," Stark said.

"Is that how it happened with Scotty?" Troy asked.

Chief Stark's head jerked back as if he'd been struck. "Watch your mouth, Kennedy," he warned. "Maybe Travis Shaw isn't the only person serving time in prison for a crime he didn't commit."

As soon as he was alone in the office, Troy called the ambulance station and asked for Jimmy Patton. "When's our next meeting?" he asked.

"Something going on?"

"Just seems like we'd better get moving if we want to have a league in operation for fall."

"My house, Saturday, lunchtime. You want to let everyone know?"

"Oh, yeah."

Troy's outrage fueled his efficiency. He went out to patrol and by the time his shift ended that night, he'd managed to contact everyone who was ostensibly interested in joining the Public Servant Bowling League of Settler Springs. When Kelly heard that

Lucas had been accused of the break-in, she went silent on the other end of the phone.

"I need to talk to Tia," she said. "She doesn't need this. Lucas wouldn't rob anyone's piggy bank! What's going on, Troy? What's he up to?"

"Finding a way to make Lucas look guilty so that people will figure he ran away because of what they're saying he did."

"How can they say he did it? I'll bet he's never been inside Mia's apartment."

"I don't think he has either, but evidence can be planted."

He wished they were having this conversation in person, not over the telephone, but it was late. She was probably ready for bed by now, and he'd be doing the same shortly, after he unwound from the day. He still hadn't heard the full account of how her lunch with Jarrod had gone; she'd just said that Jarrod believed what the Starks told him and wasn't questioning anything. She hadn't pressed the issues because she didn't want her views to get back to Mrs. Stark, but she admitted to Troy that she wondered why Mrs. Stark had been intent on Kelly going out to lunch with Jarrod.

But that wasn't what was important, not now that Lucas was both missing and accused of robbery.

"Mia will be at the meeting," Kelly said confidently. "She missed the first one because she was talking to Carrie Krymanski about rehab, but she'll be at this one. Won't she?"

"We're contacting everyone. I just wanted to let you know in advance what's going on."

"Is Stark announcing what he says they found?"

"I don't know what he's going to do. The break-in at Mia's place wasn't publicly known, and I'm not sure how widespread Stark wants it to be. Kyle pointed out that if Lucas is guilty, there should be a search for him."

"Kyle said that? I thought he stays out of the arguments."

"He always has before. But his point is a valid one: if Lucas is the thief, then why isn't there a search going on for him?"

"Because Stark doesn't want him to be found? But that doesn't make sense either, does it?"

Troy didn't answer.

"Oh, Troy, no," Kelly said, reading his silence. "You think—no, he wouldn't. He wouldn't kill Lucas . . ."

"I don't know what he'll do."

"We have to find him," she said immediately.

She made the same point the following day for lunch when they all gathered at Jimmy Patton's house. A steady rain had cancelled their Saturday run, and Troy and Kelly decided that they'd meet at Jimmy's rather than The Café. It felt odd to have a Saturday that didn't include the Trail or their usual breakfast, but he figured that, since they were an engaged couple, at least in the eyes of the town, they could spend the afternoon together and go out to eat at night. Like a date. He didn't think he'd better present it that way to Kelly, however.

It was apparent from the start that while the official reason for the gathering was to further plans for the bowling league, the real purpose was to update everyone on the Starks.

Troy took the lead. "Chief Stark told Kyle and me that it was Lucas Krymanski who broke into your apartment, Mia, and stole the money you had saved for Christmas presents for your kids. He says that's why Lucas is missing; because he ran away to spend the money and that he's probably involved with the drug dealers who supplied his sister. Stark is making it sound like Lucas uses. He's setting up what will seem like a plausible scenario: Lucas runs away because he's guilty. But if he's guilty, why isn't there a search for him?"

"I don't believe it," Mia said. Leo, sitting beside her, was shaking his head. "I think someone broke in to scare me and they stole the money because it made the break-in a robbery. Why would a kid break into my place?"

"I suppose they'll say that Lucas has drug contacts that used to be connected to your ex," Troy said. "I'm not sure how well thought out this whole plan is— they might be making it up as they go along—but they've got Lucas. That I'm sure of."

"Why?" Jimmy Patton asked. "I saw him that day when his sister OD'd. He was scared and worried for her. That wasn't the look of a kid who's in deep with the dealers who almost caused his sister's death. And I'm going to say that when I go to the library board meeting next week."

"Don't," Troy said. "Don't bring Lucas into the discussion."

"Why not? He was looking out for his sister."

"Tell Tia that, but not Mrs. Stark. If you're scheduled on the agenda for the library board meeting, focus on the quick action that saved a life."

Jimmy looked at Kelly sitting across from him. "I'm going to say that," he said. "Kelly did save a life. Despite Lois Stark's efforts to see Carrie die."

"Jimmy, if you put it that way, the Starks will start to see you as an adversary," Kelly warned him.

Beside her, Carmela was nodding grimly. "There's no telling what could happen. You have to keep the ambulance center free of any controversy while this is going on."

"What are the Starks going to do to me?" Jimmy scoffed.

"Jimmy," Kelly entreated. "Please don't go out-of-bounds on this. We need you in Settler Springs."

Troy continued on that theme. "You're the one who sees the results of what happens when people use drugs. We need to be able to connect the dots on this. Who's running this, who's supplying, who's profiting. Who killed Lyola Knesbit and why? Was Sean murdered to warn me off? Was Lucas abducted in order to make him a suspect? When Chief Stark told us that there was evidence tying Lucas to the break-in at Mia's—"

"I don't care what he says, I don't believe that Lucas Krymanski has ever been in my apartment, especially after I was at his house to talk to Carrie about going to rehab—"

Leo patted his daughter on her arm to calm her down. It was evident that she was upset and angry at the turn of events.

Troy went on. "He said that maybe Travis Shaw isn't the only one serving prison time for a crime he didn't commit."

"He's trying to make me look guilty," Leo exclaimed.

"Yes, he is." Troy kept calm, knowing how viscerally Leo would react to the accusation that he was guilty, and Travis was innocent. "So, we have to cover all the bases. And first base is Lyola Knesbit's murder. We know Travis Shaw murdered her. But we don't know why."

DEEPER INTO THE CRIMES

Carmela spoke up with an eager air. "I've been asking my friends at LifeLight about the church finances and how they do things. Or rather, how differently Lyola Knesbit did them compared to how Mrs. Stark does them. Mrs. Stark handles all the money, everything is documented. She counts the money at home after worship. Some people aren't happy about that, they think the offering should be counted in the church office like it used to be. But no one has spoken up about it. It's strange, though . . . Mrs. Stark has convinced the church Finance Committee that more giving should be done in cash, rather than checks."

"Why?"

"She said she's old fashioned, and she prefers cash. No one is accusing the accounting of being off, everyone's donations are accurate. Her records are accurate," Carmela said grudgingly. "But it doesn't make a lot of sense." Carmela shook her head. "She said they didn't have checks or electronic giving in the Bible and that's what everyone should be doing. That's just about the stupidest thing I've heard."

By the expressions on the faces of those around the table, it was clear that Carmela wasn't alone in her assessment of Mrs. Stark's theological view of giving to the church.

Troy was thoughtful. "What about the envelopes?" he said. "The envelopes that Lyola Knesbit used. Wasn't there some question about money being short for the Groundhog Day trip?"

"The money was short!" Carmela said. "I know, I counted it and we didn't have enough. We had to use the money we'd planned as profit to give the bus driver a tip." It was clear that this still irked Carmela, months after the excursion. "Lyola thought someone at the church was taking money from the envelopes."

Kelly recalled that Mrs. Knesbit had blamed Mia Shaw for the missing money. She suspected that

Carmela had also heard this but fortunately had enough tact not to mention it.

"When Mrs. Stark became treasurer after Lyola's death, she said that she wasn't going to let money be kept in the church because that was what had happened."

"That it was stolen?"

Carmela nodded at Troy's query. "She said keeping the money all accounted for would prevent anything from being stolen; no one would have access to it. Everyone went along with it."

"But no one knows who took the money?"

"No," Carmela said, resolutely not looking in Mia's direction. Kelly guessed that Carmela did not believe that Mia was guilty of stealing the money, and Kelly agreed. "The congregation just decided that, once Mrs. Stark became treasurer, they'd let her make the decision and avoid any more money being missing."

Leo didn't know that his daughter had been Lyola Knesbit's prime suspect, but his cop instincts were still in effect. "What if Mrs. Stark took the money," he said, "to create a reason for going to a different system for handling the offering income?"

Troy nodded. He'd been thinking the same thing. But if that was true, it meant that Lyola Knesbit's death on Groundhog Day was a foregone conclusion so that Lois Stark could take over as treasurer. It was still a flimsy strategy, Troy thought; churches didn't rake in the dollars. But if the Starks had an abundance of cash from drug income, then it was increasingly plausible that they needed a way to dispose of it without actually losing money. Substituting drug income cash for church offering donations would do that.

Still, it was primitive. Reasonably effective, in case anyone ever investigated the offering money and found traces of any drugs on the bills. But how likely was it that this would happen? Only if the Starks fell under suspicion and higher authorities became involved. But if the Starks maintained close ties to Representative Eldredge, it wasn't likely that they'd ever be suspects in a drug sting. Particularly if they laid the groundworks for their alibis, while getting rid of anyone who could speak against them.

It still wasn't enough to go on. But it was a start. And he noticed, from the speculative gleam in Doug Iolus' eyes, that he was thinking the same thing.

"Kelly," Troy said, his manner businesslike. "Did you learn anything from Jarrod Zabo?"

Kelly hadn't expected to be addressed at this meeting about the lunch. "Not really," she said. "He said that Representative Eldredge has plans to run for national office, for the Senate, but that's not unusual in politics. He says the Starks are generous donors to Representative Eldredge's re-election campaign. He believes everything the Starks have told him about Sean Claypool's death, about why Mrs. Stark doesn't think libraries should bring back drug overdose victims with Narcan, that the drug problems in town are problems only for certain kinds of people, like the Krymanskis—"

"That's not true!" Jimmy said angrily. "He's an idiot if he thinks that."

"He might be an idiot," Kelly said, "but he's not an accomplice. He believes what they tell him. I really don't think he's involved in any of it."

"If he's facilitating any of it, he's involved in it," Troy disagreed.

"Jarrod was never one to go below the surface," Kelly said, resenting Troy for putting her in a position where she had to speak on Jarrod's behalf rather than let him be accused of complicity in whatever the Starks were doing. "He'd believe what he's told because..."

"Because the Starks have money and let him drive their son's fancy car," Doug said succinctly, "and because Eldredge is his step up on the ladder of success."

Kelly nodded. Doug had perfectly described Jarrod's motives.

"Leo," Troy moved on, "you're recovering from an attack. Nothing was disturbed at your job site, nothing was stolen. But you were hit on the head for no apparent reason. Any thoughts on why?"

"Thoughts, sure, but nothing I can prove. I work for a security company in Pittsburgh," Leo explained to the group. "My boss wasn't happy when those interviews with Travis Shaw started showing up on the news. Shaw claims he's innocent and I forced him to confess to a crime he didn't commit."

Carmela started to speak up in support, but Troy raised his hand. It was time for Leo to speak.

"Then this happened, and now I'm off work while I go through concussion protocol. I'm fine, but my boss told me to wait before I come back. I'm not sure he wants me to come back," Leo said candidly.

"So, you lost your job here because of Travis Shaw's interviews, and now you're concerned you might be losing a second job for a reason that you can only speculate about."

"I guess," Leo said. "I'm off with pay for now, but I don't know how long that will last."

"Are you going to look for a new job?"

"I'll have to, if I lose this one. Millie and me, we aren't rich like the Starks—"

"Jarrod said the Starks have a good investment plan. I asked who their financial advisor is, but he didn't say. He might not know," Kelly told them.

"And their investment plan might not have an advisor," Jimmy said in harsh tones. "It might be what gets smuggled in through the drug routes. But as long as they seem respectable, everyone will believe the story about the smart investments. I remember when Scotty Stark was driving around in that fancy car, wondering how the heck a high school graduate could afford a car like that."

"It was registered in his mother's name," Doug reminded Jimmy. "It was in her name, but they gave it to Scotty for a graduation present."

"That was in what, May? And by the end of the year, he was behind bars for murder. But it sounds like Stark has plans to somehow prove his son's innocence, just like he has plans to prove Travis Shaw's innocence. Even though we both know that, in neither case, are those two innocent. Meanwhile, Lucas Krymanski is missing. And Jarrod Zabo is driving Scotty Stark's car."

"Jarrod said that the car goes with his position as campaign advisor," Kelly said, aware that she sounded as if she was defending Jarrod. That wasn't her intention, but neither could she allow him to be viewed as a suspect. Jarrod saw everything in terms of how it benefitted him. It wouldn't occur to him that the Starks might be offering him the forbidden fruit of temptation in the form of an expensive car.

How had she ever thought herself in love with him?

"You didn't tell them about the black pickup truck with the skull logo on the back windshield."

The rain had stopped, the sky had cleared, and Troy and Kelly, after leaving Jimmy's home, decided to spend the rest of the afternoon together in a tacit acceptance of the perks of being known as an engaged couple without having to pay allegiance to any of the obligations. There was a Greek food festival at Logan Heights; a carnival at Lenape Run; an outdoor band concert at the Little League baseball field in Armstrong, but after considering the events, both Kelly and Troy had decided that they didn't feel like doing any of them.

"We'll drive out of town and stop when we feel like it," Troy suggested, following his words by heading past the police station and out of Settler Springs. "I didn't bring up the truck because I'm not sure . . ."

"You're worried that someone will tell someone without meaning to, and it'll give away the one advantage that we have."

"That we might have," Troy cautioned. "It sounds likely that Lucas was abducted by the driver of the pickup, but we only have the word of his friends to go on. I believe them, but Stark would demolish any suggestion that this was evidence. Not that it would come to that, because all he'd have to do is remove the skull image from the windshield."

"Shouldn't we at least say that we think it might have been a black pickup?"

"Maybe. I don't know. I don't know how valuable Lucas is to Stark right now."

"You mean alive, don't you?"

It was no use hiding the truth from Kelly. "Yes," Troy said. "From what we've learned, we know that Stark needs Lucas to be seen as guilty. But that argues for needing him alive, or at least not—Stark doesn't want a body."

"It's not likely that Lucas would make a convincing suicide," she said. "Not like Sean."

She had it figured out. Troy didn't like keeping what he knew from the rest of the group, and he would definitely let Doug know. But Doug was used to keeping secrets for the safety of others. Carmela was a different matter; if she knew, she would alert everyone in her wide circle of acquaintances that a black pickup truck with a skull on the back windshield was suspected of being involved in the disappearance of Lucas Krymanski. She would do it with the best of intentions and the purest of motives, but the result would be the same, and that would put Lucas in more danger and warn Stark that the truck had to be disposed of, or altered, so that it was no longer incriminating.

"No."

They were quiet for the next few miles, each intent on pursuing thoughts which circled in a maze around the disappearance of Lucas and what they could do about it. The silence was interrupted by Arlo, who had been dozing in the back, raising his head and delivering the signature whimper that meant he needed to be taken out.

They were close to a park and Troy pulled into the parking lot, which was crowded with cars, evidence that summer picnic season was in full swing. He put Arlo on a leash, and he and Kelly walked along the pet path. The weather was warm, typical July heat and, after the earlier rain, humid. But the path was lined with trees and the shade was welcome.

They were far enough out of town that it was unlikely they would encounter anyone they knew. Kelly turned the conversation back to the subject of the investigation.

"Do you really think it's possible that Mrs. Stark wanted to be the church treasurer so badly that she'd want Lyola Knesbit killed?"

"I've said before that it's a clumsy way to launder money—substitute her own cash, from selling drugs, for the cash that's deposited by the church. But clumsy or not, it might be all she could think of. Donating generously to Representative Eldredge is another way. Letting Jarrod use her son's car . . . and trying to get you to be interested in Jarrod again . . . they aren't sophisticated tactics, but I don't know that the Starks are all that experienced in being criminals. We don't know how they got into this."

"They couldn't have afforded that car without an extra income, and it was a graduation present for Scotty, so that's only a year or so ago."

"Then they're probably novices. When the money first came in, they might have splurged—the car, for instance. Then—and this is speculation—campaign contributions to a friendly legislator."

They paused while Arlo investigated the suitability of a spot, sniffing the ground, circling, looking up, all part of his normal evaluation process.

"But they still want to look good in town," Kelly guessed. "They have an image to uphold. They've been prominent citizens in Settler Springs for a number of years. A long time, really."

"Long enough that no one would think they're guilty of anything as heinous as drug trafficking or murder."

Kelly nodded. "I always thought of them as . . ." she paused. "It sounds unbelievable now, but they were pillars of the community to me. Always generous when the library had a fundraising campaign. Mrs. Stark was invited to join the library board more than five years ago, and she seemed dedicated to promoting our work. When the Nominating Committee presented her name for the office of president two years ago, we all thought it would be a good decision. How could we not have seen what was going on? I feel like we've all been blind, and it took you coming to town, a stranger, to see what we couldn't or wouldn't see."

"It took you, Kelly, determined to prove that Lucas hadn't murdered Tyra Cardew, to reveal what no one realized. I worked with Stark and I knew there was something wrong, but I didn't know it included drugs or murder. All I knew was that he was overbearing and that Leo and Kyle accepted the rules that the police force operated on, even though they weren't fair. Now they both have another view of how things are. The change in Leo is obvious, he's not even on the force anymore, but even Kyle has new insights. He doesn't say much. I don't suppose he can take the chance, or he'd end up like Leo did. But I don't think he'll just fall in line again."

"Jimmy knows now, too. Doug knows. Carmela. Mia . . ." Kelly was thoughtful. "More people know the truth. But if we can't prove it, what they know won't matter and everyone will become cynical about a corrupt police chief because they'll figure that they can't change anything. 'Can't fight City Hall,'" she quoted. "I don't want Settler Springs to turn into that kind of town, a place where families like the

Krymanskis are always first to be suspects in any situation, and where families like the Starks are seen as innocent."

"Scotty Stark isn't innocent. He's in prison. For now, anyway."

"Until they can find a way to clear him and blame Lucas. Just like they're trying to clear Travis Shaw by blaming Leo."

Arlo, having finished his business, gazed up at his master patiently. It was time to move on, his posture seemed to say, but he wasn't going to be the one to press the issue. The park was filled with the smells of food being grilled, the vigor of activity and noise, the sounds of happy people enjoying the weather, the weekend, time spent together outside, eating and laughing. Arlo enjoyed the atmosphere around him.

It was a setting denied to the Krymanski family. Tia had a daughter who was in rehab for her drug use and a son who had disappeared. Meanwhile, she had to hold down a job to support her five children. Even though she had divorced her Krymanski husband, she'd kept his name, and his family stood by her. They would help her as much as they could, Troy knew, but they were helpless when it came to saving the children who were in jeopardy.

"Doug is still doing his surveillance at the cemetery," Troy said, his rumination taking him to this recollection. "I'll find out if he's noticed a black pickup truck among the vehicles that he's seen. He's been concentrating on photographing people, but if he knows that we need leads on that truck, he'll be looking for it."

"Do you think the truck will show up?"

"Whoever is driving it must be pretty central to whatever Stark is running."

"What if it's just the latest Eddie Kendrick," Kelly asked, "someone who does their dirty work and will be expendable if they need to get rid of him?"

Troy couldn't refute this viewpoint. "Maybe," he said. "But it's all we've got, and we have to follow it and see where it takes us. Lucas is somewhere. He's a smart kid and a resourceful kid; if there's any way to escape, he'll find it."

THE LIBRARY BOARD MEETINGS

Mrs. Stark opened the meeting of the library board of trustees.

"The agenda shows that Jimmy Patton of the Settler Springs Ambulance Center has asked to speak to the board. Jimmy, you know that you're limited to five minutes."

Jimmy's genial smile was in place. "I do, Mrs. Stark. I want to thank the library staff for saving a life. Most of you know that it's thanks to the quick thinking of your director, Kelly Armello, that a young overdose victim is now alive and undergoing rehab. Kelly administered the anti-overdose drug, Narcan—"

"We're aware of what took place, Jimmy," Mrs. Stark said. "The board will discuss whether or not Kelly should be reprimanded for disobeying my orders, which were specifically to avoid any situation in which the library can be seen as encouraging drug use among our young patrons."

Several of the board members showed discomfort at Mrs. Stark's comment. Kelly kept her expression impassive and avoided looking directly at Jimmy.

However, Jimmy was aware that his presence at the meeting would not be welcomed by the board president. "I'm sorry to hear that, Mrs. Stark. Because I've told the county commissioners what Kelly did, and we're going to present her with a commendation for her actions as a public servant responding to a need. The county commissioners agree with me that in order to fight this epidemic of drug use, we all need to be engaged in the battle."

Mrs. Stark frowned. "The county commissioners?" she repeated. "Don't they have better things to do?"

"I guess they think this is one of those better things," Jimmy said. "I'm here on behalf of the commissioners and the ambulance crew to invite all of you to attend the ceremony next month. We're tying the ceremony in with our back-to-school drug prevention program and we're encouraging the public servants of Settler Springs to be part of our campaign. I think everyone here agrees that drugs are a threat to the wellbeing of our citizens?"

He looked around the table; nodding heads confirmed his query.

"We're all proud of Kelly for what she did," spoke up Frank Serick, the retired dentist who had been on the library board since leaving his practice a decade before.

"We'll withhold any public statement, Frank, of Kelly's actions, until we've had a chance to discuss it amongst ourselves. It's not a matter for public consumption."

"Our meetings are open to the public," Frank said. "I don't care who hears what I have to say. I think what Kelly did shows that libraries aren't locked into the past; libraries have to be aware of what's going on now. Kelly wasn't afraid to do what was right, even if it meant disobeying your order. Now, Lois," Frank went on as Mrs. Stark began to argue, "I know that you have the library's best interests in mind, and I respect that. But you can't reprimand Kelly on your own, and you can't give an order like that to her without board approval. I've been bothered by that for some time and—"

"This is a matter for discussion amongst the board members," Mrs. Stark said shrilly.

"I've said what I had to say," Jimmy said cheerfully. "I hope you'll all attend the ceremony. It'll be a good piece of publicity for the library. Mrs. Stark, I hope you'll be there, and I hope Chief Stark will be there as well. Fighting crime isn't just for our men in blue anymore. It's everyone's responsibility. I'll send details to the library once we have everything worked out. Thanks, folks," he said, gathering up his papers.

He smiled at Kelly as he left the library and she knew that Jimmy was well aware that he'd made an enemy of Mrs. Stark by his comments, and by the manner in which his news had inspired other board members to challenge her authority.

It was apparent that this topic was on the minds of the board members, because as soon as the door closed behind him, another board member spoke.

"The minutes should reflect that Kelly is going to be honored by the county commissioners for her actions," said Ruby Halloway, an older woman who had been active in Settler Springs civic organizations for most of her adult life, from her years as a mother when she'd been involved in the

Parent-Teacher Organization, to her years as a member of the school board, to now, in retirement, when she was engaged with the library board. "This is a credit not only to her, but to the public library as an institution in our community."

"I think you are all being very naïve," Mrs. Stark said. The twin spots of color that showed up on her cheekbones when she was angry were visible. "The library needs to present itself as a place where inexcusable behavior will neither be encouraged nor tolerated. By making this very public overdose something to commend instead of censure, the library is at risk of becoming a hangout for other delinquents."

"Oh, come on Lois," argued Frank. "Do you really think that drug users are suddenly going to start coming in here because a girl was brought back from an overdose?"

"I think it's a risk that we can't afford to take," Mrs. Stark responded.

"The risk of ignoring the drug problem is a greater one," said Gina McCain, who taught in the high school, where her familiarity with the drug crisis was inescapable.

"We aren't ignoring it," Mrs. Stark snapped. "We are trying to preserve the library's reputation. Kelly is jeopardizing that reputation."

"I don't feel that I am jeopardizing the library's reputation, Mrs. Stark," Kelly said, expressing herself for the first time during the meeting. "If there's something in my professional conduct that fails to meet the board's requirements, I'd like to know what it is. Perhaps I should leave the meeting, so that you can all speak freely. Mrs. Stark, you're in the library every day and you have been since February. You see me perform my duties. What is it that I'm doing that is at odds with the board's vision for the library?"

"Nothing at all, Kelly," Frank said. "We're pleased with your performance and your reviews show that. You go above and beyond in your efforts to make sure that the library serves the community. If Lois chooses to be in the library every day as a volunteer, that's up to her, but it's certainly not at our direction."

"Then there's no dissatisfaction with the way in which I carry out my administrative duties?" she asked, choosing her words with care because she intended to make a point which, if she was successful, might make Mrs. Stark even more angry with her.

"Certainly not; if there were a problem, we'd have brought it up to you."

"Then I can ask why the financial management of the library's billing, bank deposits and account reconciling has been taken away from me?"

"I wasn't aware that it had been," Frank said slowly, looking from Kelly to Mrs. Stark.

Aware that she had to offer an explanation for her decision, Mrs. Stark spoke up quickly. "I'm a businesswoman," she said. "Kelly's role is to be a library director. It makes much more sense from a business stance for me to take on that burden so that she doesn't have to."

"It was never a burden," Kelly said. "I administered the library's accounts with care. I know what we need and I know what we have. If the board was displeased with my performance, I would rather that I had been told, in an open manner."

"Kelly . . ." Ruby sat forward in her seat. Like Frank, she was studying both the director of the library and the board president, sensing undercurrents that had been heretofore veiled. "Mrs. Stark's role as president should not be overlapping with your responsibilities as director. They're two clearly distinct roles."

"I took over the duties because of my background in bookkeeping," Mrs. Stark defended herself.

"Were there any discrepancies in the financial recording that led you to do so?" Gina asked.

This was tricky. If there were discrepancies, Kelly perceived that it would have been Mrs. Stark's duty to bring this to the board's attention. As she had not mentioned any issues, there would seem to be no reason for her to take the task on. The fact that the official board treasurer, Debbie Rascone, was sporadic in her meeting attendance and lax in her duties had been the reason that Kelly had had more financial responsibilities than in previous years, but this was something which the board intended to address when elections were held at the end of the year. There had not been any decision by the board to permanently authorize the president to take on the treasurer's job.

"I have a better understanding of the overall accounting practices which need to be adhered to in financial recording," Mrs. Stark said.

Was it Kelly's imagination, or did Mrs. Stark seem nervous? She had been belligerent at the start of the meeting but now she seemed to be scrambling to find her footing in the suddenly slippery terrain of authority.

Ken Lattanzi, the vice president who had accepted the position because he had been assured that he wouldn't have to do anything, rarely spoke during the meetings. When he did so now, his voice aroused looks of surprise from some of the board members.

"That's probably true," he said. "But it's too much to ask of you. You run your own business and you have a busy schedule with your other civic engagements. I move that we appoint a committee to find a solution to this problem."

"There's no problem!" Mrs. Stark exclaimed. "I'm the board member with the most financial expertise. As you say, I have my own business. In addition, I'm the treasurer for LifeLight Church. I am involved in other organizations and of course, my husband and I are actively supporting Rep. Eldredge's re-election. Nonetheless, as president of the library board, I'm uniquely suited for overseeing the library's finances. It's actually a service to Kelly, so that she has more freedom to do her job, which is to help the library meet the needs of the community."

"Which she has done, by using an anti-overdose drug which many organizations have on hand for situations like the one that happened and saving a life. Jimmy Patton wants to recognize Kelly for her actions. The county commissioners want to make what Kelly did a springboard for a vigorous anti-drug campaign when school starts. Your wish to spare Kelly work is appreciated, Lois, but it's unnecessary. I've made a motion to form a committee to resolve this issue. We need a second for the motion."

AN UNEXPECTED VISITOR

W hen Troy learned from Kelly what had taken place at the board meeting, he felt as if maybe this was a blow, however small, against the unrestrained reach of the Starks.

"I know it won't change things right away," Kelly admitted the following Saturday when she and Troy, their run at The Trail completed, were enjoying breakfast at The Café. "But the board is going to form a committee, even though Mrs. Stark was against it, to review the situation. That will tie her hands if she's using the library in any way to funnel her drug earnings through library accounts."

"What made you do it?"

"I don't know. Jimmy came, like he said he was going to, and he said nice things, which again, we knew he would. But I suddenly felt that I had to do something, to speak up. The board had no idea how involved Mrs. Stark was in controlling the library's financial operation and even though no one has any reason to suspect her, they didn't like the way she was taking over. I could sense it. So that's when I asked whether I'd done something wrong that had led the board to want her to do the finances now."

"Maybe some of the board members don't like the way she runs things?"

"I don't know. All I know is that, even though it'll take a while for any committee to come to a decision that doesn't antagonize Mrs. Stark while still ensuring that the library operations are secure, I feel like I struck a blow for Lucas. Silly, I know, because there's no connection. But I felt better than I have in months."

Troy could understand that. He'd had several of his own similar reactions when he'd stood up to Chief Stark. All the same, it made Kelly vulnerable to retaliation that could put her in danger.

"Be careful," he advised. "You've challenged her publicly and you're also setting in motion the actions that will remove her from controlling how the library money moves. She might be mad, or she might be desperate. Either way, she's a threat."

"I don't think she's going to do anything. What can she do?"

That was never a safe question to ask, Troy thought. But he wasn't sure that he could convince Kelly, who was honest and forthright and kind, that the Starks were perfectly capable of working behind the scenes to undermine her position in the town that she loved. She wasn't a Krymanski, there was no ambiguity regarding her standing in the community. But Lucas' disappearance was a reminder that there were forces at work which would not be stopped by kindness or honesty or forthrightness.

"She can do whatever any other criminal can do," he said slowly.

"Hey, you two, have you set a wedding date yet?"

Francie had returned to their booth with a fresh pot of coffee to refill their cups and her own curiosity about their engagement.

"Not yet," Kelly said, managing a smile. "With my family living in Florida, and Troy's family spread all over the place, we're trying to work out the logistics."

Francie nodded in understanding. As she poured the coffee, she said, her voice lowered, "Is there anything new on Lucas? This is really making a wreck of Tia. She's strong, you both know that, but he's been missing for almost a month now and she's starting to think . . . you know, the worst."

"I haven't heard anything," Troy said. That was true; he'd gone to the state trooper barracks to speak with Trooper Callahan, who had confirmed that Trooper Meigle was handling the disappearance and, to the best of her knowledge, had nothing to report. Troy thought he detected concern in her voice as she answered his question, but then the telephone had rung and he had left.

"Shouldn't someone have heard something by now?" Francie persisted. "How can a kid be missing and no one knows anything? And don't for a minute tell me that Lucas ran away because he was in trouble."

The rumor that Lucas Krymanski had been involved in an apartment break-in had made its way through the town. No one knew where the rumor came from or where it got started, although Troy realized that,

246

as Mia Shaw had certainly not given credence to the story, Chief Stark had to be the source.

"No," Kelly said firmly. "Lucas wouldn't do that. I wish we had some news for Tia. Good news."

"She could use it. Actually, she has had some good news. Carrie is doing well in rehab. She's doing her schoolwork while she's there and she'll be able to make up the credits for the classes she failed, so she'll have her diploma by the time she's done. She's talking about community college; there are some counselors on the staff who are helping her figure out what she wants to do."

"That'll be good. If she leaves rehab with a plan, she'll have a better chance of making it through."

"That's what Tia says. So that's good news."

"If you hear anything, anything at all from Lucas, will you let us know?"

"Sure will. And if you hear anything about a date for the wedding, you let me know. I want to make sure my calendar is clear."

After she was out of earshot, Troy said, "How many people are coming to this mythical wedding, anyway?"

"I think it would be safe to say that everyone but the Starks would expect an invitation."

"Sounds crowded."

"Then it's a good thing it's not a real engagement."

"Oh, I don't know," Troy said teasingly. "I can think of some compensations for putting up with a crowd of wedding guests. The honeymoon, for instance."

"We'd never agree on a honeymoon destination," Kelly declared. For some reason, it was easier now to enter into the engagement façade; she wasn't sure why, but since it wasn't real, she was able to play the part with more aplomb.

"Beach," Troy said emphatically.

"Europe."

"Europe has beaches."

"And museums."

Troy groaned. "No one goes on a honeymoon to visit museums."

"Don't you want to see the Louvre?"

"I've seen it."

"You have? I've never been to Europe! Did you see—"

"My parents took us when my dad was stationed in Germany. We'd go to the other countries for vacation. I saw the paintings. Statues. All of that."

"You'd see it differently as an adult."

"Beach."

"Europe has beaches," she repeated demurely, sipping her coffee.

"Europe has beaches," he agreed with a smile.

After leaving the restaurant, they separated. Troy went home to do yard work and Kelly went to the library. She had work to do to prepare for the resumption of fall programming and preferred to do it without Mrs. Stark's presence. After the board meeting, Mrs. Stark's demeanor had been silent and hostile. Carmela, having heard about the results of the meeting, could barely contain her glee, and Kelly had cautioned her against revealing too much of what she was feeling. But the atmosphere was unquestionably tense.

There were plenty of things she'd rather be doing on a Saturday afternoon, but Sundays were busy with church activities. So, she parked in the back lot so that her car wouldn't be spotted, rather than have the Starks drive by and see that she was there. Kelly didn't want to provoke an altercation, and given Mrs. Stark's show of temper, she wasn't sure if the board president could be relied upon to be calm.

Balancing the two boxes in her arms, she shut the car door with her hip. Then her keys fell to the ground. Then the boxes fell, the contents of the top box spilling onto the lot. By the time she had gathered everything back up, she was feeling almost as irritated as she would have been had she encountered the Starks.

The back entrance of the library was a serene area, with a bench underneath a shade tree and a high wall of ebullient sunflowers that greeted patrons who entered the library from that direction. Kelly often went outside to take her lunch there because it was a fairly secluded area where she could enjoy the privacy and the scenery at the same time. Today, however, she strode past the arboreal barriers, unlocked the door, and went inside.

There was always work to do in the library, but Kelly set to her task with concentration. She updated the front entrance bulletin board with the schedules for the various story times, instructing parents and caregivers that the fall programs would begin in September after Labor Day. She had new posters for the Children's Room; these she left on Chloe's desk so that she could decorate as she preferred; Kelly was careful to allow the children's librarian as much autonomy as possible over her domain. Chloe was an asset to the library and so far, she had managed to remain outside the battles with Mrs. Stark; Kelly intended to make sure that remained so. She and Carmela could deal with the imperious library board president.

Although she had intended to only stay at the library for a couple of hours, she lost track of time, something that often happened when she was alone there. There were so many temptations: a display for September Banned Book Month; updating the vacation pamphlets that the local travel agency provided; gathering books on choosing a college and careers for high school seniors were just a few of the tasks that distracted Kelly after she finished the bulletin board.

She was surprised to realize that shadows were falling outside, indicating that she'd been at the library much longer than she'd planned. Her stomach was giving her the same message. She wondered if Troy would like to get a late supper somewhere, but then she decided against it. He had said he wanted to mow his lawn and take care of some other work around the yard; by now he was probably resting from his labors, enjoying the company of Arlo while sitting on the front porch.

She didn't feel like cooking. Sloppy Joe's was closed, and she'd already eaten at The Café that day. She needed to do some grocery shopping . . .

She opened the car door, surprised that it was unlocked. She always locked her car. But she must have forgotten, she realized, after the boxes fell. That was unwise, these days. Troy had repeatedly told her that, with everything that was going on, she should never leave her car door unlocked.

She turned the key and glanced in the rearview mirror to back out of the lot, even though she could have done it blindfolded. No one else was there. Then she froze as she saw sneaker-clad feet on the back seat.

"Miz Armello, do you think we could get a pizza? I'm hungry."

29

FINDING LUCAS

K elly's emotions went from fear to joy. "Lucas!"

"Shhhh," he cautioned from his hiding place on the floor of her back seat. "Don't look down. I don't think anyone saw me come here but they'll be looking for me. I've been hiding here since you went inside. You shouldn't leave your car unlocked, Miz Armello. But I'm glad you did."

Kelly backed the car out of the lot. "Where have you been? We've been so worried! Does anyone know—"

He cut her off. "Can we get a pizza? I haven't had anything to eat since yesterday and I walked all night."

"Walked from where?"

"The lake."

"The lake! You were there? Just by the lake or at one of the camps around it?"

"At the camp."

"You were kept there, you didn't go there by choice? Lucas, we've been so worried, your mom will be so relieved—"

"We can't tell her, Miz Armello. They'll be looking for me. I got away last night and I walked back into town. I had to hide every time I saw headlights coming. I didn't know where to go, and I figured I'd sit and rest in the library back yard where it's quiet and no one would be coming. Boy was I glad to see your car!"

"Why didn't you tell me you were here when you saw me get out of the car?"

"I don't want anyone to know I'm here. They'll be looking for me, Miz Armello. I think they might want to kill me."

"We need to tell Troy right away!"

"I know, but he can't tell anyone. I came here because I knew you wouldn't let them find me."

His words, spoken so matter-of-factly, brought tears to Kelly's eyes. If he was counting on her to protect him, she had to deliver on that faith. But she needed help.

"How about if I tell him I'm going to the Pizzaria . . ."

"I can't go inside!"

This pragmatic side of Lucas was a new one and Kelly realized that his travails, combined with his worry for his sister Carrie, had brought Lucas to a point of maturity that was very different from the mischievous boy who'd been sentenced to doing community service at the library after his Halloween prank at the mayor's house.

"I know," she assured him. "But he has to be told. He has resources that we don't. How about this . . ."

She outlined a brief scenario of action and Lucas agreed to it, as long as he'd get pizza out of it. That was easy to promise. She steered her car into a parking space and took her cell phone from her purse.

I'm going to the Pizzaria for a takeout pizza, she texted. *Meet you in the parking lot.*

? was the return reply.

You know you're hungry for pizza. You haven't had it since July 4.

He got it. *Yeah, you're right. I'll order it and leave now.*

Order mine too. "Lucas, what do you want on your pizza?"

"Everything except anchovies and green peppers and olives and onions. Can I have extra cheese?"

All-meat pizza, extra cheese, extra large.

That would alert Troy if nothing else did that she was not ordering the pizza for herself.

Got it.

Kelly put her phone away.

"You know," she commented as they crossed the bridge leading from Settler Springs to Warren Borough, "a vegetable on a pizza will not kill you. In fact, it might be good for you."

"That's what Mom says. How's—have you seen her lately?" Lucas asked.

Kelly had made a point of visiting Tia Krymanski once a week and giving her a call every few days. Lucas' mother was holding up as best as she could, but the worry she was feeling could not be disguised.

"She's doing as well as she can," Kelly said. "But she's worried about you and she misses you and—this is hard on her. Carrie is doing well, though," Kelly said, relaying to him the news she and Troy had gotten that morning from Francie.

When she drove into the parking lot of the PIzzaria, which was crammed with Saturday night diners, she saw Troy's SUV parked next to an empty spot. Quickly she pulled into the vacant space, rolled down the windows halfway on the driver's side of the car, then got out of the car and waited.

Troy emerged, carrying two pizza boxes. He smiled when he saw Kelly and started to hand over one of the boxes to her. But before he could do so, Kelly leaned forward and kissed him on his lips. As kisses went, it lacked finesse, but the fact that Kelly had initiated it and that she'd done so without disturbing his hold on the pizzas made it remarkable.

"Which is mine?" she asked in a businesslike fashion.

"On top," he said.

Kelly took the pizza and, opening the back door of the car, slid it onto the seat. "There's bottled water beneath your feet," she commented.

"I know," Lucas answered. "I had a bottle while I was waiting for you," Lucas said. "Can I eat now?"

"Go ahead, it's all yours. The windows are down, so you'll be able to hear what Troy and I are saying."

Troy's gaze didn't leave Kelly's face, intent though he was on the presence of Lucas in the back seat of her car.

"So," he murmured in the contented tones of a man who had just been kissed in public by his fiancée, knowing that the sight would have been observed by anyone in the parking lot and would serve convincingly as proof that nothing more was going on other than a meeting at the Pizzaria. "What's going on?"

"I went to the library this afternoon after we left The Café. I parked in the back. I had boxes, the boxes fell, the stuff inside spilled and I forgot to lock my car door. I know, I know. But it's a good thing I did," she said, smiling as if she and Troy were discussing the wedding, or weekend plans, or a honeymoon destination, nothing as serious as the fact that a kidnapping victim had taken refuge in her car. "Because when I got into my car, someone was waiting. He said he's been held by the lake. At the camp, all this time."

Their eyes met in shared speculation, but neither asked whether the camp where Lucas had been held was the one belonging to Mayor Truvert. That questioning would have to come later, when Lucas was free to speak safely.

The sounds of the boy's eager chewing made a wordless but expressive accompaniment to their conversation, eliciting a grin from Troy as Kelly gave him a brief account of what Lucas had told her.

"We have to meet somewhere."

"But where? Lucas says they'll be looking for him."

"I think they'll kill me if they find me," Lucas said, in between swallows of his pizza.

"Where can I take him?" Kelly asked. "If they start looking for him—"

"They've probably already started looking, if they know he's missing," Troy guessed.

"They'll know," Lucas said from the back seat. "At first they stayed there with me day and night. Then they started leaving me alone at night, tied up. When they came back this morning, they'd know that I was gone."

"They? How many?"

"Two guys."

"You saw them?"

"Yeah, I saw them."

Again, Kelly's eyes met Troy's gaze. If Lucas had seen his captors, then they would be impatient to find him.

"We have to find somewhere safe," Troy said. "Somewhere they won't think to look."

He saw headlights appear in the lot, heralding the arrival of another customer for pizza. When he noticed that the headlights belonged to a black pickup truck, he put his own pizza box on the hood of his car and put his arms around Kelly's waist. He lowered his head as if he were nuzzling her ear.

"Leo's camp," he whispered.

"But he was kept up at the lake—"

"They won't expect him to be there. I'm going to let Leo know and he can drive up to his camp tomorrow."

"What about tonight, and how will we get him to Leo's?"

"You have a garage. He'll be safer if he spends the night in your car, in the garage. Lucas, you okay with that?"

"Yeah, as long as I can use the bathroom," Lucas said before diving into another piece of pizza.

"In the morning, go to church like you always do. Lock everything like you always do. Almost always do," he corrected, frowning at Kelly for her lapse. "Stick to your routine. But Lucas needs to be in the back seat of your car when you go to church."

"Can I shower?" Lucas asked plaintively. "I'm kinda dirty from all the walking. It was hot. I didn't shower the whole time, either."

It was odd to have a disembodied voice and the sounds of chewing floating up from the back seat of her car with no apparent source. It was odd, too, but in a very different way, to have Troy's arms around her and his face so close to hers.

"You can have a hot shower tonight. I wish I had a change of clothes for you, but until we can get you some, I'm afraid you're going to be wearing what you have on. What about the pickup truck?" she whispered in Troy's ear.

"Someone went in, got pizza, the truck left. Maybe it had nothing to do with Lucas, or maybe we're just a very convincing couple."

That was another thing they'd have to do, Troy thought: find out if the vehicle that had abducted Lucas was a black pickup truck sporting a skull decal on the rear window. But that would wait until they could question Lucas thoroughly.

"It'll be daylight tomorrow," Kelly reminded Troy. "He'll be visible in the back seat."

"Not for long. Your tire is going to be low on air. You'll give me a call, asking me to put air in your tire while you're at church. I'll take it to get air, leave my Suburban in the spot, come back and get Lucas in my car. Then Leo and I will go fishing up at the lake."

"Fishing?" Lucas said. "Why are you going fishing?"

"Because Kelly is going to come up after church to go swimming. It's hot out. If anyone is watching, they wouldn't expect us to be fishing and swimming if we have you."

Another piece of pizza was coming to its demise. "Okay," Lucas conceded, the syllables mashed into incoherence by his chewing.

"Kelly?" he wrapped his arms tighter around her and this time, with no pizza impeding his proximity, he lowered his mouth to hers. Her responding kiss was broken by her question.

"What if it doesn't work?"

"Shhh," he said. "We're engaged, remember?"

30

HIDING LUCAS

"Kelly, your tire looks low on air," Hayley Carpenter, who was always running late for church, had parked near Kelly. "You'd better get that taken care of before you end up with a flat."

Lucas had let enough air out of the tire earlier in the morning so that it would need attention, as Troy had directed. Kelly hadn't expected the gambit to work, but so far, it looked as if it would.

"Oh! I'll call Troy and see if he can take it for air. I don't want to drive it like that. It's really low, isn't it."

"It'll get to a station," Hayley assured her.

"I hope so. I've got a picnic basket in the back seat and it's pretty full. I've got a cover over it to keep it out of the sunlight. Troy and I made plans to go up to the lake this afternoon. He's going up early so he can go fishing. I'll give him a call now."

That had gone well, she thought; the entire story unfolding without any prompting on her part. She gave Troy the call, as agreed and, as if the request were new to him, Troy agreed to stop by the parking lot while she was inside for worship, take her car to get air and then bring it back.

When she came back outside at the end of the service, a period of time prolonged as usual by greetings from others, including from Julie Leonard, who teased that she'd heard that Kelly and Troy had enjoyed a romantic moment Saturday night at The Pizzaria, her tire was restored to full air pressure.

Kelly's blush wasn't feigned. It wasn't as if she could explain that she and Troy weren't really engaged, and they really weren't snuggling in The Pizzaria parking lot.

"The power of pepperoni," Julie joked. "It works with a man every time."

"I think I'll stay away from pepperoni this afternoon."

"Are you and Troy doing something?"

"He's up there now, fishing. I'm on my way up to go swimming. This time, I'm in charge of the lunch and there's no pepperoni."

Julie laughed. "Have fun; it's a good day for a swim. This heat wave is something. I hope it breaks before the kids go back to school."

Kelly and Julie chatted for a few minutes longer and then Kelly got in her car, this time the sole passenger, and drove home, where she changed into shorts and a blouse with her bathing suit underneath. She had told the truth when she said there was a cooler in the back seat; she'd packed it early that morning while Lucas ate a hearty breakfast. Showered and fed, he'd been fortified and ready to hide under the picnic blanket in the car. She'd have to wait until she got to Leo's camp to find out how the transfer of Lucas from her car to Troy's SUV had gone.

Kelly wished there was some way to let Tia know that Lucas was safe; it was cruel to let his mother continue to think that her son was missing, and Kelly intended to press Troy to find a way to ease Tia's anxiety.

The road that turned off from the highway to the lake had a steady flow of traffic and Kelly wondered if Troy's idea of bringing Lucas here was wise, with so many people around. When she got to Leo's camp, she pulled her car in next to the SUV and Leo's car. They were parked close to the front of the house and it was possible that Lucas could have gotten from the vehicle to the front door without being observed, at least by anyone watching from the Truvert camp, which was on the other side of the lake.

Troy had told her to just go in when she arrived; he and Leo would be fishing. Hesitantly, she opened the door and called out, "It's Kelly," and closed the door behind her.

No one made a sound. Alarmed, she looked around.

"Troy?" she called out. "Leo? I'm here. I've brought lunch."

"I'm hungry," Lucas' voice replied.

"Lucas," she whispered, "you're okay?"

"I'm in the bedroom. Officer Troy and Officer Page said to stay in here. Arlo is with me. They didn't want me to be alone."

"I'm surprised they left you by yourself."

"They wanted everything to look normal, that's why they went fishing. Officer Troy said Arlo would protect me. They'll be coming back pretty soon; they were just going to fish on the lake until you got here."

"Have you had a chance to tell them what happened?"

She went into the bedroom where Lucas was sprawled on the bed, Arlo on the floor beside him. The dog came over to her and she patted his head.

"Yeah; that's why they said to act like I'm not here. Officer Troy figures they'll be watching all of you to see if you act funny, you know, like you're hiding me."

It still seemed like a tremendous risk to leave Lucas alone in the camp with the door unlocked, but since Lucas was safe, she couldn't quibble with Troy's plan.

"What happened on the 4th?" Kelly asked. "Your friends said that a black pickup truck with a skull emblem on the rear windshield had been following you around. Was that the vehicle?"

"Yeah. I was going home. I cut through the alley, I thought it would be okay because I always do it. I didn't see the truck until it was right there—he turned off the headlights. There were two guys and one of them got out and grabbed me, put his hand over my mouth before I had a chance to yell. He threw me into the truck, and it took off like it was on a racetrack."

Kelly remembered the truck as it had speeded by that night while she and Troy were watching the fireworks. "We saw the truck. Troy tried to catch it, but the driver was going too fast."

"That's what Officer Troy said. They brought me up here; I didn't know where I was then, because they covered up my eyes. They must have given me something to knock me out because when I woke up, I was tied up and I wasn't inside the truck anymore, but I was inside someplace. It was one of the camps, but I didn't know that yet."

"What did they do to you?"

"Nothing. They kind of acted like I wasn't there. It was weird, Miz Armello," Lucas said, his eyes clouded with the memory of his captivity. "They'd untie my hands and feet when I had to go to the bathroom, and when I ate, but they only fed me once a day. I was hungry," he complained. "They didn't care. They made peanut butter and jelly sandwiches to eat and they gave me water to drink. Every day," he said, aggrieved, as if the limited menu was worse than the abduction.

"What did you do all day?"

"Nothing, there's no TV up here."

"What did they do?"

"Played cards, talked. At first they were there all the time but I think they got bored, because then they started leaving at different times. When they started leaving at night, I figured I'd better take a chance on getting out. I told them they needed to leave a candle or a lantern or something so that I could see to find my way to the bathroom. That camp has two bathrooms. One of the bathrooms is connected to the bedroom. They didn't want to do it, but I kept complaining. I guess they figured I couldn't do anything with a lantern, and if they put it in the bathroom, no one could see it from outside. No one was around anyway, at least I didn't hear anyone."

"Not even during the day?"

"During the day, yeah, but they didn't go out during the day. I don't think they wanted anyone to see them."

"People would notice the truck, wouldn't they? They'd know it belonged to the owner of the camp."

Lucas shrugged. "They didn't want to be seen. I think those camps on that side of the lake are empty; I'd hear people sometimes, but I think they were just walking around the lake or something like that."

"So what happened after they left you with a lantern? I assume they left a lantern, not a candle, or they'd have to worry that you'd burn the place down."

Lucas grinned. "Not with me inside, I wouldn't," he said. "I didn't do anything the first couple of nights. By now, they were staying away longer and longer; all night and a lot of the day, too, just coming in the evening to make me peanut butter and jelly sandwiches."

"Weren't they afraid that you'd call out to someone for help?"

"They told me not to make any noise. They said the police were looking for me because I was a suspect in a break-in in town. I guess that was supposed to scare me, but I knew I hadn't robbed anyone, so I wasn't scared. But I didn't know who else was up here, or if anyone knew them. So I waited a couple of nights. Then, Friday night, after they left, I started trying to cut through the knots. I used the metal edge of the lantern and the knots broke. Then I pulled the kitchen table over to the window and I climbed out. I stayed close to the trees so that no one would see me, and I walked all night. By daylight, I was pretty tired, and I didn't want anyone on the highway to see me, so I rested for an hour or two. Then I kept walking. I made it into town and that's when I went to the back of the library. I knew I could hide there, and I figured I'd be safe. I figured I'd find some way to let you know where I was, and you'd think of something."

"Lucas, we're so glad that you got away," Kelly said, warmed by his trust that she would somehow be able to help him. "You were brave . . . weren't you afraid?"

"Yeah," he admitted. "When they thought I was sleeping, they'd talk . . . I didn't understand all of it, but they were saying things about Chief Stark's son and how he'd be proven innocent. Sometimes they'd get on me about Carrie. I just acted kinda dumb and didn't answer. I guess they got tired of it because they finally stopped talking to me at all. Miz Armello, what's going on—"

They both heard the door open. Arlo rose from the floor and went over to the bedroom door. When it opened to admit Troy, Arlo raised his head for a pat, but he didn't leave the room and Kelly realized that the dog had been given his orders to protect Lucas, and that's what he was doing.

"Catch anything?" Kelly asked.

"Leo's getting the grill ready. Lucas filled you in?"

Kelly nodded. "Now what do we do?"

"Keep Lucas inside, for one thing, and hidden. Leo is planning to spend the next couple of days here until we figure out what we're going to do. It's not unusual for him to spend time here on his own, so no one, if anyone is watching, is going to think anything is going on. Besides, if Leo is up here, he can keep an eye on the camp across the lake."

Kelly noticed that Troy was avoiding mention of the camp belonging to Mayor Truvert, just as she had done. It wasn't the first time that the mayor's camp had been used for the wrong purposes and she wondered if that was why he had it in the first place, since, according to Leo, the mayor never seemed to use it for himself or his family.

Keeping Lucas here, so close to where he had been held captive, was both risky and logical. His kidnappers were unlikely to expect to find him here, so close to where they'd held him. But they'd be searching vigorously in town to find him and now there was an added urgency to their quest. Lucas could identify them.

31

SEARCHING FOR LUCAS

"It might work," Troy said thoughtfully.

"I can't think of anything else that would work. I know we can trust Reverend Dal to keep Lucas' identity secret and he'd be the only one who knows who Lucas really is. A week at an out-of-state church camp will get Lucas out of the area. Rev. Dal is the camp counselor, he goes every year. When I brought the idea up to him, and I explained what's going on, he agreed immediately."

"Does he realize there may be danger involved, if the kidnappers somehow find out that Lucas is there? I know, I know, it's unlikely, but you don't want Reverend Dal going into this without realizing the risks. He's got a wife and a baby to take care of."

"Olivia and the baby are going to visit relatives in Ohio while he's away. She goes every year."

Troy nodded as he considered other possible perils of the plan. Lucas couldn't stay at Leo's camp forever because Leo couldn't stay there much longer. He'd be returning to work in another week, with the half-hearted consent of his boss, now that his doctors had cleared him of any fear of a concussion from the blow to the head that he'd taken a few weeks ago. Sending Lucas off to church camp for a week would buy them some time while they tried to figure out what to do with him.

"And Tia says it's okay," Kelly added.

Telling Tia Krymanski that her kidnapped son had escaped and was safe had been a priority, but at the same time, it was risky. Tia had to go on acting as if Lucas were missing. She couldn't tell her kids the truth; kids couldn't keep a secret like that. Rev. Dal had started visiting the family to offer comfort and prayer when Lucas was missing and the Krymanskis had started going to church on Sundays. Not every Sunday, not with Tia's work schedule, but they'd been to church a couple of times and Kelly knew that Tia benefitted from the prayers. Although there were those in the congregation who were dubious about having Krymanskis in the pews, most people felt that they deserved a chance. No one knew quite what to think about Lucas being missing, but they could still offer genuine sympathy to the mother of a son who had disappeared.

Tia had agreed that she could not reveal what she knew, and she understood that everyone with any connection to Lucas was going to be under observation. A week at church camp, she had said tartly, might do him some good.

Troy laughed when Kelly told him what Tia had said about the church camp sojourn. "After being held captive, he might find a week of singing hymns not so bad."

"Oh, they don't just sing hymns at church camp," Kelly said. "They swim and canoe and they climb ropes and do a lot of physical things. At night they toast marshmallows around a fire; it'll be good. And Lucas is going to be Rev. Dal's assistant, so he'll be helping. It's a camp for kids who are ages ten to twelve, kids who come from rough situations."

"I don't think they'll be able to pull anything on Lucas," Troy said. "He might be just the assistant a clergyman needs. Good thinking, Kelly. It gives us a week to see what we can do. We've at least narrowed down some things: Carmela's information about the church treasurer operation at LifeLight was revealing. It sounds to me like they intended to get rid of Mrs. Knesbit and they called on Travis Shaw to do it because he was a native of Punxsutawney and—probably—because he knew the Starks through the drug trade. Which, if it's the case, means that Chief Stark's involvement extends beyond Settler Springs."

"Lucas is in more danger now, isn't he?" Kelly asked.

There was no use lying to her. Troy nodded grimly. "Now that he's escaped, yes, he can give a different account of what happened. Even if they insist that his prints were found at Mia Shaw's apartment, he can testify that he was held captive at Mayor Truvert's camp. There would be traces of his presence there. I imagine that Stark will have his goons clean the place to remove evidence, but Leo is up there now, and he'll notice if anything is going on. The library board is clipping Mrs. Stark's wings, thanks to Jimmy Patton. And to you."

"But we still don't have any proof. They're choosing the jury for Travis Shaw's trial, Representative Eldredge's campaign is going well, and now Lucas is in danger."

"I know. But thanks to your church connections, he's going to be out of the state and safe for a week. They'll search for him and they'll be watching all of us, but they won't find him."

"That's going to make them pretty angry, isn't it?"

"I don't imagine they're in very good moods right now."

Several days later, Troy was at home getting ready for his shift when he got a phone call that confirmed his assessment of the likely moods of Chief Stark and his accomplices.

"Officer Kennedy? This is Susan Callahan of the State Police. You asked me to call you if anything new transpired regarding the disappearance of Lucas Krymanski."

"Trooper Callahan?" Troy couldn't believe it. He'd given up hoping to hear from her on her own initiative.

"I believe there may be new information on the case," she went on in the uninflected voice that she always used. "Trooper Meigle has been very concerned today and a search is going out for the boy."

"A search?"

"Yes, I believe he is wanted in connection with a break-in and robbery in your town."

"When did the search get underway?"

"This morning."

"Is there a reason?"

"Apparently there is new evidence of the boy's presence. He's still missing but the officers are now treating his disappearance as a criminal matter."

Troy offered a silent prayer that Reverend Dal, with Lucas in tow, had already left for

Ohio. The week at camp would begin on Sunday but the minister liked to get there early to prepare for the activities that were scheduled.

"Do they have any idea where he might be?"

"The southwestern Pennsylvania area will be heavily searched, and all of his contacts may expect to be interrogated. As he is a youth, it is assumed that he would have to reach out to other adults who could help him and perhaps hide him, although of course, it would be illegal to hide a fugitive."

"Yes, well, Lucas knows a lot of people. How did he go from being a runaway to a fugitive?"

"A sum of money was stolen, and evidence connects him to the scene of the crime."

"A lot of money? To put out a dragnet like this is intended to be, I'd assume that a lot of money is at stake."

"The amount of the theft is not being released. I called to let you know, as you have asked about the status of the search."

"Thank you, Trooper Callahan," Troy said. "Thank you for letting me know."

"Perhaps Chief Stark will update you when there is more information."

"Perhaps he will."

He wondered if Kelly had heard the news. Had Mrs. Stark told her, or would the Starks prefer to catch Kelly off guard so that Chief Stark could question her to see if she knew anything regarding Lucas' whereabouts? He couldn't warn her without exposing Trooper Callahan's telephone message and, circumspect though her wording had been, he did not want to make her vulnerable to Meigle's retaliation. They were looking for Lucas; the odds are that they would search among his family, his friends. That was bound to include Kelly.

Belatedly, he wished that Kelly had not disclosed the fact that Lucas had escaped his captors to Tia. He understood her reasoning, but could Tia manage to pretend that she knew nothing?

Could Kelly keep her knowledge to herself? Would she reveal, by a misplaced word or a response that gave away too much, that she knew that Lucas was safe? Stark would certainly interrogate her. Would her conscience allow her to lie?

And what about himself, Troy wondered as he walked into the police station. Could he maintain a poker face? Stark would certainly want to probe him for information.

Chief Stark was standing in the main room of the station, his hands on his hips, as Troy entered. Kyle was engrossed in his paperwork, but it was apparent, from the set of his shoulders, that the atmosphere was tense.

"Do you know where he is?" Stark demanded.

"Where who is?"

"A search is on for Lucas Krymanski. He's not a runaway, he's a thief."

"You already said that. You said he robbed the piggy banks in Mia Shaw's apartment. Your theory was that he was using drugs, took the money to support his habit, and had left town to hang out with friends. What changed?"

Stark's gaze made no effort to conceal his dislike for Troy. Troy, his face expressionless, looked back.

"What happened?" Troy went on. "Has another piggy bank been robbed?"

"Spare me your sarcasm, Kennedy. A Krymanski is a Krymanski. We're searching every inch of town for him."

"Why weren't you doing that before? He's been gone over a month."

Stark, perhaps taken aback by Troy's aggressive responses, didn't have an answer. Without a word, he turned around and went into his office, slamming the door behind him.

32

INTERROGATIONS

Troy's cell phone was bombarded with text messages after the news that a search was underway for Lucas. Jimmy was outraged, Mia incredulous, Doug curious. There was no message from Kelly, Leo, or Tia; they knew where Lucas was now, and they all realized that silence was the best protection they could offer the boy.

Troy stopped by the photography studio to talk to Doug, but Amber said he wasn't there. He was at the Eldredge campaign headquarters, she said.

"Representative Eldredge is doing something new in campaigning," she said. "He's calling it 'Dollars to Donuts Days' and he's asking people to donate in cash."

Troy figured it was a good thing humans didn't come with antennae or his would have been shaking. "Cash? How does that work with campaign finance regulations?"

"The amounts and donor names are going to be recorded," Amber said. "I guess that's Jarrod's role in this fundraiser. They're using a roulette wheel and depending on where the arrow lands, donors will give their contributions in ones, fives, tens, twenties . . ."

"This is happening at the campaign headquarters?"

"It's scheduled for tomorrow."

"First I've heard of it. Was it in the works?"

"It's the first anyone has heard of it. I guess it's somebody's brainstorm. Doug's at the headquarters now getting the story from Jarrod."

"Maybe it was Jarrod's idea?"

Amber shrugged doubtfully. "Probably not. Jarrod likes things that are a little more highbrow. A roulette wheel and cash is not his style."

"Is it Eldredge's style?"

Another shrug. "If he brings in a lot of cash, it will be."

Troy thanked her and asked her to let Doug know that he'd stopped by and would catch him later. His second stop was at The Café. At this time of the afternoon, the restaurant wasn't busy; only a few of the booths were occupied and the diners had all been served. That meant that Tia might have time to talk.

Francie spotted him as he walked in and went over to him. "It's good to see you," she said. "Would you believe," she said, lowering her voice, "that that state trooper came in here to question Tia?"

"I can believe it. Does Tia have a minute? Is there somewhere we can talk where we won't be noticed?" He didn't want Chief Stark to know that he was here on police business. "I'll have an iced tea," he said in a normal voice.

Francie pointed to one of the empty booths in the back. "Go ahead and have a seat, I'll bring out your iced tea. I'll bet you haven't had lunch yet," she guessed. "How about a sandwich?"

Troy realized that breakfast was a long time ago. "Sounds good. Make it a burger, well done," he said. "And fries."

"I won't tell Kelly," Francie said with a grin.

Kelly knew he liked French fries; why was there any need for Francie to conceal his order? He decided it had something to do with the engagement and sat down in the booth, enjoying the air conditioning and the mid-afternoon calm in a place not known for its down time.

It was interesting that Meigle was handling this, Troy mused, and not Stark. The state police would naturally be in charge of the search, but even so, Troy was surprised that Stark was visibly taking a back seat on this effort. As the police chief of the town's force, Stark might have been expected to accompany Meigle on the interrogation. Unless Stark had been covering ground elsewhere. Troy wondered who else had been questioned about Lucas.

Tia brought out his burger and fries and slid into the opposite seat in the booth. "We're not busy right now," she said.

"Francie says that the state police were here."

It was apparent that Tia's anger had not dissipated since the visit. "He came in here, right when we're running crazy with the lunch crowd, and insisted that I had to talk to him right then. Every booth was full, we were already behind on orders, and he made sure that every person in the place knew that he wanted to talk to me."

"What did you do?"

"What could I do? We went into Glenn's office—he wouldn't mind and he's not here until later when it's time to balance the drawer—and he proceeded to tell me—Trooper Meigle, I mean—that they knew that Lucas has been seen in the area and they knew I'd helped him."

"And?"

"And I got mad," she said. "I asked him when Lucas had been seen and why hadn't anyone told me."

Troy relaxed. Tia had shrewdly opted for anger as a cover and it had probably worked. She wouldn't reveal what she knew if she was haranguing Meigle for not letting her know that he knew that her son was alive.

"What did he say?"

"He said I knew that Lucas was around here, and I was probably hiding him. So I took off my apron and I said we're going to my house right now and he can look for Lucas. I don't think he expected that, but I just started walking out of the restaurant. Everybody was staring. I don't think he liked that; I was yelling as we went out about how the police didn't have the decency to tell me that my son is alive when I've been thinking he's dead for all this time, and—" a faint smile appeared. "He didn't have any choice. I drove to my house—I wasn't riding in the state police car—and he followed and once we got there, I told him to go through the house. I showed him Lucas' room and told him that it was pretty sad that no one had bothered to check before. I opened all the drawers in Lucas' bureau, so he'd see that all his clothes were there, I showed him where Lucas kept his video games . . ."

The smile vanished. "He said they're searching for Lucas because he broke into someone's apartment and stole money. I told him that's a lie. He's making it sound like the break-in just happened, but he doesn't know that I know it was around the time that Lucas disappeared."

"You didn't let on that you knew the truth?"

"No, I just let my angry Mama Bear temper take over. I hope I did the right thing."

"You did fine."

Neither of them mentioned that Lucas was in Ohio, working as an assistant for a church camp with Reverend Meachem, who was unlikely to be one of the people that Meigle and Stark would regard as a probable contact for the boy.

"I don't know how this is going to end, Troy," she admitted. "I feel like we're stuck in some kind of terrible reality show."

"I know. But more people know now, and that's a good thing. Daylight works better than darkness."

She nodded and stood up. "You'll let me know if anything . . ."

"There's nothing to tell," he said firmly. "The state police are searching for Lucas, but at least now you know he's alive."

Tia nodded again. Troy hadn't given anything away and she would follow his lead.

He wondered if Kelly had been interrogated and how she had fared. Tia might be able to use anger to deflect her true emotions, but Kelly was wired differently. Moreover, Mrs. Stark was still irked that Jimmy Patton's appearance at the last library board meeting had led to questions regarding her role as president and whether she was overstepping the bounds of the position. How would Kelly fare under interrogation?

Kelly expected to be questioned about Lucas, and she could tell, from Mrs. Stark's manner when she came into the library later in the morning, that the questioning would come today. The news of the search for Lucas Krymanski had been made public; the reason for the search, the announcement said, was that he was wanted for questioning regarding thefts in the area.

It was a hollow accusation, but Kelly reminded herself that she didn't officially know that. When Chief Stark came into the library, Kelly was in her office. Carmela was at the circulation desk.

"Chief Stark," Carmela said with no warmth in her voice, "can I help you?"

Mrs. Stark said, "I believe he's here to speak to Kelly."

"She's in her office."

Chief Stark nodded and went to Kelly's office, closing the door behind him.

"Kelly," he said, dispensing with a greeting.

"Chief Stark? What's the matter?"

"You know that we're searching for Lucas Krymanski. He's wanted for questioning regarding a robbery."

"Lucas wouldn't steal," Kelly said quickly. She was relieved that the interrogation was finally underway; she'd been trying to maintain her usual manner throughout the morning but all she could think of was Lucas, the search, and whether she could pretend that she didn't know anything more. "He's not a thief."

"You're not the best judge of that."

"Then why are you here?" Kelly asked. "You must know that I think highly of him. I've been worried about him since he went missing. You must have found some proof that he's alive or you wouldn't be here."

"No one thought he was dead; you've all gone hysterical over this. He's a troublemaking kid from a troublemaking family and he stole money. Now we're looking for him. When did you see him last?"

"The day that his sister overdosed in the library," Kelly said immediately. "I went in the ambulance with Carrie and then I was with Tia and Lucas later that evening. I've been to Tia's house several times to see if she needed anything; she's understandably worried about her son being missing. I'm not happy that he's under suspicion for a theft I know he wouldn't commit, but I'm relieved, and I'm sure his mother is too, to learn that he's alive. We've all been asking a lot of questions since the Fourth of July when he disappeared, but we haven't been able to get any answers."

"You haven't seen him since then?"

"We don't know where he's been, how would we see him? This is all strange, Chief Stark. A boy disappears and no one seems to care. Then there's some robbery and all of a sudden, there's a manhunt? How much is he accused of stealing?"

"That's not information for the public. If Lucas Krymanski tries to contact you, it's your obligation as a citizen to notify the police. I want to make sure that you understand that. Just because you've decided to make the Krymanskis your pets, that doesn't mean that you can flout the law in their favor."

"I don't flout the law, Chief Stark," Kelly said. Her voice was cold. "I uphold it, and I respect it. I respect the law enforcement officers who protect the people of Settler Springs. Lucas isn't here; you can check the library if you like."

"If I want to search the library, I don't need your permission to do so. My wife gives a great deal of her time, not to mention financial support, to this library. It's too bad that her efforts aren't appreciated."

"Why does Mrs. Stark think she's not appreciated?" Kelly asked. His comment had nothing to do with Lucas, but she found it intriguing that he would have made the leap from one topic to the other.

"The board meeting was an insult to her."

"I'm sure it wasn't intended to be."

Chief Stark rose. "You seem to have adopted Troy Kennedy's views, Kelly. I'm surprised that someone like you, who's lived in Settler Springs long enough to know who you can trust, would be so gullible. He's turning you against the people you've known for most of your life."

Kelly stood as well. "Chief Stark," she said. "I've never needed anyone to make up my mind for me. I've always done that on my own. Lucas Krymanski isn't a thief."

"When we find him, we'll be able to prove that he is a thief, and then you and all the other people in this town who want to make the Krymanskis the good guys will be surprised. He's going to pay, this time, for what he got out of the last time."

Chief Stark left the office; he didn't slam her door shut or give way to any other signs of temper, but the air seemed to crackle with the tension he left behind.

At the desk, Carmela watched as Mrs. Stark got up from her chair and followed her husband out of the library, but not before she shut down her laptop, then closed the library ledger and took it with her.

33

SUSPECT OR RUNAWAY?

"Amber said you came by the studio earlier today. I'm sorry to be late getting back to you. I was interviewing Jarrod; you heard about the campaign fundraiser tomorrow?"

"Amber mentioned it."

"You haven't been asked to provide a police presence?"

"For what?"

"They're expecting a lot of cash to come in, according to Jarrod. It's his idea to have someone from the police force there to guard the pot, since it'll all be in cash."

"Maybe Chief Stark is doing the honors, since he'll probably be one of the donors."

"Maybe. On another note . . . when can you and Kelly come in to sign the contract for the photos? If you're going to get on my calendar for the wedding, I'll need to have an idea of the date."

Doug's businesslike segue to the subject of the wedding alerted Troy that the adroit photographer was taking no chances. It was a remote possibility that Stark or anyone else was listening in on their phone calls, but no one could guarantee that such a circumstance was not happening. Troy, conscious of the fact that since Sean's murder, he was overly vigilant on matters needing caution, was not displeased that Doug, too, felt the threat of danger.

"I'll talk to her and see when she's available."

"She's available tomorrow morning," Doug said crisply. "I gave her a call and asked. If you're free at eleven, she says she can take an early lunch."

"Eleven o'clock works for me."

Kelly texted him not long after to tell him that she'd made an appointment at Doug's studio for the following morning to go over the photographs for the engagement and wedding.

Chief Stark came by the library to ask about Lucas. I don't understand why they're only asking questions now, when he's been missing a month.

Kelly, too, was being cautious, with text messages that gave no indication that she had any knowledge about Lucas Krymanski that wasn't already known to the police. Doug's wariness was one thing; the man was a photojournalist and it was the nature of his profession to be distrustful. But Kelly was not like that and Troy felt a twinge of guilt at involving her in a situation where she had to be suspicious in order to be safe.

They think he's a suspect, that's why. Before, he was just a runaway.

Suspect or runaway, he's missing.

Kelly was right. There were two sets of laws in Settler Springs: one for people like the Krymanskis, who were judged guilty before they were tried; and another set for the people like the Starks, who were given the assumption of innocence because their standing in the town provided them with absolution. It was wrong, but as long as Chief Stark represented law enforcement in town, and Mayor Truvert was the face of the local government, it wasn't going to change.

In the meantime, he, Kelly, Leo and Tia had a secret that they couldn't share with anyone. They knew where Lucas Krymanski was, and in a few short days, they'd need to find a place to hide him.

Doug was alone in the studio when they arrived a few minutes before eleven o'clock the following morning.

"Kelly, are you going to go by the campaign headquarters to make a donation to Representative Eldredge's re-election?"

"I wasn't planning to. Why?"

"I think you might want to consider it."

"Why?" she asked curiously.

"It wouldn't hurt for people to think you support his campaign."

"I haven't made my mind up," she said. "I don't know who I'm voting for."

"The election is only three months away."

"Since when are you out beating the bushes for votes for Eldredge?" Troy asked Doug.

Doug grinned. "I'm interested in seeing how this plays out. I'm trying to figure out why, all of a sudden, the campaign is going for a strictly-cash fundraiser, given what we know about the Starks and Lois Stark's preference for cash, and why we think she has that preference. I'm wondering who's going to show up. I'm wishing I'd been at the cemetery this week, just in case something was going on. I'm wondering if the Starks are worried about losing their cash disposal system now that the library board is forming a committee to look into the issues Kelly brought up at the board meeting. I'm just a curious kind of guy."

"You'll be stopping by, I'm assuming?" Troy asked. Doug had given as tidy an assessment of the recent events affecting the Starks as a police officer would have delivered. Doing it from the perspective of journalism rather than law enforcement only highlighted the fact that, while they didn't yet have answers, the questions were falling into place.

"Oh, sure, but in a professional capacity, not to donate. What about you?"

"I'll be on duty," Troy said. "Can't mix the two."

"Why not? The Starks will."

"Mrs. Stark might make a donation while Chief Stark guards the take. Not the same thing."

"You have a point. So, when are we going to take those photos?"

"What photos?"

"Your engagement photos. It's already August . . . outdoor photos would still look nice. Lots of green outdoors. I tell you what . . . I'll give you a really good deal. We'd go out to the Trail, that's a place that has significance for you both."

"Doug, we're not going to go that far with this," Kelly said. "It's all made up."

"So take the photos anyway. You can always look back on this as a memento of a summer you'll never forget."

"You're incorrigible," she said, laughing despite herself.

"I keep getting questions from folks in town, wanting to know what's taking you two so long to make up your minds about a date. Interestingly, Jarrod also wants to know."

"Jarrod has nothing to do with any of this and no reason to ask," Kelly retorted.

"Don't go all redhead on me," Doug said imperturbably. "I'm just telling you that he asked. It wouldn't surprise me if he's planning to get you to give him a second chance."

Troy had stayed silent through this topic but the thought of Jarrod returning to a place of prominence in Kelly's life stirred him. "Maybe we should get engagement photos taken," he said. "It would lend credibility to the engagement idea."

"We don't have to lend credibility to something that's not real," Kelly said. "And Jarrod isn't going to get a second chance. He's the same person he was before and that's why I broke off the engagement. Why would I change my mind?"

"No reason at all, Kel," Doug answered. "But Jarrod doesn't know that. Have you talked to Jimmy yet?"

"No, why?"

"He's gotten a few nibbles on the Public Servant Bowling League and he's trying to find a date when we can start bowling. September is his target."

"It's August now."

"Jimmy doesn't waste time. You didn't think he was serious, did you?" Doug guessed. "He's more serious now than ever. He told the county commissioners about it and they're publicizing the idea in their local government press releases."

Troy groaned. "We're trying to break up what we think is a drug ring run by a police officer and at the same time, we're scheduling bowling tournaments!"

"No tournaments yet," Doug chided him. "First you have to prove you can bowl."

Despite the daunting problems they faced with their private investigation, both Kelly and Troy were smiling when they left Doug's studio.

"Something about this town," Troy remarked. "I guess that's what Sean meant."

It was the first time he'd mentioned Sean in a context other than his death and Kelly looked at him, waiting to hear more. "What did he say?"

"He just liked Settler Springs. I told you, that's why I came here. I'd never really settled anywhere, and I kept thinking about what he said. It's easy to forget those kinds of things when you think about what we're dealing with now. But this town meant something to him that he never forgot, even when he was in the Army, even when he was in Texas. And his dad felt it was right for him to be buried here. I never thought that was important, you know?"

"Where someone is buried?"

"Yeah. It just seemed . . . inconsequential. But knowing that Sean is buried here makes it even more important for me to do right by him and find out what's going on. For him, and for Lucas too. Lucas is living, I know that," he added hastily at Kelly's expression, "but he's been put into circumstances that a kid shouldn't be dealing with. Tia handled the interrogation. How did you do?"

"I think okay," she said. They began walking slowly, Troy toward his car, Kelly back toward the library, neither one in a hurry. "I just asked why there wasn't a search when he disappeared and there is now when he's accused of robbery."

"Did you get an answer?"

"Not really. I got a lecture, though," she smiled. "Chief Stark said I should trust the people I've known for most of my life and not let you turn me against them."

"Me turning you against them? You're sure you got the pronouns right?"

"He said I'm gullible."

They had reached Troy's car. "Gullible? You? He doesn't know you very well, does he?"

"He doesn't know me at all."

34

A VISIT WITH MRS. HAMMOND

After her conversation with Troy, Kelly decided that she would go to Sean's grave in the Settler Springs Cemetery on Sunday and put flowers there. She didn't know if the grave was being kept up, but she knew someone who would know.

It was time for a visit to Mrs. Hammond. Carmela didn't grumble when Kelly said she was going to deliver Mrs. Hammond's books to the high-rise; with Mrs. Stark at the campaign headquarters for Representative Eldredge's fundraiser, Carmela was enjoying the return to a normal workplace.

Mrs. Hammond was delighted to see Kelly and to get the books and insisted that Kelly sit down for a cup of tea and cookies. "Homemade," she explained as she put out the plate. "Ella Denver loves to bake, and she has a hard time finding people to give them to; so many of the residents are diabetic, or on some kind of diet for health."

"Maybe I'll ask her to donate some cookies for the next library bake sale," Kelly said.

Mrs. Hammond beamed. "Oh, she would love to do that. I should have thought of that myself. When is it? I'll ask her for you."

"We'll have a bake sale at the Homecoming Parade in September; I think it's the Thursday before the last Friday in the month, but I'll check the date for you to be sure. Actually, I came here for another reason. Do you and your lady friends still go to the cemetery every Sunday?"

"Every Sunday," Mrs. Hammond affirmed. "We go after church to look after our husbands' graves and we try to tidy up the ones for people we knew."

"Have you noticed how Sean Claypool's grave looks? I'm planning to go out there this Sunday and plant some flowers, but I was wondering what kind of shape it's in."

"Oh, we look after all the graves of the veterans," Mrs. Hammond assured her. "We put up little flags for the patriotic holidays; they're still there from the 4th. Sean Claypool, he was that poor young man who committed suicide a couple of months ago, wasn't he?"

Kelly didn't answer right away. Mrs. Hammond had proven her trustworthiness before in helping Troy and Kelly solve the Daffodil Alley murder; she was a keen-witted elderly lady whose powers of observation were undiminished by age. But Kelly wasn't sure that it would be fair to tell her that Troy dismissed the suicide verdict and called Sean's death a murder.

"Kelly," Mrs. Hammond said as the pause lengthened, "there's something suspicious about his death, isn't there? What is it? You're not answering me and that means there's something that I don't know. Something that other people don't know. Does it have anything to do with what we've been hearing?"

"What have you been hearing and who's been hearing it?"

"Oh, well, ever since Mrs. Krymanski spoke up at the council meeting, people have been talking, you know."

"Talking about what?"

"Wondering why nothing gets done. We're not stupid, just because we're old and we live in a senior high-rise. We saw the cars in the parking lot when that nasty man who killed Lyola Knesbit was selling drugs. We never saw a police car until your Officer Troy and Leo Page arrested him. I know that people think the Krymanskis are the town troublemakers, but Mrs. Krymanski had a point. Why isn't anything being done? Some of us are wondering if the reason that nothing is being done is because it goes up the ladder." Mrs. Hammond lifted her chin to indicate the altitude of the problem. "I never liked Chief Stark, you know," she said contemplatively. "Even before he tried to let that poor boy take the blame for that girl's murder, when it was his own son who did it. There was always something about him that was just a little too slick. I remember the police chief before him, Chief Laslo. Roy Laslo didn't care if you were a lawyer or a garbage collector; you were equal in the eyes of the law. I remember when Martin Ladderly—you wouldn't know him, Kelly, he used to be the school board president—parked his car in a no parking spot. He'd been ticketed, he'd been told not to do it, but he thought he was above the law. Chief Laslo had his car towed! Mr. Ladderly was furious, but he had to pay to get it out of the impound. Everyone was equal. That has changed.

Now," she said briskly, refilling Kelly's cup, "suppose you tell me what's the story on that young man's death? I'm not going to breathe a word of it to anyone. But if something's not what it should be, I want to know. There are elections coming up, you know; not just for Representative Eldredge, although he's certainly got a flashy re-election campaign going. School board, council, there are positions open, and I want to make sure I vote for candidates who will do the right thing for the town."

"Troy doesn't believe that Sean committed suicide. They were friends; they'd been friends since they met in the Army."

"Sean Claypool lived in Settler Springs when he was a boy. He left when his parents divorced; I believe he moved to Texas to live with his father."

Kelly wasn't surprised that Mrs. Hammond's knowledge of the town's genealogy was flawless. "That's right. They met in the military and Sean had spoken well of Settler Springs. When Troy left the Army, he decided to come here. Sean came for a visit."

"And he died here. If it wasn't a suicide, then how did he die?"

"Troy thinks it was murder."

"That's a very serious thing to say," Mrs. Hammond said, the ever-present twinkle gone from her bright eyes. "Does Troy have any proof?"

"It's hard to have proof when the police report rules it a suicide and the case is closed."

"But why would the police do that?"

"Sean had no reason to kill himself. He was enjoying his visit, re-establishing ties with his mother's family."

"The newspaper account said that he was a troubled former veteran with a history of drug use."

"He'd gotten clean. He was starting a landscaping business in Texas. He was getting treatment for PTSD. Troy would have noticed if Sean was depressed."

"Yes, I think your Troy is a very perceptive young man." Mrs. Hammond beamed. "You're engaged, I hear."

"Yes, well, we're still in the process of working out the details."

"What details? You're engaged to get married. Set a date and do it! Life is shorter than you realize, Kelly and when you meet the right one, then you don't waste time."

Kelly might have been willing to disclose what Troy suspected about Sean's cause of death but revealing the truth about her reported engagement was quite another matter. She and Mrs. Hammond chatted for a little bit longer; Kelly arranged to accompany the ladies on their graveyard visit the following Sunday.

"Oh, we'd love to have you join us. We'll see if those groundskeepers have gotten any more work done. We see them there two Sundays out of four, but for all the time they spend there, they certainly don't seem to make much progress if they're trying to clear out the lower lot. It's quite overgrown."

"Groundskeepers?"

"Yes, they've been showing up since the spring, I think. Yes, it was April, because that's the tenth anniversary of Margaret Tilden's husband's death and she was concerned that the weather would prevent the hyacinths from blooming. He didn't really like hyacinths, he said they made him sneeze, and it was their little joke that when he was gone, she would plant hyacinths on his grave." Mrs. Hammond chuckled. "That's when we saw them for the first time. They said they'd been brought in by the council to do some clearing of the lower lot, but really, they might as well not bother for all the progress they make."

Kelly and Mrs. Hammond made their plans to meet after their respective church services ended on the forthcoming Sunday, and Kelly left the apartment and returned to her car. Kelly was eager to relay what she'd learned to Troy, but first she texted Doug to ask him if he recalled anything being added to the Settler Springs budget to cover the cost of clearing out the lower section of the cemetery.

He replied that there wasn't anything about the cemetery in the budget and what was she talking about.

Someone told me that the council added money in the budget to have the lower part of the cemetery cleared of overgrowth, and that they've been working on this since April. Twice a month, on Sundays.

I covered the budget meeting; nothing about the cemetery. Maybe your source is misinformed.

I don't think so.

Why would the cemetery be a budget priority anyway? It never came up in the meetings. Trust me, I'd have remembered that.

I don't know.

I'll check my copy from the meeting last year when the budget was approved, but I'm sure there's nothing in it. The Eldredge campaign event is going over very well; big crowds, lots of cash. Every half hour, Jarrod announces a new total. Everyone cheers.

Who's everyone?

Some locals, some not. People passing by to cadge a free donut, people who are donating and have earned their donut. Expensive donuts.

Which, Kelly guessed, was Doug's way of saying that a lot of money was going into the coffers in exchange for the donuts.

THE THREADS OF THE METAPHOR

The search for Lucas Krymanski had yielded no results. Trooper Meigle and Chief Stark had redoubled their efforts to get answers from people who knew Lucas, but his friends hadn't seen him. When the pair went into the restaurant to ask more questions of Tia, she came out of the kitchen as if she welcomed the altercation. Paying no attention to the diners, she told the officers that it was their responsibility to find her son and if they had bothered to search for him when he first disappeared, they might have been more successful. Making up a robbery charge as an excuse wasn't going to bring him home safely, she yelled, and she was tired of raising her family in a town where there was a set of rules for the rich and a set of rules for the poor.

"It's not only poor people who end up with family members in prison," she'd said boldly, and no one in the restaurant doubted who she was talking about. After the officers turned around and left, the diners gave Tia a round of applause.

Neither Kelly nor Troy was in the restaurant when that happened, but the Settler Springs grapevine relayed the news to them and on Saturday, as they finished their run and walked back to their cars, they discussed what it meant.

"It's good news, in a way," Troy said. "People are seeing behind the curtain. But Stark is still in power and it looks like Eldredge is going to get re-elected. The numbers are going his way, and he raised a lot of cash with that donut gig."

"At least we caught a break with the church camp," Kelly pointed out. The counselor who was scheduled to lead the camp the following week had broken his leg and Reverend Dal had agreed to fill in for him for another week, with his assistant also agreeing to stay. That meant another week before they had to find a hiding place for Lucas.

"Meanwhile," Troy continued, "the jury has been selected for Shaw's trial, and his lawyer has had a press conference just about every day to hammer home the point that his client is a victim of police brutality."

"Can he say that? I thought that once a trial is underway, the people involved in the case have to avoid talking about the case in the media in case they sway jurors or something."

"The jurors are forbidden from paying attention. Shaw has an attorney who knows just how much he can get away with saying on behalf of his client's alleged innocence."

"At least Leo is back to work. Maybe his employer felt bad about him getting hurt. Do you think Leo meant what he said about not wanting to be the police chief?"

"Yeah, I think he meant it. It doesn't matter now, though; Chief Stark is the chief of police."

"That might change. Mrs. Hammond and her ladies have been doing some thinking since Tia confronted the council. She told me they were talking about how things used to be—"

"A favorite topic among the elderly," Troy grinned. "My neighbors still haven't recovered from the price of gas and it's been a long time since it was a quarter a gallon."

"I know, but it's not all just nostalgia. She said that the former police chief didn't play favorites. So you see, people are noticing."

"I hope so. See you at Doug's at two. And then we'll see if we can do something that has nothing to do with any of this."

It was hard to imagine that, Kelly thought as she went home to shower, change, and make lunch before the scheduled appointment with Doug, the ostensible purpose of which was to continue the discussion on the engagement photographs while actually planning out the next phase of the investigation. Ever since she'd known Troy, it seemed that their time together had been shadowed by the dark elements of crime, drugs and murder which followed in the wake of the Daffodil Alley murder on Halloween. Then, her intention had been to prove that Lucas Krymanski was innocent. Now, with so much more at stake, she felt as though she were living dual lives, one as Kelly Armello, the director of the Settler Springs Public Library, the other as the fiancée of Troy Kennedy, surreptitiously engaged in trying to uncover the roots of crime and corruption in the town.

Troy was already at Doug's studio when she arrived. Doug gave her an assessing look when she entered. "Not bad for photos," he said.

"Who said anything about photos?" She was wearing white capri pants, a sky-blue cap sleeve blouse and white sandals, ideal for summer wear but not what she'd have chosen for a photo setting.

"I did," he answered. "If I don't get some photos of you two, people are going to think you don't like my work. So we're going out to the Trail, and we're going to shoot some pictures. You can take as long as you like to decide which ones you want, but we're shooting them."

Troy, she noticed, wasn't dressed in his usual shorts and a tee shirt. He was wearing khaki trousers and a short-sleeved shirt and casual shoes. "You knew about this!" she accused.

"Guilty," he admitted. "But if we're going to play along with this charade, we need to act the part. Don't worry, I'll pay for the photos, even if the prices are outrageous," he said with a sideways grin at Doug.

"Yep," Doug said. "But you'll love the results. So come on, let's head out to the Trail and then come back here."

"I thought we were going to talk about what to do next."

"We are," Doug said as he turned out the lights. "But first, the photos."

She was surprised that, under Doug's instruction, the poses he suggested felt natural and relaxed and not at all staged. He didn't insist on anything that would make Kelly feel uncomfortable, and even when he directed them into a kissing pose, it was just Troy leaning closer, his head bent towards hers but with their faces visible, as if the kiss were only a moment away. His banter kept them laughing and when the photography was done, they returned to his studio.

Doug locked the door behind him. "Good job," he said. "Normally, I'd send the proofs digitally, but under the circumstances, I'll deliver printed copies to each of you at your workplace. It'll be more convincing. The Starks are bound to be in good spirits after the boatload of bucks that the fundraiser brought in. If they really are substituting drug earnings for honest cash, they'll have plenty to work with."

"And how do we push that along?" Kelly asked. "Troy, do you know anybody who can check on the money that goes to the campaign fund to see if there are traces of drugs on it?"

"It's not a matter of knowing anyone, although I don't. But that's a legal process, and not one that Chief Stark is likely to initiate. If we're going to find out whether what we suspect is really happening, we're going to have to be a little less honest about it. Doug, that's where you come in."

"Thanks for the compliments on my integrity," Doug said drily. "I'm all ears."

"What if you interview Jarrod and ask him if he's heard the rumors that some of Eldredge's campaign is being financed by drug lords."

Doug's eyes widened. "I suppose that if I ask, 'what rumors?' you'll ask me if I'm old enough to be in this profession."

"Something like that. I think we have to ratchet up the heat a notch or two and the only way to do that is to be a little underhanded."

"A little underhanded? That's a lot underhanded. You're asking me to manufacture a rumor so that Jarrod will react to it and presumably pass the word on to Eldredge, who will pass it on to the Starks, who will want to know the source of the rumor."

"And you, as a journalist, will say that you can't reveal your sources."

"Which is a good thing, because I don't have sources on this. Unless . . . unless I start asking other people in the political circles if they've heard anything," he said, considering the issue and its logical ramifications. "Okay, I'll think of something."

"If you need a starting point—not a source—you might reference the council meeting when Tia accused the police force of turning a blind eye to the drug problem." She went on to explain what she had learned from Mrs. Hammond. "No one is saying that Chief Stark is complicit in the drug trade, but the ladies in the high-rise were talking about how different things used to be when Roy Laslo was police chief and everyone was treated the same."

"Does this have anything to do with what you asked me about the cemetery?"

Kelly nodded. "Mrs. Hammond said that two Sundays a month, there's a group of guys doing landscaping on the lower edge of the lot. She and some of her friends go there after church to tend to their husbands' graves. She said they told her that the council is paying to have the area landscaped, but according to Mrs. Hammond, they don't make much progress."

"There's nothing in the budget, I went through my notes and checked. Not a word. So this is going on in the daytime, on Sundays? In full view? That doesn't sound like it's got anything to do with what goes on the nights I've seen cars there."

"Unless," Troy suggested, "they go there to clear out the pathway so that cars can get in and out. It's been a busy summer for mowing and clearing; my grass grows faster than I can keep up with it. If they don't want obvious signs of activity, they might want to keep the area clear. Before there's the usual traffic that you see on the nights when you go there. Which is dangerous for you to do; if you're seen there—"

"But I'm not," Doug grinned. "General Porter keeps me safe. No one sees me."

"So if we can find out if the nights when there's been cemetery action match up to the Sundays when Mrs. Hammond has noticed the landscapers . . ."

"It's not definitive," Troy cautioned.

"Maybe not," Kelly replied. "But it's something else that's happening without anyone knowing. You said yourself that if all the threads can be tied together, we might be able to figure out the loose ends."

"I doubt if I said it quite that precisely, with nary a mixed metaphor to be found," Troy said in amusement, "but thanks for the editing. Yes, that's what I think. I don't think we're going to get a final 'a ha' that puts it all together, but if we can put together enough pieces—"

"The metaphor, the metaphor," Kelly laughed.

"New metaphor. If we put together what we have, we might see an outline."

"So, what do we know?" Doug asked. "We know that Lois Stark wanted the job of treasurer and that after Lyola Knesbit died, she got it. She's asking the congregation to do their giving in cash because it's more Biblical. She takes the offering home to count it. She's taken over the job of treasurer for the library, even though finances aren't her bailiwick as board president."

"We know that someone has been able to get into Mia Shaw's apartment and that someone has a key to it. Someone planted evidence making Lucas look guilty of robbing the kids' piggy banks."

"We know that Lucas was held hostage in Mayor Truvert's camp until he escaped. We know that there wasn't a search for him until he escaped and that's when word of the robbery went public. We know that Lucas is safe."

"For the time being," Troy reminded them. "But time is running short. And we still don't have a smoking gun that will make anyone in authority pay attention to what we're asserting is the truth."

"I'm not so sure I want to see a smoking gun," Doug said. He was joking, but beneath the jocular tone was, they all knew, a candid synopsis of what it might take to bring their investigation to the tipping point.

A TRIP TO THE CEMETERY

Mrs. Hammond waved to Kelly and left her friends at the corner by the church parking lot. "If it's all the same to you," she said, "I'll ride to the cemetery with you."

"Of course, it's all right."

"Nora Halvernik just won't give up smoking and even though she doesn't smoke when we're in the car with her, the smell is always there. You'd think a woman of her age would know better."

"I suppose she feels that if she's made it this long without any ill health, there's no point in stopping smoking now," Kelly said. "Could you ride over with someone else?"

"Not many of us still drive," Mrs. Hammond acknowledged. "She's one of the few, so her smoking is one of the things we put up with. Her husband died of lung cancer; wouldn't you think that would have made her quit?"

Mrs. Hammond, despite her age, had quite a few tart observations about her circle of friends, and Kelly was laughing by the time they arrived at the cemetery.

"There they are, the landscapers," Mrs. Hammond noticed. "See them?"

"They're hard to miss. It looks like there are six or seven of them," Kelly observed. One was wielding a pushmower, a couple were picking up trash, another was trimming back bushes. "They seem pretty busy. I wonder why they work so sporadically? You said you only see them a couple of Sundays a month? Do you think they work on Saturdays and you don't see them?"

"If they do, they don't have much to show for it. If the town wants to clear out the lower lot to make room for more graves, someone needs to light a fire under this crew. I don't know who hired them, but taxpayer money is being wasted."

Kelly parked the car by the side of the road near the entrance so that Mrs. Hammond wouldn't have far to walk.

"I checked with Doug about the landscapers; he said there's nothing in the town budget to pay for cemetery landscaping. I think Art Hudek takes care of the cemetery grounds and he probably just looks after the parts that are already in use."

Mrs. Hammond leaned on her cane. "I thought that the man I spoke with said it was the council that hired him," she frowned. "I wouldn't have gotten that wrong."

Kelly knew that Mrs. Hammond had probably heard correctly; the ladies were frugal in their spending and they expected the council to do likewise when spending public money.

"I can ask him," Mrs. Hammond decided.

"Let's leave that until later," Kelly suggested. "After we've looked after the graves. Sean's grave is over there."

"Yes, I'll go with you. You can see that it's kept up nicely; we make sure that the veterans' graves aren't neglected. They served their country and we're not going to forget that, no matter how they died. It's a shame . . . I can't help but think about what you said."

Kelly and Mrs. Hammond stood in front of the gravestone where Sean Claypool was buried. As Mrs. Hammond had said, there was a pair of U.S. flags in the ground in front of his gravestone. Planted in the grass was an urn with red, white and blue geraniums.

"Gracie does that for all the veterans," Mrs. Hammond said when Kelly commented on the flowers. "You know her brother died in World War II."

"I didn't realize that Sean is buried near General Porter's tomb," Kelly remarked.

"Yes, there are a lot of veterans in this section, from most of the wars. Not the Revolution, of course, or 1812, but after that, you'll see the graves. The stones are quite worn now. Nothing like what the Porter family did for the General, but then that was the Civil War."

Mrs. Hammond spoke as if there were a certain form of etiquette observed for the different war dead. Perhaps there was, Kelly thought.

"I doubt if many people now know who General Porter was," Mrs. Hammond went on. "But he was very prominent at Gettysburg."

Kelly thought of Doug and his vigils in the cemetery, concealed within the expansive statue of the town's most renowned military hero. From that vantage point, Doug was in a perfect position to see what was going on in the lower lot.

Kelly went with Mrs. Hammond and helped her to pull weeds growing amidst the flowers that she had planted for her husband's grave. "It's been a terrible summer for weeds," Mrs. Hammond said. "No matter how many I pull, there are always more the next week. And the grass . . . of course it looks lovely, still so green, but it's always growing too. I suppose the landscapers have their work cut out for them, trying to keep it under control."

"Maybe we should thank them," Kelly suggested. "For their work."

"Not if they're being paid for it," was Mrs. Hammond's response. "If they were volunteering their labor, I'd thank them. But if they're being paid, then they're already getting their thanks. They aren't local people," she said, turning to glance down the slope where the men were working.

Kelly followed Mrs. Hammond's line of sight and then she noticed, on the other side of the road, across from the cemetery, a black pickup truck parked with other cars, probably vehicles belonging to the other workers.

Was that the truck driven by the men who had abducted Lucas? It was, perhaps, a long shot, but worth exploring.

"Maybe we should thank them anyway," Kelly said.

"I don't see—" Mrs. Hammond stopped herself and gave Kelly a shrewd appraisal. "Perhaps you're right," she said. "We've done our work here. We can meet the others at the restaurant. It's not far; we just have to turn around in that road across the street and then go out past Klaus' Dairy Farm."

"Or we can keep going out this way and we'll come out on the main road."

"Whichever you prefer, dear," Mrs. Hammond said.

Kelly wasn't fooled. She knew that Mrs. Hammond was merely holding her questions in reserve for when they were back in the car.

She held out her arm so that Mrs. Hammond could lean on her while walking down the sloping terrain. At first Mrs. Hammond demurred, but then she seemed to decide that looking a bit frail might serve them well.

"Hello, young man," she said to the tall man, not exactly young but not old, either, who sported a "Born to Raise Hell" tank top and a pair of battered denim shorts. He paused in his work.

"Yeah?"

His tone was not aggressive, nor was it welcoming. Leaning heavily on Kelly's arm, Mrs. Hammond approached him. "We'd like to thank you for your work," she said. "It's nice to see the grounds being cared for. I wish you could put in more hours, it would be very nice if this entire lower section could be cleared."

"That's not in our orders," the man said.

Kelly noticed that his baseball cap bore a skull emblem on the bill.

"I understand," Mrs. Hammond said. "Perhaps the council will be able to find more money in the budget for next year."

The man seemed to find this amusing. "Maybe," he said. His gaze swept over Kelly in a manner that she found intrusive.

"Are you all with the same company?" she asked.

"Yeah."

"We just wanted to say thank you," Kelly explained. "We'd better leave you to your work. It's been a hot summer, and I'm sure you want to finish so that you can get out of the sun."

"Yeah."

Kelly put her arm around Mrs. Hammond as if the older lady would have a hard time making it back to the car without support. Once in the car, Mrs. Hammond said, "Why are you going to go straight instead of turning? We always turn."

"I want to see if there's any image on the rear window of that black pickup," Kelly explained. "Can you look for me?"

"Of course," Mrs. Hammond responded, all indications of frailty gone as she turned in her seat so that she would be able to look at the black pickup truck as they passed it.

"Anything?" Kelly asked once they went by.

"A skull," Mrs. Hammond said distastefully. "Just like what he was wearing on his cap. I think that's disrespectful. He's in a graveyard."

"A skull? You're sure?"

"Of course, I'm sure, I know what a skull—Kelly, is that important? Does it mean something?"

"It might, but please don't say anything to anyone, not to Rosa, not to any of your friends. I'll let Troy know and he can decide."

She trusted Mrs. Hammond's discretion, but she knew that Troy had been particular about not disclosing the information about the skull image on the rear window of the pickup truck.

"I won't say a word. But after this is all solved," Mrs. Hammond's eyes were sparkling, "I expect you to tell me everything."

INTERVIEWING JARROD

Any qualms that Doug might have had about intimating to Jarrod that there were rumors of drug money funding Representative Eldredge's re-election campaign were put to rest when he read the accounts of the first day of in the Travis Shaw trial. Shaw's attorney laced every detail regarding what he described as his client's victimization with melodramatic accusations against overreaching authority, police corruption, and secret family scandals, all laying the groundwork for what was going to be a defense based not on Shaw's innocence but on Leo Page's purported guilt.

Jarrod was eager to be interviewed, as Doug had known he would be. They made plans to meet at the campaign headquarters in town the following day.

"Quite a haul," Doug said when he arrived at the headquarters. The front of the office was painted to resemble the American flag, with signs promoting Eldredge's re-election prominently arrayed in the window. Jarrod led Doug into his office, a small space barely big enough to fit the desk where Jarrod sat.

"Very good haul," Jarrod agreed, pulling out a folding chair so that Doug could sit down. "We hit on something with a little bit of novelty. People want transparency in campaign funding and that's what we gave them. Instead of fancy dinners with rich donors signing checks, we had cash, easy to account for, easy to document. The roulette wheel added a little bit of fun to the process; people aren't usually entertained by the money aspect of politics. We hope that we've hit on a new way of raising funds for honest officials to get elected."

"You think this is a better way to fund a campaign?"

"Sure, it's got everything. Transparency, which our polling finds is a number one issue for voters. They're tired of rich businessmen owning the candidates; this is something new. Spin the wheel, donate the amount. Or donate multiples of the amount. It's all honest, it's all aboveboard, every donor got a receipt. We're planning to try it again next month in another town, but Settler Springs has the distinction of being first in the state to set a new standard for election transparency."

"Representative Eldredge is in pretty good shape for re-election."

Jarrod leaned forward. He was wearing a white shirt and a red, white, and blue tie with "We, the People" printed across the fabric. "He's in very good shape. The voters are pleased with his record. In the two years that he's served, he's done more to promote business and manufacturing than his opponent has done in his entire political and private career. I don't have to tell you that our region has suffered from the loss of manufacturing since the decline of the steel industry, but under Representative Eldredge, an alliance has been formed between government and industry. The groundwork has been established during his first term. What he's asking for from the voters is a chance to build on that foundation.

Jarrod was good, Doug thought. He could deliver a smooth patter as if he were saying it for the first time, even though Doug knew that it was Jarrod's role to make each iteration of his spiel sound fresh and new.

"How'd you get into this?" Doug asked.

"It's not about me, it's about the election," Jarrod said with polished modesty.

"And an election is about the candidate and how he's packaged for the voters. It's your job to make sure that the packaging is done right, isn't it?"

Jarrod shook his head. "Doug, we go back a long way. When did you get so cynical? There's no packaging for Representative Eldredge; he's the real deal, an honest man who's doing his part to pave the way to a better future for this generation and the next."

"I don't remember you being caught up in politics when we were in school. I thought marketing was your direction. So marketing and politics, they go together, don't they?'

"For some candidates who have to put a false veneer on their agenda, it does. But my marketing background is more about giving the voters a chance to judge Representative Eldredge on his record, his merits, and his plans for the future."

"He's got a lot of local support, would you say?"

Jarrod nodded. "Chief Stark and his wife are two of his biggest supporters. They recognize what he can accomplish for our region."

"You came into the campaign late, after Keith Rigowski was demoted as head of the campaign, right?"

"Keith wasn't demoted, he was reassigned. Keith is a great guy with a lot of skills. He's more attuned to the legislative agenda and that's an important part of what we're about. People need to be able to access their candidate, to make sure that their needs are met. That's where Keith is at his best and to tell you the truth, he's Representative Eldredge's right-hand man in that role."

"He was running the campaign until his car was stolen and a man was found dead inside it. Did that play a part in getting him reassigned?"

Jarrod's ready smile faded. "No, of course not . . . that was a terrible circumstance, a tragedy, a . . . Keith had nothing to do with that, he was as much a victim of what happened as the guy who died."

"Maybe not as much a victim," Doug corrected him, "since Keith is alive, even if he's no longer the face of the campaign, and Sean Claypool is dead. But you're saying there's no connection between the death of Sean Claypool and the reassignment of Keith Rigowski."

"Of course not. I'm not sure where you'd have gotten that idea."

Jarrod hadn't lost his composure, but it was becoming apparent that he didn't like the direction that the interview had taken.

Doug continued without pausing. "Your background is marketing, not politics. Did the Starks recommend you for the job after Keith was . . . reassigned?"

Jarrod detected the meaningful pause in Dough's query. "I—they knew me from town, I grew up here, but they didn't—I didn't ask them—I got a call from Representative Eldredge's office, asking if I was interested in the job. Of course I was," Jarrod said, flashing a smile, "after all, since I planned to vote for him anyway, why not go to work for him to make sure that I could organize a campaign so that other voters would have a chance to see why I was voting for him?"

"And the Starks played no role in the choice?"

"To the best of my knowledge, no. But I'm not saying that they didn't bring my name up. They knew me. They must have known that I could give the campaign what it needed in the home stretch. If they did recommend me and that's what inspired the campaign to contact me, I'm grateful. That hometown connection is one of the things that makes this campaign so vibrant; we're not running a slick, big-city campaign. We're reaching out to every voter, and it's working. Like you said, our numbers are good, we're polling high, our engagements are well attended."

"And the campaign funds are pouring in."

"Campaigns have to have money, Doug. You know that. This latest idea was a gold mine for the campaign, and it's pure transparency. That's what the voters want."

"Transparency . . . it's what voters want, as you've noted. But isn't there a risk with cash?"

"What risk?" Jarrod laughed. "We're not worried about people donating counterfeit money, if that's what you mean."

Doug smiled as if sharing the joke. "I suppose that might be a risk," he acknowledged. "I suppose that's something the bank would check when the deposit was made."

"Probably, although I have to say, there isn't much chance of our supporters donating to the campaign with funny money."

"There are other risks, though, aren't there, with cash donations?"

"Not really. A check could bounce, but cash, that's the real deal."

"What if someone was involved in drug trafficking," Doug pointed out. "Could he—or she—donate cash without the risk of drugs being detected?"

Jarrod frowned, puzzled by Doug's assertion. "What would be the purpose?" he wanted to know. "If someone has an illegal income, they'd want the money. They wouldn't want to give it away."

"Say someone was involved with a political campaign, and they also had a drug connection. Before the funds were deposited, couldn't they substitute drug money for all the cash that was donated?"

"That's pretty unlikely," Jarrod said. "Sounds like a Hollywood movie."

"So, the money that was donated went straight to the bank after you were done recording the amounts? You were noting the amounts of the donations as they were made, as I recall."

"That's right. I wrote down the name of the donor, the amount, and then one of my assistants wrote out the receipt."

"The receipt for the amount, not the denomination of the bills."

"It's a receipt," Jarrod said irritably. "It doesn't matter to the IRS or to campaign financing regulations whether someone donates in ones or one hundreds, as long as it doesn't violate the legal amount an individual can donate. We came up with an original way to donate that captured public attention."

"And it went straight from your recording to the bank."

"It—I don't do the deposits. We have other staffers who do that. I have more than enough to do; you wouldn't expect me to go to the bank with all that money."

"No," Doug said cheerfully. "I just wondered if there was any intermediary between your role in recording the amount and the process that saw the money deposited."

He could tell that Jarrod was mystified by the question. Not uneasy, just puzzled. Which made it seem as though Kelly was right; Jarrod was probably not involved in any illegal efforts to launder money, however unsophisticated the process might be. But at the same time, Jarrod was unable to affirm that the money he had counted and recorded was the same cash that had been deposited into the campaign's account.

38

FINDING A HIDING PLACE

"She's sure it was a skull?"

"She saw it. There was a skull on his baseball cap, we both saw it. When I drove past the truck, Mrs. Hammond looked to see what was on the rear window. It was a skull. Troy, it has to be the same truck that was used to abduct Lucas."

"Mrs. Hammond isn't young," Troy said. "How close was she to the truck?"

"It was parked on the other side of the road, to our left. She turned her head and she saw it. She didn't know what to look for, I didn't give her any cues. I just told her to look and see what was there. She said it was a skull and it wasn't very respectful. I don't understand why you're making it sound as if she's a blind woman! It's the truck that took Lucas, you know it."

"We can't prove it."

"No, we can't, but Lucas can. We can ask him when he returns. He'll be able to identify the guy, too."

"And live to tell the tale?" Troy shook his head. "Did you get the license number of the truck?"

Kelly was stricken. "No, I didn't think of it! I was so determined to see if it was the truck with the skull that I forgot everything else. I'm sorry, Troy."

It was Kelly's late day at the library. She and Troy were sitting on the bench in the library back yard where Lucas had hidden after escaping his captors. Mrs. Stark had left for the day before Kelly met Troy, and they were seated together on the bench; from that position, they could see anyone coming into the library or leaving, and they could speak freely, although caution ruled their conversation and they talked in low tones as they ate the sandwiches that Troy had picked up at Sloppy Joes.

It would have been easier if there was a license plate to check but Troy saw no reason to berate Kelly for that omission. She'd managed to get the first identifying link connecting the workers at the cemetery with the kidnappers and that was a big break. The hard part would be finding a way for Lucas to safely identify the man who had kidnapped him.

Reverend Dal and Lucas would be coming home in the next couple of days. The minister was stopping to see his in-laws, where his wife was visiting. She had flown out with the baby, and Reverend Dal would drive his family back to Settler Springs. The search by the state police to find Lucas had been called off after nothing had resulted, but even if it had still been in effect, the dragnet would not have been looking for Lucas to be traveling with a young family, crossing the border from another state. The Meachems would have been willing to keep Lucas in their home after returning from church camp, but Troy knew that a minister's life was an open book. It would be impossible to keep Lucas' presence in the household a secret.

They had to find a place for Lucas where he would not be detected. And they had to find a way for him to identify the man who had kidnapped him.

"I want to see those photographs from Doug again," Troy said. "Maybe there's a shot of this guy with the skull baseball cap. It's not likely, though. He probably wore the cap to hide his face when he was at the cemetery at night."

Kelly sighed. "Where can we hide Lucas," she asked. "I wish we could ask Jimmy if he has any ideas."

"Better not to. As much as possible, we don't want to include people like Jimmy in this part of the investigation. Even if we know that Lucas isn't guilty of theft, he's wanted by the police. Jimmy's professional reputation would suffer."

"Mrs. Hammond would let him stay there," Kelly said. Then her face fell. "No, she couldn't. The high-rise doesn't allow people not on the leases to stay there. She'd lose her housing."

They both recognized the dilemma. Lucas couldn't lodge with anyone who was known to be sympathetic to him; there was every likelihood that Stark and Meigle would continue their search and they would continue to look for him among family and those who were sympathetic to his situation, like Kelly and Troy. But the pair knew that they couldn't ask outsiders, however willing they might have been, to take on the risk of harboring someone who was wanted by the police.

"Doug would do it," Kelly said. "I'm sure he would."

"Probably, but his credibility would be in jeopardy; if it didn't work, Stark would make sure his reputation as an impartial journalist would be ruined. Even if we're successful in proving that the Starks are corrupt, it'll take time for the process to go forward. He was suspended after his son was arrested, but that didn't last; there was no real investigation and he was re-instated."

"Maybe what we need isn't a person but a place."

She was right. "Maybe reading all those mysteries is an asset after all," Troy said approvingly. "You're right. A place. Somewhere where he can be hidden and stay safe."

"Now we just need to think of a place that doesn't get a lot of traffic, where no one would notice him, where he could eat, wash, use the bathroom, and not attract attention. And school is going to be starting up soon," she reminded Troy.

"Lucas isn't going to be upset if he misses some school."

"Tia will. The family needs to get into a normal routine. With Carrie's problems and now Lucas wanted by the police, they've had a lot to deal with."

"I know, I'm not minimizing what's going on. Why don't we ask Doug if he has any ideas. I'm convinced he knows every nook and cranny of this town; if there's a hiding place for Lucas, he'll find it."

"I guess it's time to choose the engagement photo."

Doug was available on Thursday evening. Troy asked for a couple of hours off so that he and Kelly could meet with the photographer. Chief Stark had no objections; despite the failure of the search for Lucas Krymanski to yield results, he'd been in good spirits since the campaign fundraiser for Representative Eldredge.

"So, she's actually going to accept you?" Stark asked sardonically. "Have you gotten her a ring yet?"

"I didn't know you followed engagement protocol so closely," Troy replied with a deceptive blandness that didn't match the razor-sharp expression in his blue eyes. "I didn't know men paid attention to things like that."

"My wife tells me things," Stark replied. "Kelly was engaged before, you know. She got a ring from Jarrod."

"She gave it back," Troy returned. "She's gotten pretty particular since then."

Stark might have responded but there was little that he could offer in rebuttal. He scowled and returned to his office.

Kyle raised his eyebrows. "You like living dangerously?" he asked in a quiet voice after Stark closed his office door.

Troy chose to misunderstand. "I'm almost thirty-three years old," he said. "I've served in Afghanistan and now I'm a cop. I guess I'm ready for marriage."

They both knew that Kyle had not been referring to marriage.

Troy arrived at Doug's studio first. Doug had printed out all of the proofs, which he'd already delivered individually to both Troy and Kelly and had placed them on the table.

"You do good work," Troy said. "Although I can't give you the credit for Kelly; I don't think she can take a bad picture."

"I like this one," Doug said. It was the photograph showing Troy about to kiss Kelly, who was looking up at him, her head tilted back and a smile on her face. They were standing underneath the canopy of leaves of one of the magnificent trees along the Trail.

"Yeah, it's pretty good," Troy said. "Too bad it's premature."

Doug arranged the photos in a different pattern. "It doesn't have to be."

The door opened and Kelly came in.

"Kel, go ahead and lock the door and flip the sign to 'Closed,' okay? I'm not expecting anyone at this hour."

"Did you tell him?" Kelly asked Troy as she sat down across from him at the table.

"Yeah, I like this one, I just wish he'd taken it a little later."

"What—" Kelly looked down to see the photograph he was pointing to. "I meant about Lucas."

"What about Lucas?"

"He'll be back tomorrow. We need a place to hide him. Somewhere that's neutral, where he'll be safe but not noticed. Where no one would be guilty of sheltering him. Any thoughts?"

"He'll need food, water . . . bathroom."

Doug made a dismissive sound. "He's what, fifteen? He's a hardy kid, he'll be fine if we find a place. We can stock it with water and some kind of food, and he'll manage."

"But—"

"Do you have a place in mind?" Troy interrupted, guessing that Doug's quick mind was already considering locations where Lucas could be hidden.

"Actually, yeah, I am . . . it's a little risky, but it's also probably the safest place."

"Where?"

"The cemetery."

Kelly protested and even Troy looked doubtful. "The cemetery?"

"The cemetery. I spend a couple nights a week there, and it's quiet. Kelly, you were there on Sunday when these supposed landscapers were working. They stay in their own area, right? And people tending graves have a specific site to visit. No one is wandering over the grounds. They'll start doing that around Halloween time, or once the junior high history teacher assigns her annual assignment to do a report on a deceased former resident."

"That's around November," Kelly said. "But where would Lucas stay? He can't sleep outside. Even if the weather is good, he can't risk being seen."

"I've done a little exploring," Doug said. "General Porter's tomb—"

"You aren't asking him to hide inside the tomb!"

"General Porter is buried in the ground. The statue over his grave is mounted on a plinth. The plinth actually is accessible; there's a locked gate—well, it was a locked gate," he smiled, "that opens into a room. Small but not cramped. I've actually started stocking supplies in there for when I spend the night. I've brought water, packaged crackers, apples . . . I can bring more. I've got books in there. A battery-operated lamp. Maybe Lucas isn't much of a reader, but we can try to find something to keep him occupied that won't attract attention. I've even got blankets and a sleeping bag inside. It's not a Marriott, but it's not bad, and for a kid, it'll be an adventure. And poor old Porter, no one visits him anymore, except me, so no one except me even knows about the hidden room."

"Better than peanut butter and jelly," Troy commented to Kelly, recalling Lucas' complaints regarding the amenities offered during his abduction.

Kelly, thinking of bathrooms and showers and dampness, realized that she'd never be able to make a case for hygiene and comfort with two men who were clearly comfortable with the rugged outdoors.

"He'd be by himself," she said. "With no way to contact anyone if there was trouble."

"I've got an extra phone I can let him use," Doug said. "If he needs help, he can call me or you or Kelly. He couldn't use it for other things, or he'd use up the charge, but he would have it if he needed it.

39

LUCAS RETURNS

It was entirely natural for her to go over in the evening after work to welcome Rev. Meachem and his family home and once inside the house, they could speak freely.

"Lucas has a real affinity for working with young people," Rev. Dal told her. They were eating supper in the family room downstairs, which had the advantage of being a room with no windows. Kelly had brought a casserole, salad, and a cake to welcome them back with a meal. "I don't know how I'd have gotten through the week without his help."

Lucas flushed with pleasure. "I liked it," he said simply. But in that phrase, Kelly sensed a deeper affirmation of the two weeks that Lucas had spent at the church camp.

Night had fallen, and Olivia Meachem had put the baby to bed, when Kelly decided that it was dark enough outside for Lucas to be able to get into her car without being detected if anyone happened to be passing by the parsonage. She drove to her house and into her garage. Lucas followed her from the garage into the house, adroitly avoiding windows in case anyone was watching from the street.

She elaborated on the information she had provided at the Meachems' house: his family was doing well, although only his mother knew his actual whereabouts; the search had been called off when there were no traces of Lucas through any of the available paths, but that didn't mean that they had given up looking for him.

"We think that we might have found one of the men who abducted you; at any rate, we think we saw the truck with the skull decal on the rear window. What did he look like?"

Lucas shrugged. She had turned on the television and his gaze continued to drift toward the screen. It had been some time since he'd lived the normal life of a teenager. With resignation, she turned on the sports channel.

"What did they look like?" she repeated. "The men who kidnapped you?"

"They just looked—my mom would have called them slobs. One of the guys, I don't know what his name was, the other guy called him AJ, he wasn't real tall but he was kind of bulky, you know, in his muscles," Lucas lifted up his shoulders to imitate heft. "He wore a baseball cap all the time; one time he took it off and I saw a bald spot. I guess that's why he wore it. The other guy was skinnier and was on his phone a lot."

"Appearance? The other guy?"

"He was skinny, kind of, and taller than AJ. He had sorta blondish hair, cut pretty short. He had a mustache."

"What was his name?"

"AJ called him 'Pal,' but I don't think that was his name. It was just what he called him, but sometimes he called me that, too, when he wanted to get my attention."

"I think we saw AJ at the cemetery, clearing some of the overgrowth at the lower part. He had a baseball cap with a skull on the bill. Does that match the cap that he wore when you were with him?"

"Yeah! He has a skull tattoo, too, on his arm, up at the top."

"Then it sounds like we might be getting closer," Kelly said. "But right now, we have to find a safe place for you."

She went on to outline Doug's suggestion that Lucas would be safe hiding inside the concealed room beneath General Porter's statue. She told him that there would be food, water, a sleeping bag and blankets for him, and a cell phone to be used in case of an emergency. Kelly was surprised that Lucas was amenable to the idea of hiding out in a tomb, but he appeared to find the idea acceptable. Perhaps, she thought, he realized that he needed a safe place to stay where he wouldn't be found, and he didn't want to risk being seen by Stark.

"I don't like the idea of you staying there," she admitted. "But I don't know a safe place where you can stay until we've made the right kind of progress."

"I'd rather be hiding in a place where friends know where I am than in a strange place with two guys who dragged me into their truck."

"You have a point. But you might be bored," she warned him. "There's no electricity so you couldn't use a laptop or anything like that. You'd have to stay inside during the day and then come out at night, and even then, you'd have to be very careful not to be seen. Doug has oiled the lock on the gate so that it doesn't squeak, and it's not in full view, but still . . . the last thing we'd need is someone thinking that there's anyone living at the cemetery."

"Kids hang out there in the woods by the graveyard all the time, after the football games," Lucas said. He didn't tell Kelly what they were doing after the games and she didn't need to ask. "Not so much now in the summer."

"You're not scared of being in a cemetery?"

"Nothing to be scared of. The dead bodies aren't going to hurt me."

"What about boredom?"

"I was pretty bored when they kidnapped me and tied me up and there wasn't anything to do. At least in the cemetery, I won't be tied up. Actually . . ."

"Yes?"

"I was wondering, Miz Armello . . . I kinda liked working with Reverend Dal at the camp. We were outside all day long doing stuff and the kids, some of them are from bad places. I could see how different they were after they'd spent time at the camp. I've been thinking that I might like to help next summer. Rev. Dal said I can, if Mom lets me, and I know she will."

"That's great, Lucas, and I know that Reverend Dal will appreciate the help. He said you did a lot of work while you were there."

"It didn't feel like work. I was wondering . . . in the evenings, when we were around the campfire, Rev. Dal would tell stories. I didn't realize at first that they were Bible stories. The way he told them, they sounded like real stuff that happened to real people."

"They did happen to real people, Lucas," Kelly said in amusement. "It's just a long time ago, that's why they seem so remote."

"Maybe. But I'd like to know more about those people. Some of them weren't so great, you know; they did bad things. But Rev. Dal, he said that even though one of them was a born liar who cheated his brother out of everything he had, and another one was a really dumb guy who fell in love with a woman who was just using him, and one woman, she was a prostitute, but she helped these two spies . . . even though they weren't the kind of people you expect to show up in the Bible, Rev. Dal said that God had a purpose for them. He wanted to make sure the kids understood that just because they don't wear the right sneakers or have perfect parents, they still have important work to do. I was thinking, if you could get me a Bible, I could read it while I'm hiding. Then, next year, I'd know more about what Rev. Dal meant when he's telling those stories."

"I can get you a Bible, Lucas. I'll get you one that's written in the kind of language we talk now, so that it'll make more sense to you."

The guest bedroom downstairs in the finished basement was always ready for use, and Kelly decided that Lucas could sleep there that night, rather than in the garage. She didn't know how long he'd have to sleep beneath the statute of General Porter, but at least he could have this night of comfort in a real bed. There was a television in the room and as she closed the door, she saw Lucas holding onto the remote control as if he'd discovered a long-lost friend.

To think of Lucas asking for a Bible so that he would know the stories Rev. Dal had shared with the kids at the church camp . . . it made Kelly wonder if, amidst all of the corruption and violence that seemed to surround them, the senseless deaths of Lyola Knesbit and Sean Claypool; Carrie Krymanski's near-fatal overdose and the grim tally of drug deaths that Jimmy Patton had witnessed; the cruel pranks harassing Mia Shaw and the vicious campaign against Leo Page's integrity, there was still a divine plan to bring something miraculous out of the wretchedness. It was far too soon to ascribe a spiritual transformation to Lucas, she knew. But still, it was a victory amidst so many defeats.

40

ENGAGEMENT COMPLICATIONS

Doug promised to look after Lucas as much as he could. Kelly had confidence in Doug's resourcefulness; nonetheless, she reminded him that the threats to Lucas came from Chief Stark but also from Lucas' youth. Doug assured her that he'd make it clear to Lucas that his safety depended upon his own discretion.

"He's probably gotten a crash course in self-preservation after his kidnapping," Doug said.

"He's had a growing-up summer. First, looking after his sister as much as he could, and now this. I want to see Tia and talk to her, but Troy said not to tell her where Lucas is staying."

"Better that way. Just so she knows that he's safe. And he is. It's been over a century since General

Porter was responsible for protecting civilians," Doug said with a grin. "Now he's earning those stripes all over again."

Kelly smiled. "You have a point."

Troy was sympathetic to Kelly's concerns and admitted that he shared them.

"I don't know if I could have spent time in a cemetery like that when I was his age," he said when he and Kelly were at The Café, in their usual booth, at their usual time on Saturday. "Doug plans to go out there more at night to do some surveillance and probably to make sure Lucas is okay. Now that we have a face—we think—and Lucas would recognize him, we're a little closer to tying some of the knots tighter."

"The metaphor holds," Kelly said.

"I hope. We hope. Doug's theory, and it's a good one, is that the Starks are going to be of two minds right now: the cash roulette fundraiser went extremely well, so if they're worried about Mrs. Stark losing the authority to oversee the library's finances and it goes back to you, they'll still have an outlet for their earnings. Once LifeLight hears that the library is standing up to her, that congregation might decide to do the same. The Starks will need a way to launder their own money and the re-election campaign might just be it. I had an interesting talk with Trooper Callahan yesterday." Although he was speaking in low tones already, his voice dropped even lower and he kept his eyes on the entrance to the restaurant as he talked. "She said that Trooper Meigle has been out a lot, doesn't say where or why. That's a lot of freedom for a state cop. She also said that he's in a foul mood when he's in the office."

"Does she think he's looking for Lucas?"

"She wouldn't go that far. She's very cautious and not given to speculation. But she did say that Chief Stark stops there more than he used to. Stark used to wait for Meigle to come to him. It sounds like he's getting a little bit antsy. Which probably means that Lucas is in the best possible place. That's not somewhere they'd look for him."

Kelly sighed. "Do you think we're coming to some resolution on this?"

"I hope so. Leo testifies next week at Shaw's trial."

"Do you think Chief Stark is concerned?"

"I don't know that he has anything to be concerned about. There's nothing tying him to Shaw or to Mrs. Knesbit. If Leo can keep calm and answer in a straightforward manner, he can make a convincing case. He knows that."

"I thought that you and Carmela would have been subpoenaed to testify."

"I did too, but Shaw's attorney is pinning everything on Leo, and I guess the prosecution agrees. Leo was acting chief at the time, so whatever happened would be under his authority."

"And Mia?"

"She wasn't subpoenaed. Again, I thought she would be. All I can guess is that the defense didn't want to give the prosecution a chance to ask leading questions about Shaw's connections, and the prosecution didn't want to give the defense a chance to discredit Mia on the basis of her past drug history."

"It's kind of funny; Carmela didn't want to testify, but now that she hasn't been subpoenaed, I think she's mad at being slighted."

Troy laughed. "Carmela tells me that we should schedule an April wedding."

Kelly made a face. "She's really bought into this whole engagement thing. She told me the same thing. She said it would be better to do it before the

Memorial Day program or summer reading because then I'm too busy."

"Well, speaking as the husband-to-be in this 'whole engagement thing,' if we were getting married, I'd make sure we were on our honeymoon for Memorial Day, because there's no way I'd want to have to go through all of that again." He sobered. "I talked to Sean's dad today. I told him about the grave and how it's being taken care of. He seemed to find that comforting."

Kelly put her hand over his. "When we unravel all of this," she said. "you'll be able to prove that Sean didn't commit suicide."

Francie came over to bring their checks, noticed the gesture, and raised her eyebrows. "Well," she said, "it looks like you two are getting along just fine. Oh, I saw the photos and they came out great!"

"You saw the photos?" Kelly asked.

"I stopped by the studio to schedule my daughter's senior picture and they were out on the table. I like the one where Troy's about to give you a nice, big kiss, Kelly."

"That's the one we both like," Troy answered before Kelly had a chance to.

"Very romantic. Very ooh-la-la!"

"How's Tia?" Kelly asked, detouring the topic.

"She's hanging in there. It's a long time to go without a word about Lucas."

"Has Stark been back in to question her?"

Francie shook her head with a grin. "I think she scared him off the last time," Francie said. "I was surprised, but since then, different people who were here that night have told me that they're glad she spoke up. I think that Tia giving the council an earful at that meeting might have made people think."

"Might have," Troy agreed noncommittally. "Tell her we said hi, okay?"

Troy asked Kelly if she had any plans for the afternoon. He was disappointed but not surprised when she said that, with the new school year about to start, she had to work on her fall programming schedule. Mrs. Stark was still coming to the library, just as she had done earlier, but she came in an hour later and left an hour earlier. It was an improvement, but not enough of one and Kelly preferred to work on projects without Mrs. Stark's disapproving presence.

Troy nodded. He felt the same way about Chief Stark. "You know," he commented as they left the restaurant and went to their respective cars, "I'm sure that people in town are wondering why we don't kiss goodbye when we leave each other."

"Oh, kissing has to wait for the ring," Kelly said, trying to conceal a grin.

"Oh, yeah, the ring. Anytime you want to go ring shopping, Kelly, just say the word."

He almost sounded serious. She looked up at him curiously. He was smiling, but not as if he were making a joke.

For the rest of the afternoon, as she worked at the library to develop the various after-school programs that would get underway once the students were back in their classes, Kelly was reminded of that smile. If she didn't know better, she'd have described it as the smile of a man who was happy to be engaged, one who was looking forward to being married. Of course, that was impossible; Troy had given no indication that he wanted to be married. He seemed to find the subject of their engagement a matter of great amusement; he had handled it, from the beginning, with much more equanimity than she had, Kelly realized.

That was the trouble. She took marriage seriously. Troy Kennedy didn't. Their engagement was a ploy concocted by Doug Iolus so that they would be able to meet and discuss the investigation without being suspected of doing so by Chief Stark.

She must have been crazy to have gone alone with it, Kelly thought as she went through the stacks to pull out the titles that would be book report topics for the middle school students in September. Disentangling themselves from this engagement was going to be difficult, especially since everyone in town seemed to have an opinion on the couple's supposed marital plans.

And how was she going to explain it all to her parents when they came up for Thanksgiving? The only consolation she had was that by then, perhaps the investigation would be resolved, Lucas would be safe and his family would be back to a normal routine again, the Starks would be called to account for their deeds, Leo would be exonerated, Travis Shaw would be in prison for the murder of Lyola Knesbit, the plot to murder Sean Claypool would be exposed, Mia Shaw's harassment would be revealed, and Settler Springs could be rid of the foul influence that drugs and corruption had sponsored.

It was a lot to ask for, Kelly realized. What they were trying to accomplish was much more important than her discomfort over a fabricated wedding engagement. They'd already achieved a lot, even if it hadn't yet yielded the results that were needed to prove that Chief Stark and his wife, along with Mayor Truvert, were criminals.

Unbidden, the lyric of one of the hymns they'd sung last Sunday came to mind:

This is my Father's world. O let me ne'er forget

That though the wrong seems oft so strong, God is the ruler yet.

41

THOUGH THE WRONG SEEMS OFT SO STRONG

"I just thought you'd like to know that those landscapers were there again today," Mrs. Hammond said.

"Okay, Mrs. Hammond, thanks. Doing the same thing as usual?"

"Oh, yes, the very same. One of them was smoking and would you believe that Nora Halvernik went right up to him and said she expected him to make sure he didn't leave any cigarette butts behind. Nora, a smoker herself! But she says she's always respectful of other people's property."

"What did he say? The landscaper?"

"He didn't look very happy about it, but he said he wouldn't leave any butts there."

"Do you know which one it was?"

"It wasn't the one with the skull that we talked to. It was a tall man who looked like he couldn't weigh one hundred pounds soaking wet."

"Anything else about him that you remember?"

"He had facial hair," Mrs. Hammond replied. "A scraggly looking mustache. He doesn't look as though he shaves regularly. Kelly, is all of this important?"

"It might be. You didn't tell anyone anything, did you?"

"Certainly not! There isn't really much to tell. But you promise that you'll explain it all to me after it's all solved?"

"I'll tell you whatever I know," Kelly promised.

After that call ended, she texted Doug.

Mrs. Hammond and the graveyard ladies weren't very happy. The landscapers are there and one of them is smoking. One of the ladies told him that he'd better not leave any cigarette butts around.

It seemed absurd, in a way, to use such elaborate messages when communicating with Doug and Troy in order to avoid revealing their real meaning.

Maybe Troy was right, Kelly thought, and she was reading too many mysteries and was acting on them. But Troy's sense of caution had reinforced the ways in which they communicated and maybe it was better that way.

She drove by Troy's house to deliver the message in person that she'd texted to Doug. He was in his back yard, grilling hamburgers. He smiled as soon as he saw her.

"Kelly, now this is a good surprise. Can you stay for lunch?"

"Sure, but I didn't bring anything."

"As long as you don't object to hot dogs, hamburgers, buns, and pickles, I can offer you a pretty good lunch."

She smiled and sat down on the bench while he grilled. "Mrs. Hammond called to let me know that the 'landscapers' are there again. I texted Doug so he'd know."

"We'll see if they show up on a Sunday before there's a delivery at night. Has Doug responded?"

"Not yet, but he doesn't always answer right away."

"I think we can bet that he'll be out there tonight. Would you hand me that plate? These are done."

Troy put the grilled meat on the plate. While Kelly was slicing tomatoes and onions, he cut open the buns and placed them on the grill so that they'd be toasted. Troy had a cooler filled with ice by the bench; inside were cans of soda and bottles of water.

"It's a little less fancy than when you're doing it," he said as he handed her a bottle of water, "but I'll learn."

"This is perfectly fine," she answered.

"Yes," Troy said softly, "it's perfectly fine."

He had that look in his eyes again, the one she'd noticed yesterday, the one that made it seem as though the man she knew was the same as the fiancée who'd been created. Confused, Kelly looked away. "At least it's not raining today. It would be pretty hard for Doug to stay at the cemetery if it were raining."

"Not if he went into the tomb room," Troy said.

"That would defeat the purpose of being at the cemetery to watch what's going on."

"Maybe I'll take a ride out there tonight," Troy said.

"Be careful," she said with a sense of urgency that seemed out of place.

Troy looked at her curiously. "Don't worry," he said. "I know how to take care of myself."

He turned the conversation to other topics, ones which had nothing to do with the Starks or the investigation. He was going to get a shed for the back yard; he'd acquired so many new lawn tools that he needed a place to keep them. When he first rented the place, the owner of the house assured him that by mid-August, the rains had stopped and the ground was so dry that he probably wouldn't need to mow any more. "Here it is, almost Labor Day, and I'm mowing like it's May."

"It's been a pretty wet summer," Kelly agreed. "One of the neighbor kids does my lawn and he's putting a down payment on a car. A used car, but still, his first car. I think he's made the down payment just with the lawns he's mowing this summer."

"I can mow it for you," Troy offered.

"Oh, I could do it myself," Kelly said. "I used to, but Austin started his own mowing business this summer and we all want to see him do well. He's a good kid and a hard worker."

The conversation continued in that vein, casual and light. Yet, as they chatted about the lawn and the weather and kids going back to school, Kelly could not dispel a sense of apprehension. Just as they finished eating, the sky, which had been cloudless just an hour before, suddenly went gray and drops of rain fell down. Kelly hurried and brought everything inside while Troy closed the grill and brought the cooler into the house.

"You don't have to go," he said. "Arlo is going to think you just came for the eats."

She smiled and patted Arlo to reassure him that she'd stopped by to visit him as well as to have lunch. "I'd better be going," she said. "Work tomorrow. You'll—you will be careful if you go to the cemetery?"

"I'm always careful," Troy said. "You know that."

She did know that, but as she waved good-bye and drove away, she could not explain the longing that she felt as she saw Troy standing on the curb while he watched her leave.

The rain ended almost as quickly as it began, but by that time, Kelly was already home. Doug had texted while she was at Troy's house.

I'll see how it looks, he'd texted. Those ladies won't be happy if the grounds are messy.

That was all, but she knew that he'd be checking on Lucas, and probably bringing a treat of some kind for the boy to enjoy. She wondered how Lucas was faring with the Bible she'd given him. She'd told Reverend Dal what Lucas had told her about the stories he'd listened to, and how he wanted to know more of them so that, next year, he'd be more familiar with them. Reverend Dal had looked pleased. Lucas Krymanski, he told Kelly, had something in him that, if nurtured, was going to nurture the gifts of the Spirit.

Kelly felt the same way but she was still troubled by that odd, inexplicable sense of anxiety and she was unable to settle down, as she usually did on a Sunday afternoon, to rest on the sofa while she planned out her work schedule for the coming week.

Dusk came and brought with it the soft gray shadows of summer evening. As darkness fell, she felt the sense of melancholy that she always experienced, every summer, when she realized that the days were slowly getting shorter and the night was claiming more minutes. The lightning bugs with their bright illumination were giving way to the chirping of the crickets who belonged to the autumn. Then the cold and frost would come, and the insects would retreat entirely. The leaves on the branches would burst forth in the brilliant fall colors, painting the tree-lined streets of Settler Springs with gorgeous shades of yellow, orange, red and bronze, until they too, would surrender to the cold, barren winter.

Kelly wondered why she was reacting this way. She enjoyed all the seasons, knowing that each one brought its own unique character to the landscape. Why, then, was she suddenly reluctant to accept that summer was preparing to give way to its successor, as it did every year?

She knew that she ought to just go to bed. A good night's sleep would drive away these silly fancies. But she remained on the sofa, looking out the window into the darkness, as if there were something concealed that was waiting to be detected.

42

SCENES AT THE CEMETERY

Doug was relieved when the rain turned out to be no more than a brief shower. He was interested in finding out whether or not the Sunday activities on the part of men who called themselves landscapers would have any follow-up action that night with nocturnal traffic in the cemetery. He also wanted to make sure that Lucas was okay. The boy didn't lack for courage, that was for sure.

As soon as dusk fell, Doug set off on his trek to the cemetery, his backpack loaded with items that he thought might make Lucas' stay in General Porter's hidden room a little less Spartan. Although he knew that he was a familiar sight on foot, and that no one in town would think twice at seeing him walking anywhere, Doug found himself keeping to the shadows, as if he needed to conceal his presence. He wasn't sure what had cast the peculiar spell over him. Maybe it was the onset of fall, he thought as he approached the cemetery, entering by an overgrown foot path that was seldom, if ever, used anymore. It, like the hidden room beneath General Porter's statue, belonged to another time in the history of Settler Springs.

He was glad to note that General Porter's graveyard bore no traces of any live occupancy; Lucas was keeping his presence in the room private. Staying silent, Doug moved within the swaddling bands of shadow as he approached the gate. He announced his presence with the code that he and Lucas had settled on: two snaps of his fingers which could be heard in the quiet night air. Then he opened the gate and entered the hidden room.

Lucas was standing, a baseball bat in hand, poised to defend himself had it been necessary, just as Doug had instructed him. He relaxed when he saw Doug, who sat down on the blanket Lucas had spread on the cement and began to empty his backpack. Lucas raised his hands in a mute cheer when he found the bag of potato chips and the bottle of soda. Doug had adhered to Kelly's insistence that Lucas could not live on junk food during this time, so he'd brought the boy bread, beef jerky, individual containers of fruit and pudding along with plastic utensils, so that he would have a little bit of variety. But Lucas was a kid, Doug didn't forget that, which was why he always brought something that belonged to the favorite teen food group, junk food.

Food delivery accomplished, Doug prepared to commence his outside vigil, night camera at the ready, so that he'd be able to watch and see if cars began to arrive.

"You want to come out?" he whispered to Lucas, who immediately put down the bag of chips and the soda and nodded.

Kelly wouldn't like it, Doug knew. Troy wouldn't like it either. But Doug had spent quite a few nights during the summer, right here, protected by the height and span of General Porter's tomb, and it only seemed fair to let Lucas have some respite outside. The air was turning cooler, but Lucas had on a flannel shirt, jeans and a dark hoodie, which he pulled over his head so that he, like Doug, blended into the opaque night.

Lucas' sharp young eyes spotted the vehicle as soon as Doug did as it drove slowly, headlights off, down the road and onto the path at the lower end of the lot. Lucas drew in his breath and then slowly exhaled. Doug didn't react at all, except to grip his camera. Then, turning to Lucas, he handed him a second camera, miming for him to look through the lens.

"See if you recognize anyone," he said. "If you do, shoot. No flash."

Lucas nodded in understanding. Gradually, another vehicle came, and then another. It was a processional, grim in its purpose. Doug aimed and shot, aware all the time that, at his side, Lucas was very intent on what was going on. Was it because of his sister's addiction that Lucas was paying such close attention? Did he expect that he would recognize a face, see someone who had sold his sister the drugs that had caused her to overdose and that could have killed her had Kelly not administered Narcan? Doug didn't know and wasn't going to ask, not now, when silence was imperative. But he thought that, one day, he'd like to interview Mr. Lucas Krymanski.

Then Doug felt Lucas tense next to him. Lucas pointed to the vehicle that was just now turning onto the road.

"Troy," Lucas whispered.

Doug jerked his head. The big Suburban was hugging the side of the road, so far invisible to the cluster of cars further down by the lower lot. Its headlights were off.

"Stay here," Doug said, cupping his hand over his mouth so that the sound wouldn't travel. "Keep shooting, stay low, below the surface. No one can see you. No one should come this far up. If you see anyone coming this way, get back into the room and close the gate and shut the door. Don't come out unless I signal."

"What are you—"

Doug shook his head. He wrapped his camera inside his jacket so that it wouldn't make noise. Then he took off in a crouch, crossing the graves in a weird posture that kept him out of sight while allowing him to move quickly. He crept down the slope until he came to the Suburban, now parked by the side of the road. More cars would be coming soon; someone would wonder why a car was parked there.

Doug crawled around the back of the SUV until he came to the driver's side. Slowly, he stood up. But no one was in the car. Doug felt panic; was Lucas wrong? Was this not Troy's car?

He heard nothing, saw nothing, but with no warning, there was a gun pressed against the back of his neck. Doug felt a purposeful hand move to the front of his jacket and stop at the camera concealed inside.

"Doug."

"What are you doing here?" Doug whispered. "They'll see your SUV, they'll know."

"They don't know my car. I'm going further down where I can see what's going on."

"Don't do it. It's not safe."

"I've been in worse situations in Afghanistan. You go back and make sure Lucas is safe."

Once again, Doug saw no movement and heard no noise, but he knew that Troy was in motion. Should he follow Troy or go back to look after Lucas and continue with his usual routine when at the cemetery, which was to use his camera to record the participants in the transactions taking place below?

He decided to follow Troy, or at least to head in that direction. Lucas was safe as long as he stayed with General Porter, Doug decided. And Doug had made sure that Lucas had the cell phone on him that Doug had given him. If necessary . . .

Closer, closer, moving within the dark circumference of shadow, Doug advanced toward the cluster of cars, the absence of headlights making the night seem even more devoid of light. He still couldn't see Troy, but he supposed that was the intention of the police officer's military training, to strike without being seen.

Cars were still arriving, but the ones that had already finished their business were leaving; some turned around to go back the way they had come, others were going straight out, where they would connect from the cemetery road to the main highway. Some, he realized, would not wait to use the drugs they had just bought; they would inject immediately, risking the threat of death for the chance of brief ecstasy. People like Stark were profiting on the deadly roulette that addicts played with their lives. And that, Doug knew, was why Troy was advancing in the darkness, because, now that he was so close to the source of the poison, he could not turn back.

There were fewer cars now. It seemed as though there had been more the last time Doug had been present while the selling was going on. He wondered why. It didn't matter, though. The results would be the same.

Every time a car passed him, Doug was conscious of his vulnerability. Only the cover of darkness and the fact that, once they'd acquired the drug they sought, an addict didn't care about anything but putting it to use, gave him the courage to keep moving forward.

The black pickup truck was still there.

"Hands up, police!" Troy's voice came out of the darkness like a supernatural presence, heard but invisible.

Then, behind him, Doug heard the sound of a vehicle making its way down the road. He hoped that Troy was well hidden, because this vehicle had its lights on and it wasn't showing any hesitation at all. Then the car stopped suddenly, and he realized that it was a police car. Doug crouched down on the ground and took out his camera.

"What's going on, AJ?"

Troy's voice, sounding unperturbed, even though, Doug thought, he had to recognize that it was Chief Stark speaking. "You're under arrest!"

Stark followed the sound of the voice with his gun. Another officer got out of the car on the passenger side and started shooting. Doug stolidly continued to aim his camera at the two visible police officers.

He watched and aimed and clicked as the pickup truck suddenly peeled out of the pathway and down the road.

"Did you get him?" asked the other officer, running over to Stark.

They were both heading to the other side of the road. Stark bent down into the darkness.

"I got him," he said. "We aren't going to have to deal with Kennedy's interference anymore."

"Let's get out of here."

Doug's camera continued without pausing, following the police car as it drove away. He pulled out his phone and called the ambulance center directly, not wanting to risk a 911 call behind heard by Stark and his accomplice in case they returned.

"Yeah?" Jimmy's voice, puzzled that someone had called the ambulance center's direct line.

"Jimmy, bring an ambulance to the cemetery. Troy's been shot."

Doug crossed the road. He nearly tripped over Troy's sprawled body. He pressed his hand against Troy's chest and felt blood. Too much blood, and too close to his heart. But he could feel a heartbeat. Maybe it wouldn't be too late. Maybe . . .

He heard footsteps running. Abandoning caution, Lucas had run down from General Porter's tomb.

"Is he alive?"

"He's been shot. Jimmy is coming with the ambulance."

Lucas took the phone out of his pocket. "I better let Miz Armello know."

43

KELLY'S VIGIL

Hospitals were part of Reverend Dal Meachem's field of battle and he spent a lot of time in them. But he wasn't usually in them on Christmas Day. The nurses, recognizing him and knowing where he was going, nodded a greeting.

At least it wasn't ICU, Reverend Dal thought as he went into the room.

Kelly was sitting there, talking to the still, unresponsive form in the bed.

"The trial is expected to get underway in January," she was saying. "The Starks can't get bail; their lawyer tried, but the prosecutor says they're flight risks. They've found out that Chief Stark had a steady supply of people to work for him. Travis

390

Shaw coordinated the names from people he knew who were on parole. Everything from selling drugs, to—to stealing the car that Sean was murdered in, they did it. One of them was responsible for hitting Leo over the head that night; it was to scare him. A day doesn't go by without something new about what they were doing—oh, Rev. Dal," she said. "I didn't know you were here. I always tell him the latest news. Sometimes I repeat what I already told him," she admitted. "But I want him to know that it worked, that—"

She stopped talking. He knew why. She didn't want to cry, not because she feared crying in front of her pastor, but because she didn't want Troy, or whatever senses of his were active despite his unconscious state, to hear her crying. Because, he knew, she feared that if he heard her crying, he'd know how seriously injured he was and how bad his wounds were and how he might not recover.

"Your parents are worried," he said. "They called me. They said that you barely ate any of your Christmas dinner and then you came straight to the hospital."

"I need to be here," she said. "I can't let him be alone on Christmas day. His family just left on Monday. They didn't want to leave, but they all have their lives. I promised that I'd stay in touch with them and let them know if—I'll keep them updated. You shouldn't have come here today, what about the baby and Olivia?"

"They're fine and this is where I need to be. But Olivia would be mad at me if I didn't insist that you go down to the cafeteria and get something to eat. She's worried about you. Your parents are worried about you. They say you're not eating, you're not sleeping—"

"I'm not hungry."

"Go down to the cafeteria," he said firmly. "Get a sandwich and a cup of coffee. Sit down. Take a bite and chew it. Swallow. Take a sip of coffee. Don't come back up here until you've finished them. Do it, Kelly. You're no good for Troy or for yourself if you don't."

"I'm not hungry—"

"Maybe not," he said. "But I'm here and I'm going to pray with Troy. I promise that he'll be in God's hands while you're gone."

She didn't want to leave, and Reverend Dal knew that she came here every day, whether she came after work or early in the morning on the weekends. In the more than three months since the shooting that had shocked Settler Springs, Kelly's steadfast presence at Troy's bedside had not wavered. While the town reeled from the revelation that the police chief and his wife were the masterminds behind one of the largest drug rings in existence in western Pennsylvania, an operation so far-reaching that it had ended State Representative Elderedge's campaign after word got out that he had used his influence to protect them from the law, Kelly had followed a routine which took her to work, to the hospital, and to church.

As Reverend Dal bent his head and leaned over the railings of the bed, he wondered how much Troy, in his present state, was able to understand of what Kelly told him. Did he know that his actions, although they had nearly cost him his life, had been caught on camera by Doug Iolus, whose swift action the night of the shooting had gotten the ambulance to the crime scene without delay? Doug's photographs, and the evidence he had provided, had been damning and as a result, Roger Stark was in jail. So was Trooper Meigle, the state policeman who had been Stark's partner throughout.

Stark had hired a skilled lawyer for himself and his wife, but the newspapers were already following up on the evidence against him: the death of the church treasurer who was in the way of Lois Stark's ambition to use the office as a way to funnel drug money through church deposits; the murder of military veteran Sean Claypool, who had been killed and had not committed suicide, because he was a friend of Troy Kennedy; the connivance of Representative Eldredge with Travis Shaw to unleash a public relations campaign that made Leo Page appear to be the villain; getting Jarrod Zabo the position in Eldredge's campaign so that he would be able to try to get back with Kelly and turn her against Troy; the vicious pranks played against Mia Shaw to frighten her . . .

Reverend Dal sighed. Evil was pervasive. But good was stronger.

"Father in heaven," he prayed, "You are here in this room with your son, Troy, and your daughter, Kelly. Heal him of his wounds, Lord, wounds he received in the service of others. Give your daughter Kelly the strength that she needs as she waits for the man she loves to be restored to health and to her heart. You know that she is faithful, Lord, and you know that these two have endured much. Their cause was just, and together they have brought good out of evil and justice out of corruption. But you know all this, Lord, and you—"

Rev. Dal was not in the habit of interrupting his own prayers, but he sensed a stirring where, moments before, there had been only stillness. He opened his eyes and saw Troy's gaze upon him.

"Troy! Praise God!"

Troy could not answer; he was breathing thanks to the ventilator and Rev. Dal could see the man's confusion and irritation at his intubated state. Rev. Dal rang for the nurse; Troy was still in a weakened condition, but he didn't want to risk him pulling the tube out.

The nurse came quickly. When she saw Troy's open eyes, her own eyes widened in amazement. She saw Troy's agitation.

"I'm going to get the doctor. We'll have to sedate him to keep him calm; he can't come off the ventilator yet. Can you keep him calm until then?"

"I'll do my best. After you've reached the doctor, can you send someone down to the cafeteria for Kelly Armello?"

The nurse nodded. "She's been here every day; she deserves to see him with his eyes open before we sedate him."

The nurse followed through on her promise. The doctor had just entered Troy's room when Kelly ran in behind him.

"And to think I was complaining that I had to work on Christmas day," the doctor said as he checked Troy's vital signs. "Officer Kennedy, you've just delivered a Christmas present for all of us."

Troy looked at them wonderingly and jerked his head.

"No, we can't take the tube out yet," the doctor said, his voice soothing but firm. "We're going to give you something to make you relax. Pretty soon, you'll be able to breathe on your own and when we're sure that you're all right, we'll take it out. And then you can talk."

Troy's eyes fell upon Kelly. Tears were spilling from her eyes, but she was smiling as she reached for his hand. He followed the direction of her hand, looking puzzled.

"You're in the hospital," the doctor said. "You were shot in the line of duty and you've been here awhile. Your fiancée will be able to fill you in on all the details and you can ask all the questions you want to ask her. But right now . . ."

Troy's eyelids flickered, then drooped, then finally closed as the sedative took effect.

"His heartbeat is steady," the doctor said. "I can't say he's out of the woods, but it looks like he's holding his own. He'll be able to appreciate that Christmas tree you decorated," he said, nodding at the small tree on the windowsill. "He might even wonder where his presents are. But he's gotten the best present."

"I've gotten the best present," Kelly corrected the doctor. "I didn't know if he'd ever open his eyes again."

"Neither did we," the doctor said frankly. "You must have put something extra powerful in that prayer, Reverend. Now, he's not all better yet. He's going to need a lot of physical therapy to gain back even minimal strength. But he's young and he's healthy. I'd say your fiancé is going to be able to be a husband sometime in the new year, but not right away."

Troy, however, had different thoughts. Once he was off the ventilator and breathing on his own, sitting up in his bed and then sitting up in a chair beside the bed, he wanted to know how soon before he could go home.

"You can't even stand up on your own," his nurse told him. She had been an army nurse before returning to civilian life and her blunt manner perfectly matched Troy's impatience. "You want to have this pretty thing carry you across the threshold?"

After she left, Kelly pulled a chair close so that she could sit next to Troy. "The therapist said you're doing really well," she told him.

"That's what he told me too, but it doesn't feel like it. I don't want to be an invalid."

"And you aren't going to be. Just a week ago, you opened your eyes. Now you're sitting up in a chair and you're getting therapy twice a day. You're doing great. Do you remember what happened?"

"I remember getting out of the Suburban and walking. I don't remember anything after that."

"Stark and Meigle shot you. The guy in the black pickup truck drove away, but Lucas was taking photographs the whole time. So was Doug. There's so much evidence that there was no chance of bail. Jimmy drove you to the hospital, and I met the ambulance there. They operated . . . well, you've had a few operations. The bullets hit major organs, and there was a lot of blood loss, but you hung on. The surgeon said you just wouldn't let go of living."

Troy raised his finger to wipe away the tears that were falling from Kelly's eyes. "I wouldn't let go of you," he said. "I can't explain it, but living meant you. Dying meant not having you. Kelly, I know our engagement was just for pretend, but I knew even then that what I felt for you, what I feel for you now, is real. I want us to be married."

"Is that a proposal? Because if it is, my answer is yes. And if it's not, why isn't it?"

"It's a proposal," he said, leaning his head against the high-backed chair. He detested the way weariness suddenly overcame him every day and he hated being weak. He'd just proposed marriage to the woman he loved, and he didn't even have the strength to kiss her. What kind of husband was he going to be?

"Then I accept. When can we get married?"

He felt his eyes closing. Sleep was pressing upon him.

"As soon as I'm able to . . ."

When Troy confronted the doctor to demand a timetable for his recovery, the doctor said that

Troy's body hadn't caught up with his will yet, and no, he couldn't be released.

"Then we'll get married right here," Kelly declared. Since Troy's recovery, Kelly had been rejuvenated and her inherent spirit and optimism had returned. Troy wasn't used to having somebody do his fighting for him, but Kelly was determined.

"We're going to get married right in this room," she told him. "I've already contacted your family. Doug said he wants to be your best man; he says that since he's responsible for us being engaged, he's the logical choice. The Public Servants Bowling Team is coming; in fact, they're bringing the food for the reception that we're going to have in the patients' lounge. Mia is coming. The Krymanskis are coming; Carrie and Lucas both will be there. Mayor Page is coming—"

"Mayor Who?"

Kelly grinned in triumph. "Once the council found out that Mayor Truvert had been involved in everything the Starks were doing, they fired him and he's being charged with accessory to kidnapping, corruption, all sorts of things. The council asked Leo if he'd take the job, and he accepted, with one condition: when you're recovered, he wants you to be named the chief of police."

"Who's chief now?"

"The position is open for the time being. The council hired a new police officer, he's fresh out of the academy. Kyle thinks he's going to work out. They're all waiting for you to come back."

Troy's hands tightened around Kelly's fingers. "I never thought, when I decided to move to Settler Springs, that I'd find a home I didn't want to leave. Is Reverend Dal going to do the wedding?"

"Of course. He said he has to, since it was when he was praying that you opened your eyes."

"Then I owe him a lot."

"We owe God a lot," Kelly corrected him gently.

Troy waited, then nodded. "I guess we do. Maybe it's time I started paying on that debt."

"It's already paid, love," Kelly said, leaning closer to her husband-to-be.

The nurse paused at the door. It was time to check the patient's blood pressure and temperature, but she decided to come back later. It was plain to see that Officer Kennedy was on the mend.

THANK YOU FOR CHOOSING A PUREREAD BOOK!

We hope you enjoyed the story, and as a way to thank you for choosing PureRead we'd like to send you this free Special Edition Cozy, and other fun reader rewards…

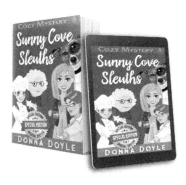

Click Here to download your free Cozy Mystery
PureRead.com/cozy

Thanks again for reading.

See you soon!

If you loved this story why not continue straight away
with other books in the series?

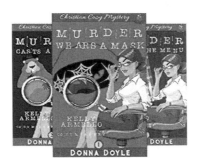

Murder Wears A Mask

Murder Casts a Shadow

Murder Plans The Menu

Murder Wears a Medal

Murder Is A Smoking Gun

Murder Has a Heart

OR READ THE COMPLETE BOXSET!

Start Reading On Amazon Now

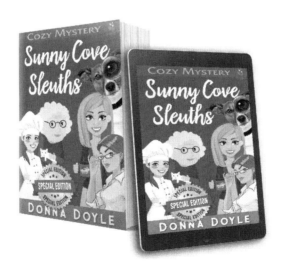

At PureRead we publish books you can trust. Great tales without smut or swearing, but with all of the mystery and romance you expect from a great story.

Be the first to know when we release new books, take part in our fun competitions, and get surprise free books in your inbox by signing up to our Reader list.

As a thank you you'll receive this exclusive Special Edition Cozy available only to our subscribers...

Click Here to download your free Cozy Mystery
PureRead.com/cozy

Thanks again for reading.
See you soon!

Made in the USA
Coppell, TX
15 November 2023

24291644R00238